THE MARQUESS MEETS HIS MATCH

Laura Martin

MILLS & BOON

First Published in Great Britain 2022
by Mills & Boon, an imprint of HarperCollins*Publishers* Ltd,
1 London Bridge Street, London, SE1 9GF

www.harpercollins.co.uk

HarperCollins*Publishers*
1st Floor, Watermarque Building,
Ringsend Road, Dublin 4, Ireland

The Marquess Meets His Match © 2022 Laura Martin

ISBN: 978-0-263-30162-5

03/22

MIX
Paper from
responsible sources
FSC™ C007454

This book is produced from independently certified FSC™ paper
to ensure responsible forest management.
For more information visit www.harpercollins.co.uk/green.

Printed and Bound in Spain using 100% Renewable Electricity
at CPI Black Print, Barcelona

For my boys. Everything I do, I do for you.

Chapter One

Bath—1812

Glancing over her shoulder as if she were about to commit a crime, Charlotte crept through the door that led to a sunny patio and quietly closed it behind her. From here it was only a brisk walk across the lawn until she was out of sight of the house and then it would be easy to sneak into the stables.

She wasn't sure why she felt quite so guilty about slipping away. Her hostess, the effusive Lady Mountjoy, had insisted she freshen up and rest until all the guests arrived and so it wasn't as if Charlotte should be somewhere else.

Even so she walked quickly, only slowing when she was hidden by a hedge that separated the lawn behind the house from the rose garden. It was a sunny day and for a moment

Charlotte paused, taking a moment to inhale the sweet scent of the pink blooms and listen to the buzzing of the bees as they flew from flower to flower.

There was a gate in the wall that led to the stable yard and, as Charlotte made her way through, a carriage rolled past, forcing her to step back for a minute. The yard was a bustle of activity with grooms and stable boys running backwards and forward seeing to the new arrivals and it was perfect cover for her to sidle into the stables unseen.

Inside the air was cool on her skin and the familiar farmyard sounds and smells comforting. She wished she could grab one of the gleaming saddles, prepare a horse and gallop back through the Somerset countryside to her home.

'You wouldn't mind, would you?' she murmured to the beautiful mare as she stroked her nose. The horse tossed her head and Charlotte smiled at the idea of the animal answering her.

A ride through the fields sounded much more appealing than spending the next few weeks closeted with the simpering young ladies Lady Mountjoy had no doubt invited to her little gathering.

Charlotte closed her eyes and remembered the reluctant promise she had given her mother.

'Yes, I will try my hardest to get Lady Mount-joy to choose me. Yes, I do understand how marvellous it would be to have a London Season.'

It wasn't her dream, but she had promised her mother she would try.

Knowing she should return to the main house, she dawdled a little longer, stepping from stall to stall and admiring the horses Lady Mountjoy kept in the spacious stables. Her family had not been able to spare a horse for her to keep while she stayed at Rowlings Hall, but now she had met Lady Mountjoy she doubted the older woman would begrudge her taking one of these fine mares out for a ride every so often.

Charlotte was about to tear herself away and make the walk back to the main house when she heard the low rumble of voices at the stable door. She expected a groom to enter and perhaps lead a horse into one of the empty stalls, but as she turned to look she caught sight of a tall figure in the doorway. His back was to her at that moment and he was addressing someone outside in the stable yard, but even so Charlotte knew exactly who it was.

Her stomach felt heavy and immediately she began to look around, trying to find another way out, any way that meant she didn't need to go past Lord Overby.

The stable only had doors at one end and Lord Overby was standing right in the middle of them. About halfway along the block, opposite one of the stalls, was a ladder leading up to the hayloft above and for a moment Charlotte considered hiding in among the hay until Lord Overby had disappeared. She took a step towards it before remembering the brand-new, expensive dress she was wearing and her mother's instructions not to do anything to ruin it. Scrabbling about in the hayloft would probably count as endangering the expensive satin they really couldn't afford.

Her eyes flicked to the window at the opposite end of the stables to Lord Overby. It was narrow and high, but there was a bucket to stand on conveniently placed underneath. She was quite slender with narrow hips and years of working on the family farm meant she would have the strength to pull herself up, but she risked someone seeing her clambering out of the window of the stables and reporting it to Lady Mountjoy. It might be enough of a transgression to get her sent back home immediately. While going home was what she wanted, she didn't want to be sent back in disgrace and disappoint her family.

'I'll take him in and rub him down,' Lord Overby said, addressing one of the grooms. 'If you could see he gets some hay and is ready for riding again today. I expect I will want to take him out later this afternoon.'

At most she had five seconds to make the decision. He was already half turning, listening to what the groom was saying but ready to step into the cool of the stables with the horse he was leading. If it was anyone else she would just walk past, but Lord Overby was the last person she wanted to encounter. She doubted she would be able to be polite to him. There was something about the man that made her want to revert to a nine-year-old version of herself and she had images of him greeting her in that cool, supercilious tone and her not being able to resist sticking her tongue out at him.

Charlotte hitched up her skirts, upended the bucket and climbed up on to it. She gripped hold of the bottom of the ledge and stifled a grunt as she pulled herself up and threw one leg through the opening so she was straddling the wood of the window. Now all she had to do was twist, pull over her other leg and slip down on to the cobbles below.

Twisting, she felt something pull at her hip and in dismay she glanced down to see her skirt was stuck on a nail protruding from the wall. In panic she looked up. Lord Overby had finished talking to the groom in the yard and was turning to enter the stables. In a couple of seconds he would be inside and one glance in her direction would reveal her half in and half out of the window, balanced precariously and in a decidedly unladylike manner.

There was nothing else for it. She wrenched at her skirt, but the material was too thick and nothing gave.

'Miss Greenacre,' Lord Overby said, his tone only slightly surprised as if he wasn't completely taken aback to see her climbing through a window. 'Is there a problem with the door?'

Charlotte summoned a smile through gritted teeth.

Lord Overby walked his horse into a stall and started to remove the saddle and bridle and Charlotte stared in amazement. Any other gentleman would rush to her side immediately, offering assistance. Lord Overby seemed in no hurry and, instead of acknowledging her further, murmured quietly to his horse as he went about his work.

He was going to make her ask for his help.

Trying one last time to free herself before she gave in and addressed Lord Overby, Charlotte felt the material give a little, but not enough to allow her to clamber in or out of the window— her dress was still pulled too tight over her legs.

Biting down her distaste at addressing the man in the stables with her, she dug her fingers into the wood and called out.

In normal circumstances Robert wouldn't have left a young lady in such a predicament. If it were anyone else stuck half in and half out of the stable window, he would have rushed to assist them immediately, but it was Miss Greenacre and where she was concerned his chivalrous tendencies seemed to desert him.

Besides, he suspected the only reason Miss Greenacre was climbing out of the window was to avoid him. That alone meant he felt a little justified in making her actually ask for his help.

'Lord Overby, would you be so kind as to help me? My skirt is stuck.' He could tell the words came through gritted teeth and had to smother a smile at her reluctance to ask for assistance.

'Of course, Miss Greenacre.' Without rushing, he put down the saddle he'd just removed from his horse, Washington, and ambled over to inspect the position the young lady had got herself into. 'Not the most practical attire to wear for scrambling round the stable yard,' he observed. The dress she wore was very different from the clothes he had seen her in before. It was made of pale pink satin with little puff sleeves and a white sash tied into a bow at her back. 'It suits you.'

She grimaced and instinctively he knew she felt more at home in the breeches and shirt he had seen her in the last time he'd visited Willow Tree Farm.

'Can you hurry up and release my dress?'

'Let's see,' Robert said, taking his time and crouching down to examine where the offending nail was. He grinned as he heard Miss Greenacre tut at how long this was all taking. 'I'm going to unsnag it now—make sure you don't fall. I'd hate to have to explain to my aunt how one of her guests had ended up with a blow to the head and covered in manure on the first day of her stay.'

Reaching out, he released the hem of her dress from the nail and then stood.

'Thank you,' Miss Greenacre said grudgingly.

'I live to assist,' he said with a mock bow and began to turn away.

He'd expected her to slip back into the stables, to put her feet back on the bucket she had positioned beneath the window and then step down to the ground. That would be what any sensible person would do. Perhaps it was too much to expect from Miss Greenacre.

Out of the corner of his eye he saw her start to swing her other leg over the windowsill. At the top she wobbled and his instincts kicked in. He lunged forward, grabbing her by the waist as she lost her balance and pulled her back down into the stables. She was small in build, but even so the momentum was too much as she was coming from too high a height. Robert felt all the breath being forced from his lungs as she hit his chest and he stumbled backwards, arms wrapped around her, cushioning her fall as he hit the ground.

For a long moment neither of them moved. Robert was too winded, too shocked by the force of the impact. By the way Miss Greenacre remained completely still, he assumed she felt the same.

He glanced up, groaning at even the slightest movement, to find her lips an inch from his. Slowly he became aware of the curve of her waist under his hand and the sweet smell of roses in her hair. This was much closer than he had ever expected to be to the frosty young woman, but it wasn't as entirely unpleasant as he had imagined.

'What did you do that for?'

He blinked. 'Excuse me?'

'I was doing absolutely fine until you came and grabbed me.'

'You were falling out of the window.'

'I would have regained my balance.'

'Nonsense. You would have fallen backwards out of the window and cracked your skull.'

Miss Greenacre pulled a face, but didn't protest any more. She was straddling him, her hips pressed against his, and suddenly she looked down, becoming aware of the position they were in. Quickly she scrabbled to her feet, brushing herself down and backing away until her body hit the door of one of the stalls.

Slowly, painfully, Robert sat up and then managed to struggle to his feet. His tailbone had taken much of the impact and he knew he would have a bruise developing over the next couple of days, but at least there were no more serious injuries than that.

'I didn't realise you would be here,' Miss Greenacre said, watching him as he brushed himself down.

'Lady Mountjoy is my aunt. She requested my assistance with her little project.' He shrugged. He couldn't think of many worse ways to spend a couple of weeks, sequestered with simpering young ladies trying to convince his aunt they were the right choice to take to London. He'd agreed on the condition that she didn't ask him to get overly involved in the decision process of selecting which debutante would get a Season. 'Why did you decide to come?'

Although he had been the one to suggest Miss Greenacre as a possible candidate for his aunt's little experiment, he had doubted she would accept the invitation.

'My mother,' she said by way of explanation, not elaborating any further.

Robert moved back into the stall and began to rub down Washington.

'I'm sure we will not have to spend too much time together,' Miss Greenacre said, turning to leave.

'Haven't you heard? My aunt has paired us for most of the activities.' He didn't know if they had been paired for any of the activities or not, he wasn't privy to all of his aunt's plans for the next few weeks, and he knew he shouldn't tease the serious young woman, but the temptation was too great. The look of horror on her face would be enough to offend most men, but Robert just grinned again and turned back to his horse.

Chapter Two

❦

Charlotte was still fuming twenty minutes later as she made her way back to the house. She had decided against returning immediately, thinking a walk around the garden would give her time to clear her head and calm down, but instead it had allowed her to dwell on every second of the encounter with Lord Overby, getting more and more worked up with each passing minute.

'Horrible man,' she muttered to herself as she ascended the steps that led to the terrace. She'd disliked him for years, ever since an encounter when she was only nine or ten. He'd been riding near the perimeter of his land in one of the places it bordered their estate while Charlotte was helping her father mend one of their drystone walls. She couldn't remember his exact words, but he'd said something about her helping her father *'like a son'*, insinuating from his tone that she was a second-rate helper. Charlotte had always felt her parents would have preferred a boy, not that they had ever said anything to confirm her suspicions, but even when she was younger they could not afford as much help on the farm and estate as was really needed. A strapping young lad to ease some of the burden of the physical work would have been more use to them than her. It had meant Lord Overby's words had cut her to her core and made her feel inadequate. Ever since she had tried to avoid him.

That dislike had changed into something deeper, something approaching hatred when he had tricked her mother into selling some of their land.

'There you are,' Lady Mountjoy called as she bustled out of the French doors. 'Come my dear, everyone is gathering in the drawing room. We're quite the party.'

Charlotte allowed the older woman to take her by the arm, whisking her back into the house and through the spacious hallway into the drawing room. There was a hum of chatter, a buzz of excitement and Charlotte had to remind herself to smile. She *was* lucky to be here.

'You must know Miss Lucy Freeman,' Lady

Mountjoy said, depositing her with a pretty young woman dressed in a pure white cotton dress, much more appropriate for the scorching weather than Charlotte's satin.

'A pleasure to meet you,' Miss Freeman said with a friendly smile. Charlotte only had the chance to respond with her name before Lady Mountjoy spun away and called the whole room to attention.

As the assembled guests fell silent Charlotte took the opportunity to look around. The drawing room, like the rest of the house, was large and beautifully decorated. The walls were covered in a light blue wallpaper and spaced at equal distances were cream half-pillars. There was an intricate gold leaf design trailing along where the walls met the ceiling. It was an opulent room, but not garishly done. Lady Mountjoy clearly had taste alongside her vast fortune.

'I am so happy to see you all gathered here in one place,' Lady Mountjoy said, clapping her hands together in joy. 'When I first decided I wanted to host this little party and then champion a young lady through her first Season in London, I half suspected I would never see my plans come to fruition.'

'You do have a lot of plans, my dear,' Lord Mountjoy murmured quietly, but his deep voice carried across the room in the silence. Charlotte blinked. She hadn't noticed the husband of her hostess standing quietly in the corner of the room. He was smiling warmly at his wife and seemed to fade into the background as she started talking again.

'I am so thankful all of your families are as excited about the idea as I am. We shall have such fun these next two weeks, all of us together. Of course I cannot take you all to London with me as much as I wish I could, but I hope you will find the next few weeks fun and helpful in preparing you for the most exciting years of your lives.'

Charlotte glanced at the other young ladies in the room, three more besides her and Miss Lucy Freeman. That made five. Five young women all vying for Lady Mountjoy's favour, all wanting to be that special one selected to have a London Season, something she doubted any of them would experience without Lady Mountjoy's intervention. All of them wanting it except her.

'I have invited a number of young gentlemen to stay with us as well, most arriving later in the week to allow us to get to know one another first. Although my nephew Lord Overby is here with us already.' She looked around the room as if seeking him out, frowning at his absence. 'Although none of you has had to journey too far, I know the hustle and bustle of travelling can be exhausting. I suggest you take the afternoon to rest and we can continue getting to know one another this evening at dinner.'

Lady Mountjoy beamed at her guests and then stepped back to show she was done with her little speech.

'I think she might be the kindest woman I've ever met,' Miss Freeman said quietly to Charlotte, beaming at their hostess.

Charlotte watched as a stunningly beautiful young lady she didn't know hurried over and cornered Lady Mountjoy and she wondered if the other ladies invited to compete for the prize of a London Season would treat this as a competition. At least she didn't have to worry about that.

'I don't quite understand *why* she is doing this, Miss Freeman,' Charlotte said, turning back to her companion.

'Please call me Lucy. I think we're going to be spending a lot of time together.' Lucy linked her hand through Charlotte's arm and they began to very slowly stroll around the perimeter of the drawing room. 'Lady Mountjoy told my mother than she loved the excitement of the London Season so much when she was escorting her daughters while they were looking for husbands that she wanted to do it all over again.'

'I can't think of much worse,' Charlotte said quietly.

'You aren't excited for a London Season?'

'I can't quite imagine it.' She smiled, trying to deflect her new friend from probing further. She could hardly come out and say she would rather be at home milking the cows or mending a perimeter wall on the farm.

'What can't you quite imagine?' A gruff voice came from behind her. Charlotte spun too quickly and stumbled as she realised her body was a little too close to Lord Overby's.

'A London Season.'

'I'm sure London can't quite imagine you either, Miss Greenacre,' Lord Overby said as he bowed his head in greeting to Miss Freeman.

Charlotte was sure it was meant as an insult as Lord Overby couldn't know that she would rather be dragged through a flaming fire than fritter away six months of her life waltzing through ballrooms.

'A provincial young lady from Somerset? Surely wide-eyed young debutantes from the far-flung counties are exactly what you expect at the start of the Season.'

'*You* are not a typical debutante, Miss Green-acre.'

Even Miss Freeman's eyebrows raised at the direct way Lord Overby was addressing her.

'I don't think you have the first idea what I am, Lord Overby.'

He smiled, a slow, wicked smile that made her feel a little nervous, and then took a step closer. Against her better judgement Charlotte found she was holding her breath, waiting for his next words.

'Oh, I see you, Miss Greenacre. Your expressions are so easy to read it is like perusing the morning gossip column.' His breath tickled her ear and she felt a shiver of anticipation. With a little jolt of horror she quickly pushed it away. Lord Overby was the last person she wanted to feel anything but distaste for.

'Stop taunting poor Miss Greenacre,' Lady Mountjoy said as she bustled over, her eyes shining with the excitement of the afternoon.

Charlotte blinked. *Poor Miss Greenacre* wasn't how she wanted to be known among this group, among any group. Her family might have been down on their luck for the last five years, but she hated the idea that she was pit-ied. It went against everything she strived for.

'Come, you must try to put the past behind

you. My nephew has a wicked sense of humour, I know, but he is a good boy.'

Despite her indignation at being cornered like this, Charlotte had to suppress a grin at Lord Overby being called a good boy by this eccentric older woman. He didn't seem to mind and gave Charlotte a bland and infuriating smile that made her want to surreptitiously kick him in the shins.

'He is the one who suggested I invite you after all,' Lady Mountjoy continued. 'Of course as soon as he said your name I knew you were the perfect choice. I knew your mother when she was a young woman—she's a little older than my children, but not by much. We'd lost touch over the years, but I was delighted for an excuse to reach out.'

All the background sounds, the chatter of voices and rustling of dresses seemed to fade away and her eyes locked with Lord Overby. She wanted to reach out, to grasp him by the lapels on his jacket and shake him, to ask him what she had ever done to deserve to be tormented by him in such a fashion. First there had been the farmland he'd stolen and now this.

Innate good manners meant she was just about able to stop from launching herself at the man, but she hardly heard Lady Mountjoy excuse herself or Lord Overby also murmur his excuse to leave. In a matter of seconds she was left alone with Miss Freeman, who looked entirely bemused by the exchange.

'Lucy, would you please excuse me?' Charlotte said, not taking her eyes off Lord Overby's retreating form.

'Of course. Perhaps I can knock on your door before dinner and we can come down together.'

'That would be marvellous.'

Quickly she strode from the room, not wanting to be caught up in the small talk among the other young ladies in the drawing room. She was curious as to who they all were and how they had come to be here, but that was far overshadowed right now by her need to catch up and confront Lord Overby.

The man was quick—he'd already disappeared by the time she had made her way into the grand entrance hall. After a moment's thought she headed towards the library and the doors that led out into the garden. Lord Overby struck her as the sort of man who spent most of his time outside. Her assumptions were right. As she hurried into the library the door to the terrace clicked shut and she caught a glimpse of Lord Overby's retreating form on the steps down to the garden.

Determined to catch him up, she broke into a run, praying no one had followed her to see such undignified behaviour, flung open the door and called out before Lord Overby disappeared among the bushes.

'Lord Overby, wait.'

She saw him pause, but for a moment he didn't turn round and she wondered if he were contemplating pretending he hadn't heard her.

'Lord Overby,' she shouted even louder.

This time he turned around, a mildly irritated expression on his face. 'Miss Greenacre,' he said, still not making any move towards her, 'Three encounters in one hour. I am privileged indeed.'

'What did your aunt mean?'

A frown crossed his face and Charlotte realised she was going to have to be clearer. In her anger she was not coming across well.

Taking a breath and exhaling slowly, she forced herself to walk down the steps and over the grass until she was a few feet from the man. With a calmness she didn't feel inside she looked up at the Marquess and smiled, although it might have appeared more of a grimace.

'In the drawing room your aunt said you were the one who suggested she invite me. What did she mean?'

'Exactly that.'

'Exactly what?'

Lord Overby regarded her as though she were of questionable intelligence. When he spoke next his words were slow and drawn out.

'I suggested she invite you as one of her *deb- utantes*.'

'Why on earth did you do that?'

He looked puzzled by the question.

'Is it not enough that you steal our land, the land my family has owned for generations? Or that you wait until my father is dead, our fam- ily unable to defend ourselves, to strike? Now you decide to subject me to *this*.' She gestured in the general direction of the house behind her.

'A house party,' he supplied.

'Exactly.' She knew she sounded a bit ridicu- lous, but if it hadn't been for the invitation from Lady Mountjoy she would be back home en- suring the harvest was brought in on time and overseeing the purchase of what livestock they needed to see them through winter.

'My aunt enquired as to whether I knew of any local young ladies who were from good families without the funds to give them a Lon- don Season. You fit that description so I gave her your name…' He paused and made a point of waiting until she met his eye before continuing. 'There was nothing more to it, no hidden meaning, no malicious thought.'

Charlotte felt much of the indignation ebb out of her and after a moment she looked down, gently scuffing at the ground with her shoe.

'I know you do not like me, Miss Greenacre, and I have no problem with that, but we will be forced to spend some time together over the coming weeks. Perhaps you can decide to accept my assurances that I do not wish you ill.'

He was sounding so reasonable that Charlotte felt a pang of remorse at immediately thinking the worst. Then she reminded herself what he had already done to her family, what he had already taken from her and she felt her jaw clench and her teeth begin to press together.

'I suggest that other than for arranged activities we do our utmost to keep out of each other's way,' Charlotte suggested curtly.

'Excellent idea.'

'Good.'

'Wonderful.'

She wasn't sure if he was mocking her—he was a difficult man to read. The expression in his deep brown eyes was neutral with no hint of malevolence or ridicule.

'Right,' she said, feeling a little awkward. 'Good day, Lord Overby.'

'Good day, Miss Greenacre.'

Chapter Three

With a sigh Robert sank into a chair and closed his eyes. He'd forgotten how exhausting it was trying to pretend he was enjoying himself. Of course he was often in London for the Season, but he barely ever accepted an invitation to a ball or a dinner party. Only the invitations issued by his closest friends would entice him to enter the melee of a ballroom when the young ladies and their mothers were husband hunting.

He owed Lady Mountjoy his presence though—his presence and at least the pretence he was enjoying himself. His aunt had been a rock throughout the difficult times in his life, much more so than his flighty mother, Lady Mountjoy's sister. When she had asked him to help make this house party a success he couldn't refuse.

Slowly he inhaled, the fresh scent of the citrus trees rejuvenating him a little. This was his favourite room of the house, even in the stifling heat of summer. The garden room, filled with luscious and overgrown tropical plants, had been a jungle when he was a boy and now some parts were too dense to forge a path through, but in the middle was a table surrounded by comfortable chairs overlooking a pond filled with colourful fish.

For a moment he let his mind wander back to the conversation he'd had with Miss Greenacre that afternoon. She'd been almost shaking with indignation and rage when she had asked him why he had put her name forward as a possible debutante who might appreciate a London Season. When he had reassured her there had been nothing malicious he'd been telling the truth. His aunt had asked and Miss Greenacre's name had popped into his mind. He knew a little of her family's struggles over the last few years since her father had died. Although the farm and estate they owned was doing better than they had for a long time, he doubted there would be money for a London Season for Miss Greenacre.

With a wry smile he had to admit there was more to it than neighbourly concern. There was something about Miss Greenacre that intrigued him. She was so frosty towards him, but he saw how hard she worked to do her bit on the farm and around the estate. She certainly wasn't like other young ladies in how she spent her time. They were neighbours, even if he didn't know her well, and he hadn't seen any harm in suggesting her name to his aunt so he might see who his neighbour really was as well as giving her an opportunity she might not otherwise have.

He started as the door to the garden room clicked open and then a moment later closed. From his position he couldn't see who had entered. All of the guests should be getting ready for dinner and Lord and Lady Mountjoy had retired for a late-afternoon rest before the festivities of the first evening commenced.

Through the leaves of the plants he saw a flash of pale blue and immediately knew it was Miss Greenacre. She was the only debutante who would be creeping around the house rather than spending the time choosing a dress or tidying her hair before dinner.

'Don't worry, we'll find a place for you,' she murmured and for a moment he thought she must be talking to him. There was no one else there with them. Slowly she made her way through the garden room, pushing aside low-hanging branches. 'We'll find somewhere nice and warm and snug and safe.'

Now she had walked a bit further into the room he could see she was addressing a bundle in her arms. Puzzled, he leaned forward, wondering whether to announce himself. In a few seconds she would see him anyway, but first he wanted to know who she was speaking to.

'I will never let anyone hurt you.'

He jolted in his chair, shocked by her words. Surely she couldn't have a baby wrapped up in the blanket in her arms? It was a preposterous idea, yet there didn't seem to be another explanation.

Clearing his throat, he stood and saw the expression of sheer panic on Miss Greenacre's face as she realised she was not alone. Quickly she pulled the bundle tighter in to her chest, her eyes wide and furtive and her body tensing as if deciding whether to stay or to run.

'Good afternoon, Miss Greenacre,' he said, resisting the urge to crane his neck to get a better view of the bundle.

'Good afternoon,' she managed to stutter, backing away from him into a large exotic fern.

He helpfully held up one of the oversized leaves, allowing her to step out. The bundle in her arms wriggled.

'What do you have there, Miss Greenacre?' His tone was sharper than he intended, but if she had a baby cradled in her arms then this was an insurmountable scandal.

'I can't tell you.'

Her face had lost all colour and she looked as though she might be sick at any moment.

'I think you're going to have to.'

'I can't,' she whispered.

Moving slowly so as not to startle her, he stepped forward and very gently pressed her arms down so he could see inside the bundle.

In the last minute he'd convinced himself there was going to be a baby in the bundle. Even though the thought that she could have smuggled one into the house, or kept an infant secret for any amount of time, was ridiculous, he couldn't see what else she would be talking to and trying to hide.

As he looked at the pink face wrapped in a blanket he felt the relief and mirth bubble up inside him and explode in a bark of laughter.

'Don't laugh,' Miss Greenacre said, pulling the bundle back towards her chest.

'I thought you had a child in there.'

'A child? A human child?'

'Yes.'

'How…? Why…?' She started, then shook

her head. 'You thought I had a child of my own? Or had stolen someone else's?'

'I hadn't got that far in working out what you were doing.'

'That's preposterous.'

He raised an eyebrow and motioned at the bundle. '*That* is preposterous.'

Slowly Miss Greenacre loosened her grip on the blanket and Robert could see the folded-over ears and little pink snout of the piglet she had wrapped up.

'I have so many questions I barely know where to start,' he said, trying to suppress a smile at the huff she gave.

'I really don't have time for questions. I need to find somewhere to keep Arnold.'

'Arnold.' He felt his eyebrows shoot up even further. Any more surprises and they would be in his hairline.

'That's his name. Don't look like that. It's perfectly normal to give animals names. I will wager you have given your horse a name.'

'Yes. Washington. But he's a horse, not a pig.' He shook his head. 'I think we're getting distracted, although I do have a lot of questions about the origin of this piglet's name. Perhaps our conversation can circle back round once you've explained why you're creeping through the house, cradling a piglet in your arms like a baby.'

'I need to find somewhere to keep him while I'm staying here. I thought he would be fine in my bedroom…'

'You thought you would keep a pig in your bedroom?'

'Arnold often comes into my room at home,' she said, a look of defiance in her eyes. Before this conversation he'd thought Miss Greenacre strait-laced and a little dull, but now he wasn't sure if she was fascinating or mad. 'But he was unsettled by the unfamiliar surroundings and made a bit of a mess.'

'Ah. Hence the search for new lodgings for Arnold.' He narrowed his eyes. 'You brought the pig from home?'

'Yes.'

'Why?'

Miss Greenacre sank down on to one of the metal chairs, her arms relaxing a little, and Arnold started to wriggle and squirm in the blanket. Cautiously she looked over her shoulder and then set him on the floor, smiling at the happy squeal as he trotted off to explore the garden room.

'He's the runt of the litter. His mother had thirteen piglets and he couldn't fight his way in for any milk. It was either kill him or...' She trailed off, shrugging.

'Or hand-rear him.'

Miss Greenacre nodded. 'Don't think I'm soft hearted,' she said suddenly. 'I am perfectly capable of doing what needs to be done on the farm.'

'But not to Arnold,' Robert said quietly.

'He is adorable.'

The little piglet seemed fascinated by the different sights and smells and was happily rootling among the exotic trees.

'I understand why you brought him, although surely it would have been easier to ask someone at home to look after him in your absence, but I'm struggling to imagine *how* you brought him.'

'Oh, that was easy. I bribed the boy driving the cart to keep Arnold hidden up front while I said farewell to Mother and when I first arrived here, then I ran out to get him once I had slipped away from Lady Mountjoy.' She looked at him, her eyes narrowing. 'You're going to tell someone.'

'Do you really think that little of me? To risk poor Arnold's safety...'

'Don't jest. This is a serious matter.'

Robert managed to get his smile under control and nod with what felt appropriate gravitas for the situation. 'There wasn't anyone at Willow Tree Farm that could look after him?'

Miss Greenacre pulled a face that was halfway between a grimace and a scowl.

'My mother thinks I get too attached to the animals, what with it being a working farm. She's told me too many times I can't keep saving them from slaughter.'

'Ah.'

'I didn't want her to find out I was asking one of the farm hands to keep Arnold safe when she would tell me it wasn't the natural order of things to hand-rear him rather than let him take his chances with the rest of the piglets.'

'Ah. May I be of assistance in finding Arnold alternative lodgings for the duration of his stay with us here at Rowlings Hall?'

'Do you know of anywhere?'

'Does it have to be inside?'

Miss Greenacre shook her head. 'As long as it is secure. He's only little and can slip through the slightest hole.'

'There's a spare stall in the stables, I'm sure we can make it comfortable enough with some fresh straw. I'll show you.'

He watched, trying to suppress a chuckle of laughter Miss Greenacre started to chase the piglet around the garden room. Arnold was fast and obviously thought he was engaged in a thoroughly enjoyable game, squealing and slipping from his owner's arms again and again. After watching for a few minutes Robert waited for the piglet to turn in his direction and then swooped down and caught him firmly around the middle. The pig wriggled but calmed as Robert lifted him up and brought him closer to his face.

'Good afternoon, Arnold,' he said, giving the squirming piglet a gentle stroke. 'Why don't we find somewhere nice for you to sleep tonight?'

He handed the pig back to Miss Greenacre, who gave him a look of grudging appreciation, waited for her to wrap it up in the ridiculous blanket again and then opened the door leading to the garden.

It was a hot afternoon. The flowers that lined the borders were drooping in the sunlight and the normally perfect grass looked a little brown in the heat. In other circumstances Robert would linger, taking a moment to appreciate the sights and smells of the garden. In the last few years he had forced himself to slow down, to take the time to notice the little things in the world that made it a better place. It had been this attitude that had finally helped him move on from the trauma of his personal life, each day focusing on the little things until everything else became a little less painful, a little less raw.

Today he could see Miss Greenacre was on edge so he quickly led the way through the garden towards the stables. Earlier the stable yard had been alive with activity, but with all the guests now arrived and settled in the house it was much calmer with just a couple of stable boys polishing a saddle lethargically in the shade.

'In here.' He motioned for Miss Greenacre to go ahead of him into the stable where he had found her climbing out of the window earlier in the day and couldn't help but smile at the memory. She might not like him and he had always found her to be irritable and far too quick to judge, but Miss Greenacre had made his first day at Rowlings Hall anything but dull.

They made their way past Washington's stall and he paused for a moment to stroke his good-tempered horse on the nose, before going all the way to the end of the stable. There was a small, unoccupied compartment at the end with a couple of brooms leaning up against the wall.

He watched as Miss Greenacre tried the door,

closing it to ensure there were no little holes Arnold could slip through to escape.

'What do you think?'

'The grooms won't let him out by mistake?'

'Peter,' he called, waiting until one of the stable boys came running inside. 'Here's a coin for you if you make sure this pig is kept safe in this stall while Miss Greenacre is a guest here.' He handed over the shiny silver shilling. 'There is another one for you at the end of her stay if the pig is well cared for.'

'Yes, my lord.' The young stable boy grinned and pocketed the shilling. 'I'll go and get some pig food from Home Farm.'

Robert went to fetch some straw and once the stall was prepared Miss Greenacre gave the piglet in her arms a little squeeze and then lowered him to the floor.

For a long moment they both stood side by side, watching the animal rooting around in the straw and exploring his new home.

'I'll come visit you tomorrow,' Miss Greenacre said as they turned to leave.

Silently they started to walk back towards Rowlings Hall.

'Thank you,' Miss Greenacre said eventually. He glanced at the young woman next to him and saw how much it had cost her to be civil, but the thanks she was giving him were genuine.

'You're welcome. I would never want to see an innocent little creature in distress.'

'It was good of you to help me.' She paused, as if about to say something more, then gave him a fleeting smile and hurried on ahead of him into the house, disappearing upstairs to the guest bedrooms.

Chapter Four

～～～

Pinning back a stray strand of hair, Charlotte looked at herself critically in the mirror. Her cheeks were flushed, her hair difficult to control and her dress, although new, looked crumpled from being packed in a trunk for the journey over here. She didn't look like a debutante who was ready to be the darling of the London Season.

As much as she didn't want to be the one chosen by Lady Mountjoy, she also didn't want to be a laughing stock among the other young ladies. Although she didn't know them, she imagined they would be charming and full of poise. They wouldn't be sitting in front of their mirrors worrying about the little hairs that framed their faces curling in the wrong direction or spilling something on the dresses they had been laced into.

There was a firm rap on the door and Charlotte crossed the room to open it, expecting to see Miss Lucy Freeman standing outside. Instead there was one of the other young ladies, a striking, petite young woman with raven-black hair and piercing green eyes.

'Good, you haven't gone down yet. I heard Lucy saying she would call on you to go down together and I thought I might have missed you.' She smiled confidently before continuing, 'I'm Eliza, Eliza Stanley.'

Charlotte stood back as the young woman strode past her into the bedroom, flopping down on the edge of the bed and looking around critically.

'You've got a bigger room than I have and a better view—' she ran her hand over the bed-covers '—although I'm pleased we don't have to share. Knowing my luck, I'd be with that ghastly Miss Huntley.'

'Miss Huntley?' Charlotte said, feeling as though a whirlwind had invaded her room.

'Yes, you know, Miss Huntley. Tall, slim, blonde and beautiful, and a tongue that could cut through three-day-old bread. Although I'm sure she'll be sweet as anything whenever Lady Mountjoy is around.'

'Oh.' Charlotte didn't really know what to

say. She didn't have many friends her own age. Since her father's death she had been kept busy on the farm and even when her mother suggested she spend the evening at the Assembly Rooms she had shied away from the idea.

'You're Charlotte, right? Miss Charlotte Greenacre, aged twenty-one. Never had a Season. Lives on a small estate ten miles from Bath. Two younger sisters, father deceased— sorry about that.'

Charlotte blinked. She didn't even know the names of the other young ladies here, let alone any details about their lives. Although she supposed she had been a bit distracted, firstly silently moaning about finding herself here in this situation and then secondly by the Arnold situation.

'How do you know all that about me?' Charlotte came to perch on the bed beside Eliza.

'I talk. To *everyone*. The maids, the grooms, the other guests. Lord Mountjoy is a kind old man, too, and holds a wealth of information— I spent half an hour with him this afternoon.'

'Oh.'

There was another knock on the door and Charlotte rose to answer it, this time finding Lucy standing outside.

'Lucy,' Eliza said, 'Good. Now you're here we can go down to dinner.'

Charlotte allowed Eliza to take her arm, chattering the whole time, and lead her and Lucy as if they were old friends down the stairs.

'So why are you here?' Eliza asked as they reached the drawing room. Lucy had already stepped through the door so Charlotte couldn't pretend the question wasn't directed at her.

'What do you mean?'

'Well, take me—I was desperate to escape the life my father had mapped out for me. Marriage to some respectable local gentleman three times my age. Five children before I'm twenty-five and then a life of dull drudgery raising the babies and pleasing my husband thereafter.'

'That does sound a bit grim.'

'Just a bit. My mother is good friends with one of Lady Mountjoy's daughters so when she wrote asking if I wanted to spend three weeks with her here to see whether I would be a good fit to take to London for a Season I jumped at the chance.' She smiled, full of enthusiasm. 'Think, a whole six months of dinner parties and balls and dances and gossip and intrigue.'

Charlotte nodded her head, trying to mirror Eliza's excitement. Hopefully Lady Mountjoy would see Eliza was a much better choice to take to London. She would make the most of the opportunities the older woman was offering.

'So how about you? Why are you here?'

'My father was a moderately successful land-owner,' Charlotte said, surprising herself with her candour. 'Then when he died my mother struggled with the upkeep of the estate. We get by, but there is no money for a London Season, no money for a decent dowry even, so when Lady Mountjoy approached my mother she was very keen I take the opportunity.'

'And you?'

'Me?' Charlotte looked around to check no one else was listening. 'I'm a country girl at heart. I feel a bit out of place in Bath, let alone London.'

'You might surprise yourself,' Eliza said, flashing Charlotte a dazzling smile. 'Once you try it you might find it is a life you want.'

'Perhaps.' In truth, Charlotte couldn't imagine wanting anything but the rolling green hills that surrounded her farm. She loved paddling her feet in the cool water of the stream that ran across the bottom of their property and climbing the trees that bordered the fields. She loved taking her tools to fix the perimeter walls and spending long afternoons helping the local farrier shoe their horses. She couldn't imagine anything in Bath or London that could beat rural Somerset life.

'Good evening ladies,' Lady Mountjoy said, beaming at the group of assembled young women. 'We have half an hour before dinner. I thought it would be nice if we had some music. As I'm sure you are aware young ladies are often called upon to play the piano or sing at informal gatherings among friends and it is a skill you will need if you do come to London. Who would like to go first?'

Miss Huntley stepped forward before anyone else even looked as though they might move and smiled beatifically at their hostess.

'I love to play the piano, Lady Mountjoy, and have been told my singing voice is like an angel's.'

Lady Mountjoy motioned for Miss Huntley to take a seat at the piano.

Miss Huntley took her time, adjusting her position and spreading her fingers out on the keys and then began a gentle piece that fully demonstrated her musical abilities. For a moment Charlotte was enthralled, unable to take her eyes off the young woman as she played and sang. Everyone else was the same, watching with wide eyes as Miss Huntley entertained them. At the end of the piece Lady Mountjoy led the applause.

'What musical talent you have, my dear.'

'I've practised for two hours a day since I was seven years old,' Miss Huntley said. 'I believe if you want to excel at something then you need to put in the hours of practice. So many people moan that they have no musical talent, but in reality I think they're lazy.'

'Not everyone can be as blessed as you with their voice though,' Lady Mountjoy admonished gently.

'No, I suppose not.'

Beaming at the other young ladies, Lady Mountjoy seemed to be waiting for the next volunteer, but no one wanted to go directly after Miss Huntley. The comparison wouldn't be a favourable one.

'Miss Greenacre, I would love for you to play for us,' Lady Mountjoy said eventually, her eyes locking with Charlotte's.

Charlotte's skin prickled and she felt a cold dread wash over her. Her lips managed to curl into something that sort of resembled a smile and she managed to keep her head from shaking from side to side violently.

As she walked over to the piano she silently cursed her younger self for always sneaking off instead of practising the piano. Her father had loved to play and one of her fondest memories of her childhood was lying in bed listening to her father play for her mother after dinner. Still, none of his talent had filtered down to her and she had found it hard to sit still for her music lessons.

She sat, running her fingers over the cool ivory keys and trying desperately to settle on a piece that wouldn't embarrass her too much. Already she had decided not to sing—the other guests hadn't done anything to deserve being subjected to her out-of-tune warbling.

Closing her eyes for a moment, she tried to recall her father's favourite, the tune she had often drifted off to sleep listening to.

She began, immediately going wrong and needing to pause, to take her fingers off the keys and take a deep breath before starting again. This time she got thirty seconds in before making a mistake, but forged on, hoping no one else had noticed. By the end of the piece she felt her dress damp with perspiration and her heart exhausted from thumping so hard in her chest, but at least it was done. Hopefully Lady Mountjoy would not ask her to play again, not when they had a musical prodigy in the form of Miss Huntley.

There was a light smattering of applause, and with her cheeks flushing Charlotte rose from behind the piano.

'What did I miss?' Lord Overby said as he came through the door as Charlotte was about to step away from the piano stool.

'Miss Huntley and Miss Greenacre have been playing for us,' Lady Mountjoy said, smiling warmly at Charlotte. 'They were wonderful.'

'I am sorry to have missed it.' He eyed Charlotte thoughtfully as if not quite believing she had any musical talent. 'Perhaps you might indulge me and play again.'

Charlotte couldn't help herself, she screwed up her nose, gave Lord Overby a look as if he was suggesting she might like to murder one of her young sisters and shook her head.

'No, thank you,' she said abruptly.

Miss Huntley was smiling a sickly-sweet smile at the Marquess. '*I* would love to play for you, Lord Overby. Perhaps you could help me with the music.'

Charlotte watched as Miss Huntley glided back to the piano, taking her time to sit down and then look up at Lord Overby, who had come to join her with an expression of coy innocence.

'She is so in love with herself,' Eliza whispered as she moved across to stand next to Charlotte.

'She can play very well,' Charlotte conceded.

'What do you know about the handsome Marquess?'

Charlotte looked at the man standing beside Miss Huntley, ready to turn the pages of a piano piece she had chosen. She supposed if you looked at it objectively he was handsome. He was tall, taller than most men of her acquaintance, and slim but with broad shoulders and strong arms. His hair was dark blond with a few lighter streaks showing how much time he spent in the sun as did the hint of a tan on his skin.

'He owns some land near to ours,' she said with a shrug. 'Apart from that not much.'

'What about *the scandal*?' Eliza asked, leaning in and saying the last two words in an exaggerated whisper.

'What scandal?'

Eliza looked at her askance for a moment. 'I can't work out if you're trying to be discreet or if you actually don't know.'

'I don't know.'

'Good. I hate it when people pretend they're above a little bit of gossip.' She dipped her head to better hear Eliza's hushed whisper. 'I'll tell you all I know later when we're away from so many ears, but the short story is the superior Lord Overby was married, but the marriage wasn't a happy one. He was in the process of trying to divorce his wife when she left him in spectacular fashion and then mysteriously died a few months later.'

'You don't mean…?'

'There's been much speculation, but Lord Overby is a very private man. No one knows all the details.'

Charlotte glanced over to the piano where Lord Overby stood looking the very picture of respectability. She couldn't imagine him being involved in any sort of scandal, let alone a big one involving divorce and a dead wife.

'You wouldn't believe it looking at him, would you?' Eliza murmured.

For a long moment she studied him, feeling her pulse quicken as he glanced up directly at her and held her eye for a second. Quickly Charlotte looked away, knowing her cheeks would be turning pink and hoping that everyone else was too enthralled with Miss Huntley's playing to notice.

Chapter Five

The evening was balmy, almost tropical, reminding Robert of the long, hot nights he'd spent walking along the beach when unable to sleep on his honeymoon. His late wife, Amelia, had told him she wished to travel, so he had arranged for an almost year-long tour of Europe, making it as far as Greece. It had been a miserable time, despite his best efforts, and he'd had a lot to think about on those evening walks.

Now whenever there was excessively warm weather, whenever even the evening breeze blew hot, he was transported back to the unhappiest years of his life.

Sighing, he tried to push the thoughts from his mind. It was all history now, part of his history, inescapable in many ways, but history all the same.

Resting back in his chair, he looked up at the house. It was in darkness, all the windows just dark rectangles and no hint of movement. Soon he would retire to bed, too, but he had never needed much sleep, much preferring to stay up until the early hours of the morning and then rest for a few hours before dawn.

He was sitting on one of the benches in the garden of Rowlings Hall, surrounded by fragrant summer flowers. There were white and pink lilies behind him, giving off the most sweet smell, and he took a moment to breathe in and enjoy them, trying to distract himself from the thoughts of his late wife still crashing round in his head.

As he was about to get up he saw the flicker of candlelight in one of the downstairs windows. It was there for a second and then it disappeared. Frowning, he stood, wondering who could be up at this time. All the servants would be fast asleep to be ready for the early start expected of them. He doubted his aunt or uncle were wandering around the house in the middle of the night. Perhaps one of the guests couldn't sleep. Knowing that was the most likely scenario, he didn't rush, not wanting to barrel in and scare whoever it was, but he did want to check nothing untoward was going on all the same. Lord and Lady Mountjoy had countless expensive paintings and ornaments and pieces of jewellery. He knew a few country houses that had been broken into while fully occupied in the middle of the night and some of the best pieces stolen. It took someone with unshakeable nerves or completely desperate to do something so risky, but it wasn't unheard of.

As he stepped back into the house, turning to lock the door behind him, he listened carefully. After a few seconds he heard the quiet creaking of floorboards and then the opening and shutting of a door. Walking as silently as he could, he followed the sounds, allowing his sense of hearing to lead him down the set of servants' stairs to the warren of passageways below that led to the kitchen.

Everything had gone quiet as he stepped into the huge kitchen, the cavernous room filled with shadows. Out of the corner of his eye he saw a flash of movement and instinctively put an arm up to defend himself. The object flying towards him stopped a few inches from his face and he heard an indrawing of breath.

'Were you trying to knock me out with that pan, Miss Greenacre?'

Slowly, not making any sudden movements, he reached up and took the heavy saucepan from her hands. As his fingers wrapped around the handle they brushed against hers and he felt she was trembling.

'Did I give you a fright?' he said, a little softer.

'I was coming to get a drink,' she said, her voice sounding young and uncertain in the darkness. 'And then you started following me and I knew you weren't a servant because you came from outside rather than upstairs.'

'Ah. I was worried you were a burglar. I saw the candlelight.'

'From outside?'

'I couldn't sleep. Well, I haven't tried. It's a warm night and I was enjoying the cool air in the garden.'

Carefully he set the saucepan on the side and turned to face in the general direction of Miss Greenacre. He could tell by the tension in her voice she was still on edge and didn't want to scare her any more.

'Do you have a candle?'

'Yes, but I blew it out when I heard you coming downstairs.'

'I'm sure there will be a tinderbox somewhere. Can I have the candle?'

'Here.'

He reached out into the darkness, planning on taking the candle, but Miss Greenacre was a little closer than he had anticipated. His hand brushed against the cotton of her nightgown and he couldn't help but feel her warm skin underneath. She inhaled sharply and then clattered backwards, letting out a yelp as she bumped into one of the kitchen worktables.

'Not how women normally react to me,' he murmured, wondering if Miss Greenacre was so jumpy with all gentlemen or if it was just him she distrusted so much.

She thrust the candlestick out again and this time Robert was able to see the glint of the metal in the darkness. He took it and started to feel his way around the kitchen until he found the great fireplace and sitting on top the familiar shape of a tinderbox.

Half a minute later the candle was lit and a soft light illuminated the kitchen.

'There,' he said, glancing at Miss Greenacre. She was standing with her arms wrapped around her protectively despite the full-length cotton nightdress she was wearing. It buttoned up to below her chin and swept all the way down to her ankles. 'I'm not going to launch myself at you,' he said with a sigh. 'You're hardly my type.'

Her eyes grew wide, but he wasn't sure if it was from indignation or surprise at his comment.

'Hardly your type?' she repeated, her tone clipped.

'Exactly.' He knew he shouldn't, but she had been annoying him all day with her hostile looks, even when he had been doing his best to be conciliatory. 'You're the last person in this house that I'd consider for a little bit of late-night fun.'

'The last person?'

'Well, maybe that's a very slight exaggeration. Lord Mountjoy *really* isn't my type.'

'I dread to ask what *is* your type? No doubt buxom and eager to please.'

'You do have a poor opinion of me, don't you?' he said quietly. 'I always hesitate to speak for my fellow man, but I think men put much less stock in appearances than women do.'

Miss Greenacre snorted. 'Nonsense. You're saying that if there was a choice between a beautiful woman like Miss Huntley or a woman with a snaggle tooth and wandering eye, you'd choose the second?'

'No, of course there has to be an attraction between a man and a woman, but that attraction isn't based purely on what she looks like.

A physically beautiful woman with a horrible temperament instantly becomes less attractive.'

'And me? What makes me the least attractive person to you in this house?'

He paused, wondering if he had gone too far. The last thing he wanted to do was feed some deep-seated insecurity in this young woman. She had enough to battle with in her life without some man telling her she was unattractive.

'As I'm sure you have been told many times, Miss Greenacre, you are a very beautiful young woman. When you smile, properly smile, it lights up the room and I expect when you have your Season many young gentlemen will write you poems about your eyes and your hair.' He cleared his throat, glad of the flickering light in the kitchen. 'What makes you not my type is not your appearance or your personality. It is simply your clear dislike of me.'

'Oh.'

Even in the darkness he could tell this had shocked her. For a long moment she was silent, then she raised her eyes and met his, straightening slightly as she did so.

'Well, that's very clear,' she said eventually.

There was a tension in the air between them and Robert knew something needed to break it, but he wasn't sure what. If he walked away now, returned to his room and went to bed, things would be awkward between them when they next ran into one another.

'You wanted a drink,' he said quietly, 'What would you like?'

Miss Greenacre looked momentarily surprised at the change of subject, but quickly nodded in appreciation of moving on.

'I was going to see if I could heat some milk. I am struggling to sleep and when my little sisters find it hard to drop off I always make them a cup of hot milk.'

'You don't normally find it hard to sleep?'

She shook her head. 'I'm always busy at home, there's so much to be done, physical jobs, tiring jobs. Today I've sat in a cart, sat on my bed and sat for some very delicious but very lengthy meals, then sat in the drawing room after dinner.'

'Perhaps rather than a glass of milk you should try to round up some lost sheep or ask the estate manager if there is a fence to mend.'

'Are you mocking me, Lord Overby?'

'Good lord, no. I would never mock anyone who works hard, especially for the sake of their family.' He shrugged. 'But in lieu of hard physical labour let me find you the milk.'

He took the candle and rummaged through

the kitchen until he found the milk, brandishing the bottle in front of him. Miss Greenacre took it and then deftly set about lighting the stove, pouring some milk into a saucepan and heating it. It was hardly a culinary masterpiece, but Robert was impressed. Despite her talk about working on her family's land he knew the Greenacres still had servants and he had expected her to struggle to light the fire to heat the milk. She seemed comfortable in the kitchen, looking through the bottles of herbs and spices to find some cinnamon and dropping it in to the warming milk and repeating the action with a spoonful of sugar.

After a few minutes she took two mugs and poured in the milk, taking time to make sure the fire was out underneath the stove and everything was made safe. Then carefully she pushed one of the mugs towards Robert.

'Thank you,' he said, surprised she had thought to make him one, too. Perhaps it was her way of trying to make peace with him after their rocky start.

She took a long sip of hot milk and closed her eyes, smiling as she appreciated the taste.

'That's good,' Robert said.

'Isn't it.' She gave him a half-smile, but it

was better than her normal frown when she saw him.

'I should get to bed, or I'll frighten the other young ladies with my dark rings and pasty complexion tomorrow.'

She picked up the candle and then hesitated. 'Do you need a light?'

He shook his head, watching as she turned away. She was holding the candle out in front of her and as it shone back through her nightdress it made the cotton appear almost invisible, revealing the outline of her body underneath. For a long second Robert could see the curve of her waist and, as she walked, the pert roundness of her buttocks. A better man would have looked away immediately, a better man would have called out, telling her to hold the candle further from her body, but Robert found his voice stuck in his throat and his eyes refusing to blink.

Then she was gone, disappearing up the stairs and out of sight.

'Control yourself,' he muttered. '*That* is a very bad idea.' Even so, he knew the image of her walking away in a sheer nightgown was not something he would be able to easily forget.

Chapter Six

There was a hum of excitement as Charlotte made her way downstairs to join the assembled group. She was pleased to see what she was wearing didn't look too out of place. It had been a whole new experience going dress shopping with her mother a few weeks earlier. Over the last few years new dresses had been thin on the ground as they had needed to economise and channel their money into the shrinking estate. On a couple of occasions she had received bundles from her cousins—lovely, generous young women who'd sent her the dresses they had worn the previous Season. A lot of adjustment was needed for these to even vaguely fit as they were both tall and of bigger build than Charlotte, but she had ended up with some passable dresses.

Three weeks earlier, when they had received

the letter from Lady Mountjoy confirming she would be inviting Charlotte to stay, Charlotte's mother had arranged a trip to the dressmaker in Bath. They'd spent upwards of four hours choosing fabrics, taking measurements, discussing designs. The amount of money her mother had spent on clothes for her made her feel nauseated and could have been much better spent paying for food for their livestock. Her mother had disagreed.

'It's an investment,' Mrs Greenacre had said, her expression serious. *'An investment in your future. In all our futures.'* She'd gestured over at Charlotte's two little sisters, angelic-looking twins who had been only three months old when their father had died.

Pushing the thought from her mind, she smiled and joined the rest of the young women who seemed to be waiting for Lady Mountjoy.

'Charlotte, you're here,' Eliza said, linking her arm through Charlotte's and bending her head in close. 'I hear we're going to the Pump Room.' The young woman's eyes were sparkling with excitement and her cheeks were flushed. Here was someone who would thrive in London, who would appreciate the intrigue and opportunities of society.

'I have always marvelled at the architecture

in Bath. I love gazing at the beauty of the Corinthian columns and the crystal of the chandelier,' the quiet young woman, Miss Jane Ashbrook, said while pushing her oversized spectacles further up her nose.

'That's not the point of going to the Pump Room,' Miss Huntley said, a sneer curling her lip. 'Surely even you know that.'

'You're wrong.' Eliza rounded on Miss Huntley with a smile that didn't reach her eyes. 'Bath is considered one of the most beautiful cities in England and plenty of people visit for its charm as well as to take the waters.'

For a long moment Miss Huntley and Eliza stared at one another and Charlotte wondered where their animosity came from. They had only spent a short amount of time cloistered together, surely not enough for the two young women to develop such a dislike for one another.

'I for one won't be wasting my time gazing at columns and brickwork,' Miss Huntley said, 'and, Miss Ashbrook, I only have your best interests at heart when I suggest you don't either. We can't all go to London with Lady Mountjoy and she's hardly likely to select someone who would rather talk about buildings than the intrigue of the day.'

Eliza turned to Charlotte and Lucy and rolled her eyes, but thankfully they were saved from any further argument but the arrival of Lady Mountjoy.

She descended the sweeping staircase as if she were making a grand entrance at a ball, dressed in a purple and red dress that had more frills and feathers than Charlotte had ever set eyes on in her life.

'Ladies,' Lady Mountjoy said, bestowing her smile on them one by one, 'I trust you slept well and are excited about our trip into Bath. One of my favourite activities is to visit the Pump Room and take the water, as well as a nice cup of tea.'

'Drinking that foul water is entirely optional,' Lord Overby said as he sauntered into the hall from the direction of the library.

'Don't listen to my wicked nephew. The water is perfectly palatable and has no end of medicinal properties. Now we have the carriage, which will carry five at a squeeze, and Lord Overby has kindly volunteered to take someone in his curricle.'

Charlotte glanced at Lord Overby, remembering the truce they had seemed to have reached in the kitchen the night before. Still, she didn't particularly want to spend half an hour alone with him on his curricle. Quickly she fell into step with Eliza and made sure they were towards the front of the group as they left Rowlings Hall.

'Miss Greenacre, have you forgotten your bonnet?' Lady Mountjoy called and with dismay Charlotte realised all the other young women were properly protected from the sun by the brims of their bonnets. She didn't think Lady Mountjoy would approve of her explaining that she actually *liked* the feel of the sun on her face and quickly hurried back inside, hoping that one of the other young ladies might like the idea of riding with Lord Overby. He was an eligible bachelor, a very wealthy and influential man, although she knew the young ladies were all keen to impress Lady Mountjoy and that meant spending time with her, not her handsome nephew.

As she stepped back into the sunshine, bonnet pulled down on her head, she saw that all the young ladies were crowded around Lord Overby's curricle. It would seem she didn't need to worry. Even the quiet Miss Jane Ashbrook was admiring the brightly painted frame and the two strong horses that looked ready to dash at the slightest provocation.

'Why don't you take Miss Greenacre?' Lady Mountjoy said as Charlotte came to join them.

She opened her mouth to protest, but knew it would be unforgivably rude to refuse to ride with her hostess's nephew, especially when every other young lady would be eager for the chance.

'Miss Greenacre,' Lord Overby said, holding out his hand for her.

She placed her fingers in his and allowed him to help her up, adjusting her skirts around her as she sat on the padded bench.

'You look like you'd rather be wading through a crocodile-infested swamp,' Lord Overby commented quietly as he climbed up beside her. 'Is it my company you wish to avoid or my aunt's you covet?'

Charlotte snorted, her eyes widening as she realised how she'd responded to him and a hand flying to cover her mouth and nose.

'Your aunt seems to be a wonderful person,' she said, choosing her words carefully. 'Of course I would like to get to know her better.'

'But not to further your chances of going to London with her?'

'No.'

'You're not even a little tempted by the opportunity?'

'What could London possibly have that compares to Somerset?'

'The vibrancy of a city, the buzz of all those people coming together.'

'Sounds terrible.'

Lord Overby regarded her for a long moment. 'I concede there aren't many places in the world that I know that I love as much as these rolling hills, but London does have a certain charm of its own. Do you not have the urge to travel at all, to see what the rest of the world has to offer?'

Charlotte looked down at her hands. Six years ago, before her father had died, she'd had all sorts of dreams. The walls of her bedroom had been covered with hand-drawn pictures of India and Egypt, of temples in Greece and the canals in Venice. She'd been determined that she would not have the life of a provincial wife and mother. She was going to do something *more*.

Then the wasting disease had started to take her father, reducing him as every day passed, eating away at his once-healthy body until he looked like a living skeleton. When he'd died she had lost her innocence, her childhood and many of her dreams.

'When I was younger I used to pore over the

books my father brought back from London. There was a set of travel journals and each time my father visited a bookshop he would bring me back the next one.'

'What changed?'

Charlotte felt the tears well unbidden in her eyes and sniffed, turning away for a moment.

'I grew up,' she said harshly. It was the truth. Once her father had died she'd had to push away her dreams and focus on helping her mother keep their family afloat. It had seemed important to work hard and keep the estate and the farm, where her memories of her father were all grounded. Once or twice her mother had mentioned they should think about finding somewhere smaller and it had been Charlotte's emotional protests that had put that suggestion to bed. She couldn't bear to think of never walking the fields she had walked with her father again or never hopping on the stepping stones across the little stream. Everywhere on the estate had memories tied up in it, memories of happier times.

'Growing up isn't always all you think it will be,' Lord Overby said quietly.

'No.'

'Sometimes it can be hard to remember

the person you were before, when you were younger, more innocent.'

In her life everything was separated into before and after. Before her father's illness and after. Before she'd dreamed and laughed and lived a carefree existence. After, she and her mother had struggled and she'd lost a part of herself—it seemed as though it had died with her father.

If she thought rationally, she knew it hadn't been solely her father's death that had put them into a spiral of bad fortune. The farm had been struggling anyway, with a few bad harvests and poor years. They'd been just about coping and then her father had fallen ill and suddenly he wasn't able to run things any more. With his death their creditors had also been less forgiving, thinking her mother couldn't run the farm successfully on her own and they'd had to pay off the few small debts they had as well as trying to save the estate and farm.

She felt Lord Overby's eyes on her and sat a little straighter. She had never confided how she felt about the direction of her life changing and she wasn't about to start now with the man next to her.

He must have sensed her stiffness, her desire to move on. Giving a flick of the reins, he encouraged the pair of horses forward and Charlotte felt the lurch of the curricle as they started to move.

'Have you ever driven a curricle?'

'No. I drive the cart at home, although the horses we use for that are older and much slower than your pair.'

'I don't think there is anything more thrilling than racing at speed in a curricle. Although I did promise my aunt I wouldn't do anything to traumatise you.'

Charlotte scoffed. 'I hardly think you could traumatise me with a curricle and two horses.'

'That sounds rather like a challenge. It is a good thing I am too much of a gentleman to respond.'

'So we're going to trot along at a sedate pace like two grandmothers going for a Sunday afternoon ride.'

He turned and raised an eyebrow at her and for the first time she sensed a hint of fun underneath Lord Overby's stiff exterior.

'If we pick up the pace a little, can I be assured you will not hold me responsible if you do find it too scary?'

'I won't.'

He let out some of the tension in the reins and the horses responded immediately. They were on the wide, flat road heading out of the village, perfect for a racing curricle.

'We could go a *bit* faster,' Charlotte said, placing one hand on her bonnet to stop it flying off in the wind.

Lord Overby grinned at her and she was momentarily struck by how he was even more attractive when he smiled.

'Hold on,' he cautioned and let the horses go at full gallop.

Charlotte gripped the edge of the curricle with her free hand, loving the sensation of the wind whipping her hair and the fields speeding by on either side of them. She felt a wonderful freedom, as if for once she was not tied to anything, free to go wherever she wanted, do whatever she chose.

They continued at speed for a couple of minutes until the road narrowed and Lord Overby pulled on the reins to slow the horses.

'That was incredible,' Charlotte said, her heart pounding in her chest.

'Even the hundredth time you let the horses run it still gives you a thrill.'

She looked up at Lord Overby and saw the sparkle in his eyes, the colour on his cheeks, and realised he had enjoyed the ride as much as her. After a moment she became aware of how close she was sitting to him, how their legs were pressed together, how his arm brushed hers as he adjusted the reins. She felt her pulse quicken as he brushed against her again and had to stop herself from leaning in closer.

Trying to compose herself, she desperately sought to ignore the heat that was rising up inside her. Even if she tried to deny it she couldn't escape what she was feeling: attraction for the man she was supposed to dislike above all others.

It's purely physical, she told herself. He was a handsome man with a toned physique—many young ladies would feel this way when they were in close proximity to him, she was sure.

He seemed oblivious to her little crisis, adjusting his position every now and then and not even seeming to notice the contact between their bodies.

'Would you like to take the reins?'

'Me?'

'You said you often drove your horse and cart at home.'

'I do. You'd trust me with your curricle?'

He shrugged, handing the reins carefully to her and showing her how best to hold them. As he adjusted the position of her hands his fingers seemed to caress her skin and she felt an intense heat sweep through her body. Trying to focus on the horses and the instructions he was giving her was harder than it should be, and she felt her body swaying ever closer to his. 'Are you ready?'

She nodded, watching as he released her hands and let her be solely in charge of the curricle.

It took a moment for her to recover some of her equilibrium and to allow the exhilaration to sweep over her. Slowly she started to release the reins, to give the horses more freedom and urging them forward until it felt as though they were flying along the road. She successfully navigated a shallow bend and was able to keep the pace as they passed a carriage travelling in the opposite direction.

'That was incredible,' she said as she handed the reins back to Lord Overby after having to slow as they started to meet more carriages as they neared Bath.

'You're a natural.'

She beamed. Her first loves were animals, but she could definitely find space in her heart for high-speed races.

Chapter Seven

'Tell me everything about the curricle ride,' Eliza said as she hopped down from the carriage.

'It was rather thrilling. We went at such a speed and Lord Overby let me take the reins for a while. It is the fastest I've ever travelled, much faster than by ordinary carriage.'

Eliza looked at her askance for a moment. 'Yes, yes, yes, but what about Lord Overby?'

'Lord Overby?' Charlotte tried to feign innocence and hoped that her cheeks were not reddening at the mention of his name. The moment in the carriage, as overwhelming as it had been, was just that—a moment. A moment of madness, a moment where her spirits had been high and her judgement impaired.

'Yes, he is looking rather delectable today,

isn't he? And you got to spend a whole half an hour alone with the eligible Marquess.'

'We talked about the horses and the curricle.'

Eliza rolled her eyes and gave Charlotte a friendly tap on the arm. 'Really, Lord Overby is wasted on you. Think what an opportunity he presents to you to practise your charms on him if you get chosen to go to London.'

'I hardly think I'll be the one selected to go to London.'

'Don't be so sure. Although Lady Mountjoy says she can only take one, I spoke to her lady's maid, who informed me she is keen to take as many of us as possible with her for a Season. Can you imagine?'

Charlotte felt a wave of nausea overtake her. She'd been quite confident that she wouldn't be Lady Mountjoy's choice for a debutante to take to London when it was all five of them competing for one spot, but if Lady Mountjoy was planning on taking more, then it was less of a certainty she'd be left behind.

'Shall we go in?' Lady Mountjoy said, gathering the young ladies around her.

'I shall join you a little later,' Lord Overby said, nodding to his aunt before sauntering off.

Charlotte caught herself before she turned

to watch him leave, instead staring resolutely ahead.

With Lady Mountjoy leading them they entered the Pump Room. Despite the relatively early hour it was already busy.

For a moment Charlotte felt a little overwhelmed. Despite living in Somerset for all her life and visiting Bath on a number of occasions, she had never set foot in the Pump Room. Before her father had died she had been too young for an outing such as this and afterwards they had needed to conserve their money for much more practical uses.

'It's beautiful,' Jane Ashworth said, pushing her spectacles up her nose and looking all around her. 'It's so light and airy, yet so regal.'

'It does look fit for royalty,' Charlotte murmured and was pleased to see the quiet Jane Ashworth smiling at her.

'What do we do?' Eliza whispered, clearly not wanting to let on to anyone else that she felt as out of place as Charlotte.

'Shall we walk, ladies?'

Slowly, feeling a little bit ridiculous, Charlotte fell into step with Eliza on one side and Lucy on the other. In front of them Lady Mountjoy was arm in arm with Jane Ashbrook and Miss Huntley.

'Do we walk?' Lucy murmured, looking around her.

Charlotte tried not to stare at the other people in the Pump Room, slowly promenading around the perimeter. There were some chairs set out and a few of the older women present were sitting and talking rather than walking.

'I think we just walk,' Charlotte said, 'and then we drink.'

'Is it me or does anyone else find this a little bizarre?' Eliza asked quietly.

'When you think about it, a lot of what we do seems a little bizarre,' Lucy said.

'Like the obsession with balls and dancing,' Charlotte said.

'I love balls,' Eliza exclaimed a little too loudly, quickly dropping her voice. 'Don't tell me you don't, Charlotte. Balls are so much fun.'

'I'm not the best dancer.'

'You don't need to be,' Eliza said quickly.

'I agree with Eliza here,' Lucy said after a moment. 'Too much of the time the focus is on impressing people or finding a husband, but if you take that away and focus on enjoying yourself they can be so much fun.'

Charlotte had only attended a couple of balls and been to the Assembly Rooms in Bath a grand total of three times. On all occasions she'd felt out of her depth and couldn't wait to return home.

'Ah, ladies, who would like to try some of the healing water?' Lady Mountjoy had a glass in her hand and a young woman in the dark dress and white apron signifying someone who worked there was holding a tray of glasses.

They all dutifully took a glass and Charlotte peered at the clear liquid. It had a faint metallic smell to it and she had heard rumours that it had a distinctive flavour. She took a small sip first of all, letting the liquid rest on her tongue before swallowing it. It was cool with an underlying heaviness that she knew meant it had been pumped out directly from the natural spring.

'What do you think?' A low voice came from behind her. She felt an involuntary shiver of anticipation run up the length of her spine and she found herself standing a little taller as she turned around.

Lord Overby stood there, glass in hand, his face screwed into an expression of distaste, but all the same he took a second sip.

'There's a spring at the back of our house. It runs down to meet the stream at the edge of our property—' she took a deep breath and managed not to grit her teeth as she continued '—the stream that runs on at the border between our property and yours. This water tastes like the water when it first bubbles up from the spring.'

'Don't say that too loudly,' Lord Overby said with a smile, 'otherwise you'll have all the sick and infirm of Somerset coming to try out the healing properties of your spring.'

'It didn't help my father.'

'No,' Lord Overby said quietly, placing a hand on her arm. She stiffened for a moment, not expecting such consideration from him.

'I'm not sure the other young ladies are quite as accepting of the taste as I am,' she said, keen not to dwell on a memory that could reduce her to tears in public.

They looked around as Lady Mountjoy began to extol the healing properties of the water as the rest of the group took the tiniest of sips.

Charlotte suddenly felt the overwhelming urge to giggle and tried desperately to press her lips together to stop it.

'Something amusing you?'

'Just this, the whole situation. Your aunt is so generous, inviting us all to have the opportunity that may very well change our futures, and everyone is so keen, but as yet no one knows how best to behave around Lady Mountjoy. Would she prefer a young lady who is docile and does what she is told or a spirited young Miss who has a hint of rebellion?'

'Docile is a bit dull, isn't it?'

'But is docile the best path to London?'

'I know what path you will take,' Lord Overby said.

'You know no such thing.'

He raised an eyebrow at her and she felt a bubble of irritation at his superior expression. 'I told you yesterday you're easy to read, Miss Greenacre.'

She let out a quiet snort. 'You know nothing about me or how I will react.'

'That sounds like another challenge. Let me show you.'

'How?'

'Take a walk with me—my aunt won't mind. In fact, she's probably rubbing her hands together in glee, thinking she is matchmaking.'

'Me and you?' Charlotte said a little too loudly, aghast at the idea.

'Never fear, I have never been good at doing what others expect of me. You're safe.'

As she had the evening before when he had told her she was the last person he would think about in an intimate fashion, she felt a hint of disappointment. She might not want a London Season and she certainly did not want to be courted by Lord Overby, but she didn't want to be seen as unmarriageable.

'While we walk you give me some different situations you have found yourself in and I will tell you how I think you reacted. If I am right, I get a point—if I am wrong, then you do.'

Charlotte leaned her head to one side and considered. Lady Mountjoy was now regaling the other young ladies with tales of her youth in Bath society—she would hardly miss them.

'Fine. But you won't win.'

'And the prize—' for a moment Lord Overby paused and looked into her eyes, seeming to move closer even though his feet stayed in the same spot. Charlotte had the wild notion that he was going to suggest a kiss and felt a wave of desire roll over her, her eyes flicking to his lips and wondering what they would feel like on hers '—a favour to be claimed whenever the winner chooses.'

She tried to ignore the disappointment she felt as she nodded her agreement. The suggestion of a kiss would be ridiculous.

Taking his arm when he offered, she began to walk with him around the room, Lord Overby smiling in greeting to a few people he recognised.

'What's your first scenario?'

Charlotte made herself concentrate, made herself ignore the firmness of his body as it brushed against hers.

'A couple of years ago I was thrown from my horse when out riding a few miles from the estate. It was on a road, with carriages and carts passing much of the time. I'd sprained my ankle and hurt my wrist. What do you think I did and who do you think helped me?'

Lord Overby took a moment to think about it. 'There would have been plenty of people happy to help you home,' he said quietly, 'but I don't think you asked anyone. I think you got back up on to your horse, sprained ankle and all, and rode the uncomfortable few miles back home, probably sitting astride and giving passers-by defiant looks daring them to say something about your riding position.'

Charlotte remained quiet. It was unsettling how accurate he was with this description. She let out a little harrumph and chose another anecdote.

'When my little sister Lizzie was three she got stuck up a tree and refused to even try to climb down when I was supposed to be looking after her. What did I do?'

'First of all, I am forced to enquire whether your little sister is some sort of acrobat, climbing high enough in a tree at three years old that you weren't able to simply reach up and pluck her down.'

'She is a bit of a terror,' Charlotte said fondly.

'I wonder who she learnt her tree climbing skills from?'

She knew he was picturing her attempting to climb out of the window in the stables when he had first arrived at Rowlings Hall.

'You're stalling. What do you think I did?'

'I think you climbed up there with her and sat and talked for a while, then managed to coax her down when you climbed down by telling her you were off to do something more fun.'

'How…?' she spluttered.

'I told you, you're easy to read. And you have a strong personality. Strong personalities make it easy to predict what someone is going to do.'

'You make me sound like a caricature of a person.'

'I never said it was a bad thing. You're strong minded, strong willed. Many people would think they were positives.'

'Hmmm. Fine, I have one more for you and you definitely won't be able to guess this one.'

'Try me,' he said with a challenge in his voice. It reminded her that although Lord Overby was on his best behaviour, no doubt at the request of his aunt, he was a calculating man who liked to win.

'What did I do after I overheard you talking to my mother about buying our land?'

Lord Overby stiffened beside her and stopped walking, slowly turning to face her and waiting until she met his eye.

'And here I was thinking we were having a pleasant morning together, trying to put the past behind us.' His voice was low, dangerous, but despite herself Charlotte felt an illicit thrill, a pull of attraction to the man standing opposite her. He shook his head and for a moment she thought he was going to walk away without answering her. Instead he took a step towards her so they were standing a little too close. Charlotte felt her body sway involuntarily and had to tense her muscles to stop the movement before she made a fool of herself.

'Does that mean you don't have an answer?'

Lord Overby sighed and passed a hand through his hair, looking around as if wishing he was anywhere but here and with anyone but her.

'I suspect you made an effigy of me and proceeded to torture it in a number of inventive and cruel ways,' he said, meeting her eyes and daring her to challenge him. 'Now, if you will excuse me, I think I will take my leave.'

Charlotte watched him, feeling self-conscious as he strode away leaving her alone in the middle of the Pump Room. It had been an unnecessary question, she knew that. Lord Overby had been making an effort to be pleasant, to try to put her at ease when he knew she felt uncomfortable.

'You're a coward and a fool, Charlotte Greenacre,' she muttered to herself. She knew the reason she had asked him that question was to try to push him away, to distance herself from him because of the unbidden surge of attraction she was feeling. For so long Lord Overby had been a distant figure she had been able to blame for some of her family's misfortunes. He was the last person she should feel any desire towards.

Still, it didn't excuse that question.

Quietly she returned to the rest of the group, slotting in next to Lucy and silently thanking the young woman as she looped her arm through Charlotte's as if she had never been away.

Chapter Eight

In much better spirits than he had been an hour earlier, Robert sauntered down Gay Street back towards the hubbub of central Bath. He'd grown up in Somerset; he knew Bath much better than he knew anywhere else in the world. Sometimes walking through these streets transported him back to his youth. Those years when he was young and carefree, before he had married, before he had brought Amelia and all her drama into his life.

'Robert darling,' Lady Mountjoy called from outside the Pump Room a few minutes later. She and the young ladies were gathered round the carriage, looks of concern on their faces. 'We can't find Miss Greenacre.'

'What do you mean?'

'Well, after you left we went for tea and cake and then for a stroll around Bath. She was with us until ten minutes ago and then suddenly she wasn't.'

'Don't panic,' Robert said calmly, 'It's hardly a den of iniquity. It's Bath. She probably got distracted looking at some of the sights.'

'We did pass that beautiful street, a real example of perfect modern architecture, on the way back to the carriage,' Miss Jane Ashworth said earnestly. 'Perhaps she lingered a moment too long and didn't realise we'd moved on.'

'I will find her, Aunt, don't worry. You take the rest of the ladies back to Rowlings Hall and I will hunt down Miss Greenacre and bring her back in my curricle.'

Lady Mountjoy gripped his arm. 'Thank you, Robert, I can't bear to think of her out here alone. I gave her mother my word I would treat her as I would my own daughters.'

'We will be back with you at Rowlings Hall within an hour or so,' Robert promised.

He assisted the young ladies and his aunt into the carriage, trying to ignore the openly flirtatious look Miss Huntley gave him. After waving them off he looked around, wondering where a young lady like Miss Greenacre might take herself on an afternoon in Bath.

It was unlikely she would have popped into a dressmaker's or stopped to admire pretty ribbons in the window, and he doubted she would be overly impressed by the architecture as Miss Jane Ashworth had suggested.

'Animals,' he muttered to himself. 'That woman likes animals and nature.' Where would she find animals in the middle of a city?

Ten minutes later he had the answer.

'What do you think you're doing?' he growled as he strode up to her on the riverbank. 'My aunt is at her wits' end.'

'I got lost,' Miss Greenacre said, her face a little pale and drawn.

'Lost? A lost person doesn't just stand there admiring the cygnets.'

She looked at him, a flare of defiance in her eyes. 'I have been wandering the streets for the last fifteen minutes, but when I realised I was hopelessly lost I made my way back to where I last saw Lady Mountjoy and the others.'

'Fine. We should get back to Rowlings Hall.'

They walked in complete silence through the streets until they reached the Pump Room. It took a few minutes for his curricle to be brought round from the yard he had left it in and the horses to be fetched from the nearest inn's stables.

He offered a hand to Miss Greenacre, but

she ignored it, pulling herself up into the curricle and adjusting her position on the seat so she was as far from him as possible.

Robert vaulted up next to her and then urged the horses forward, moving slowly through the streets of Bath and only picking up the pace when they were a good distance from the city.

He could see Miss Greenacre shooting him glances every now and then, but whenever he turned in her direction she was looking resolutely forward.

'Right,' he declared, pulling on the reins. 'Enough.'

'What are you doing?'

He jumped down from the curricle and secured the horses and then reached up to help her down. She hesitated, but must have seen the determined look in his eye and slid from the bench of the curricle.

He'd chosen the spot on a whim, but the road was quiet and the fields on either side tranquil and bathed in afternoon sunlight.

'I think we need to clear up a misunderstanding,' he said quietly but firmly.

Miss Greenacre looked at him warily.

'Before yesterday I can count on one hand the number of times we have conversed,' he said, levelling a serious gaze at the young woman standing in front of him. 'Yet you have a poor opinion of me.'

He watched as she fidgeted a little, swaying from side to side in minuscule movements and scrunching her hands in the material of her dress.

'As far as I know I have never done anything to wrong you personally, yet you continue to treat me as though I were the devil himself. Is this to do with your father's land?'

'Our land,' she corrected him quietly. 'My father's, my mother's, my little sisters' and mine.'

'Your land,' Robert corrected. 'You said the other day you think I stole your land.'

'I do not accuse you of being a thief, Lord Overby, not directly, but you're not much better than one.'

He raised an eyebrow, forcing himself to keep calm. 'That is slander, Miss Greenacre.'

'You waited until my father was dead before you approached my mother to buy our land, knowing she was in mourning and inexperienced at dealing with the minutiae of running an estate.'

'I didn't approach your mother,' he said slowly, hoping that she would actually hear his words and believe him so they could finally move past this animosity. 'At least not to suggest I buy some of your land.'

'Yes, you did.'

He shook his head, ignoring her indignant tone. 'I didn't. After your father passed away I came to pay my respects and give my condolences to your mother when I returned from London a few weeks later. I told your mother to let me know if there was anything I could do for her to help at such a difficult time…' He shrugged. It had been an innocent act, one born out of neighbourly concern and nothing more.

'No,' Miss Greenacre said slowly, shaking her head. 'You came and told my mother you wanted to buy some of our land. No doubt you phrased it differently, to make her think it was an act of kindness, but you suggested it all the same.'

'You give your mother too little credit. She approached me a few weeks later with the offer of a parcel of land. She explained that without your father she would struggle to keep the estate running. If she sold part of the land, she would be able to keep the rest.'

'My mother wouldn't have done that.'

'It was a shrewd move. Rather than struggling with land she couldn't afford to work she sold it and used the proceeds to ensure the rest of the estate and farm remained viable.'

'No,' Miss Greenacre said stubbornly, but he could see the flicker of doubt in her eyes.

'I had no real interest in the land. My estate was already plenty large enough for my needs, but I had the funds and your mother was very frank in her approach to me. She said this was her best chance of keeping some of the estate for you and your sisters.'

'No.' Charlotte shook her head again. 'It wasn't like that.'

He fell silent, allowing her some time to take in everything he'd told her.

'Why didn't you say anything before?'

Robert shrugged. 'It wasn't my place. I didn't know what your mother had told you and what you'd pieced together yourself, but I thought it better that I be the villain, the one who had stolen the land from you, than your mother.'

'She never said much at all, just that you bought the land from us and we would be keeping the rest.'

Robert kept quiet and watched as she frowned and screwed up her face as if trying to reason through everything.

'You really did it to help us?' she said softly after a few moments.

'Yes. Your mother had three children and an estate to run, I couldn't refuse her request for help.'

'I should thank you.' She couldn't quite meet his eye as if remembering all the times she'd been rude or surly towards him.

'There's no need. Your mother thanked me at the time and I didn't do it for thanks.'

'I'm sorry,' she said, ever so quietly, but it was an apology none the less.

'Perhaps we can put some of this mistrust and animosity behind us now.'

'I'd like that.'

They stood a few feet apart, neither wanting to be the first one to move, the first one to break the moment of their truce.

Charlotte felt overwhelmingly foolish. All these years she had hated this man for something he hadn't done. All the times she had cursed his name, blamed him for the loss of their land, when in fact he had probably saved them from losing everything. She thought of her mother poring over the estate accounts, trying to make things balance in the months after her father's death. If she really thought back carefully, things had eased once Lord Overby had bought the parcel of land from them.

She glanced at him again, wondering at his calm demeanour. She supposed her anger towards him had barely even registered, it was insignificant in his world, but even so he had risen above it.

Closing her eyes for a moment, she wondered if she had got Lord Overby wrong in other ways. She thought back to that moment she had first become aware of their neighbour—as a young girl out on the estate with her father. She'd thought he had meant to dismiss her worth and what she could bring to the farm because she was a girl and not a physically stronger boy, but perhaps that had been her own insecurities rearing up, twisting his words into something that would confirm her suspicions that a son would be more useful to her parents.

'I suppose we should get back,' Charlotte said eventually. 'Lady Mountjoy will worry otherwise.'

'They won't have been home long. It takes much longer in the carriage than the curricle, but you're right, we should get back.'

She climbed up first, settling her skirts around her before Lord Overby jumped up beside her. The horses were raring to go, pulling at their bits and eager to pick up speed on the empty road. Lord Overby allowed them into a trot, but no faster, conscious of the bends in the road not too far away.

Charlotte felt on edge, as if she was filled with a nervous energy. Her skin prickled in the warm afternoon air and every tiny movement set her muscles tensing and contracting.

'Did you know your father used to have a curricle much like this?' Lord Overby said as he relaxed back on to the bench, allowing the horses to lead with only a small amount of guidance from him.

'No.'

'He and my father were friends. I can remember when I was a young boy, before you were born, they often raced their curricles. They would start at our front door and the course would be twice down the long drive and back.' He was smiling at the memory.

'*My* father?' Charlotte clarified, incredulous. Her father had always been a force of nature, but all the same she couldn't really imagine him young and carefree enough to race a curricle.

'Yes. From what I could tell he loved that curricle—and the horses, of course.'

'I wonder why he got rid of it.'

'I think it must have been soon after you were born.' Lord Overby shrugged. 'And curricles are not cheap to maintain, especially with a fine pair of horses like your father had. Although I don't know for sure. When my father died my mother sent me to live with various relatives until I was older and more interesting.'

Charlotte considered his words for a moment, trying to picture a younger version of her father, laughing and carefree as he raced his friend in their curricles. She was aware her father had endured a few bad years on the farm around the time when she was born—it had led to a few small parcels of land being sold off, so she supposed that was why he had needed to get rid of his curricle.

'How old were you when your father died?'

'Eleven.'

'Were you close?'

'Yes. Very. He was the sort of person who loved life, every experience, every person he met.'

'I'm sorry he died when you were so young.'

'These things happen. I still have one parent alive and determined to live life to the full.'

She saw the flicker of tension around his eyes and wondered what his mother must be like to cause so much stress to her son.

It felt odd to be sitting side by side with this man she had hated for so long, talking as if they were perhaps not friends, but certainly friendly acquaintances. Glancing up at him, she felt something stir inside her, a heat that washed over her body and threatened to overpower her. Charlotte had the urge to move towards him, to feel the firmness of his body against hers, to wrap her arms around him.

Silently she shifted in her seat, hoping he wasn't aware of the feelings that raged through her. It would be mortifying if he knew. Surreptitiously she looked over at him, drawn to the curve of his lips and imagining how his mouth would feel on hers. The desire took her breath away as she conjured up the warmth and intensity of his kiss and she felt a shiver run down her spine as she imagined those lips trailing lower…

'Is something wrong?' Lord Overby said, looking at her strangely.

She shook her head, not trusting herself to speak. With a steadying breath she banished all inappropriate thoughts of Lord Overby from her mind. He might not be the cad she had thought him, but that didn't mean she wanted anything more than a companionable truce with him, or with any man when she thought about it. Her focus was the estate and the farm and building something she could be proud of for her and her sisters in the future.

Chapter Nine

~~~

It was getting late when Robert saw Miss Greenacre sidle to the edge of the drawing room, glance around surreptitiously and then slip out of the door. She was an interesting character to watch, her face always alive with emotion, and she seemed to find it difficult to hide any thought that passed through her head. He'd seen her start to fidget about ten minutes ago and every so often had found his gaze wandering back to her even though he should be listening to what Miss Jane Ashworth was saying. Miss Ashworth was quiet and serious, sincere in her manner and interesting to talk to, but even so he felt his concentration slipping as his thoughts kept returning to Miss Greenacre.

'Would you excuse me, Miss Ashworth?' he said when their conversation trailed off for a moment. The young lady smiled and nodded, sitting back in her chair and not seeming to mind that he was leaving her on her own.

Quickly he strode from the drawing room, following the path he knew Miss Greenacre had taken. He told himself he was following her out of concern, but deep down he knew there was another reason, too. Although his aunt's estate should be a safe place, it was growing dark and away from the house anyone could wander on to the land unchallenged. It was a good reason to follow her, but he also had this compulsion to see her, to talk as they had earlier, to be in her company. Carefully he pushed the idea from his mind, not wanting to examine what it might mean.

She was heading for the stables, her evening dress billowing out behind her as she walked, and he marvelled at how quickly she could move. Most young ladies were taught to stroll slowly, to never look as though they were in a hurry, but Miss Greenacre darted everywhere as if her feet were on fire. Even so she moved gracefully, as only someone who was light on their feet and sure of their step could do.

After a moment she disappeared into the stables and by the time Robert had followed her in she was already down the very end, leaning over the last stall.

'Hello, my little darling,' she crooned as she bent down to pick Arnold up. The piglet snuffled and snorted in excitement at seeing her and wriggled in her arms.

'I should have guessed this was where you were creeping off to.' Robert spoke softly, so as not to make her jump, but she looked startled by his presence all the same.

'I'm surprised you didn't think I was smuggling another baby into your aunt's house.'

'*Nothing* would surprise me when it comes to you, Miss Greenacre.'

'I wanted to check on Arnold before bed, make sure he had everything he needed and wasn't too lonely.'

'Do pigs get lonely?'

Miss Greenacre shrugged. 'I think most creatures get lonely if left alone long enough. And pigs naturally live in groups, or at least the sows and their babies do.'

Robert stepped forward and gently stroked the piglet behind the ears, seeing how he stopped wriggling at the contact.

'I half expect him to start purring. He reminds me of a cat.'

'You're much more affectionate than a cat, aren't you, Arnold?'

Robert glanced up. He was standing too close

to Miss Greenacre, even though their bodies were separated by the piglet. All it would take was one step forward, one quick movement and she could be in his arms.

Desperately he tried to dismiss the thought, even though he knew it had been building all day. As they'd sat side by side in his curricle earlier he'd been acutely aware of Miss Greenacre's closeness, the warmth of her body, and ever since he'd had this overwhelming urge to pull her to him even if his rational mind knew it would be disastrous.

His eyes flicked to her lips, wondering what it would be like to kiss her. Everything about her was soft and he knew instinctively her lips would be like the most expensive velvet brushing over his.

Robert cleared his throat, stepping away. Miss Greenacre was a pretty young woman, but she was hardly the right choice for a dalliance. He wasn't that sort of man and Miss Greenacre was respectable even if her family had fallen on harder times of late. She wasn't the sort of young woman you could kiss in the stables and then both walk away, however much he wanted to in this moment.

Miss Greenacre looked up at him and for an instant he got the impression she wanted to be kissed. Her eyes were dark and inviting and her lips had parted ever so slightly. Her cheeks were flushed and he wasn't sure if he was imagining it, but he thought her breath was coming a little quicker, her chest rising and falling faster than it normally would.

Without thinking about the consequences, he moved back towards her, taking her elbows in his hands. He felt mesmerised, as if not quite in control as he looked down into her eyes.

He felt her sway towards him, her body brushing against his. Carefully he took hold of Arnold and placed the piglet back in his stall and then turned back to Miss Greenacre. She was still standing in the same position, arms held as if she were cradling something.

'Miss Greenacre...' he said, wanting to check he wasn't wildly mistaken in what she wanted.

'Charlotte,' she said with an upward twitch of her lips, 'my name is Charlotte.'

'Charlotte,' he murmured as he stepped towards her again and this time there was nothing to come between them. He took his time, his gaze dancing over her lips, her eyes, her body. Then, when he was certain he'd taken every last bit of her in, he kissed her.

Robert tried to remind himself it was likely to be her first kiss, tried to be slow and gentle, but as his lips met hers the desire consumed him and he couldn't hold back. A surge of yearning ripped through his body and he had the urge to tumble her down among the hay and run his hands over every inch of her body. He kissed her long and hard, feeling her entwine her fingers in his hair as he mirrored the movement in hers.

Her body was warm and soft under his hands and, as he trailed his fingers down her back, he felt her press her hips into his. Robert hadn't been celibate since the messy situation with his late wife, but he hadn't felt desire like this for a very long time.

Slowly, as if reluctant to break the connection between them, Charlotte pulled away, biting her bottom lip in a manner that made him want to kiss her all over again.

They were both breathing hard, both looking a little stunned at what had happened, and it was ten seconds before Charlotte would meet his eye.

'I'm sorry,' he murmured. Never had he felt more insincere in his life. He wasn't sorry he had kissed her even if he knew it wasn't right. 'I couldn't help myself.'

'A moment of madness,' Charlotte said quietly, but he could see the flicker of a question in her eye as if she were waiting for him to confirm why he had kissed her before showing her reaction to it.

'Exactly.' He gave a little half-smile and with great effort managed to step a few paces away.

Robert felt torn. Part of him wanted to pull Charlotte back into his arms and tumble her down on to the soft hay and damn the consequences, while the other part of him was screaming for him to make his apologies and leave as quickly as he could. The young woman in front of him seemed nothing like his late wife, but he had vowed never to become entangled with anyone else again. He'd learnt his lesson the first time. Amelia had taught him that you couldn't judge a person on their superficial traits. She had been charming for the first few months of their courtship, only showing her true personality after the wedding.

Pushing thoughts of his late wife from his mind, he turned his attention back to Charlotte.

'I should get to bed,' she blurted out, trying to edge around him. 'We have a busy day planned for tomorrow and I don't want Lady Mountjoy to think I'm not grateful for the opportunity to be here.'

He knew he should say something to her, to explain why he had kissed her, to check she really wasn't too upset by the situation, but before he could find the words she had slipped past him and fled the stables, leaving him feeling as though he had handled the whole situation poorly.

Charlotte waited until she had rounded the corner of the stables and then set out at a run, not caring if anyone saw her dashing through the gardens and across the lawn. There was still a hum of conversation from the drawing room, but she couldn't face going in and pretending that nothing had happened, nothing had changed.

Everything had changed. She couldn't quite believe Lord Overby had kissed her, but what had shocked her more was her reaction. She'd felt this deep, visceral pull, as if nothing could have made her step away from him no matter how bad an idea kissing him had been. Objectively she knew he was an attractive man and now she had realised he wasn't at all responsible for her family's bad fortune it was as though the barrier had been removed that blocked any attraction.

Shaking her head, she tried to banish from her mind the memory of his hands running down her back and caressing her skin through her dress. It was just a kiss, a moment that had got out of hand. She didn't want to desire Lord Overby, she didn't want to desire anyone, and he'd made it clear it was a mistake.

She scoffed. Of course it was a mistake for him. He was a marquess, one of the most influential men in the country, and she was the mildly irritating young woman who lived on the small estate bordering his.

'Charlotte, we missed you in the drawing room,' Lucy said as she appeared in the hallway as Charlotte began climbing the stairs.

'Did Lady Mountjoy notice?'

'I'm not sure. People have been drifting off to bed for the last twenty minutes, though, so perhaps not.' Lucy looked at her with her head on one side. 'Have you been outside?'

Looking down, she realised there were pieces of hay stuck to the bottom of her dress from the stables.

'I felt a little warm so took a walk over to the stables to see the horses.' She smiled, hoping her voice didn't betray the panic she was feeling. 'We have a farm and I always go and see the animals when I feel a little overwhelmed.'

Lucy came up and linked her arm through Charlotte's, seeming to accept the explanation. 'It is a little overwhelming, isn't it?'

Charlotte nodded as they walked together along the corridor to the bedrooms. They paused outside Charlotte's door and Lucy seemed to hesitate.

'May I confide in you, Charlotte?' she asked quietly.

'Of course—why don't you come in?' She was slightly taken aback by the request, but Lucy looked worried and it would be good to focus on something other than the barrage of thoughts about Lord Overby that was threatening to overwhelm her.

Charlotte sat on the bed and Lucy took the chair by the window, both silent for a few moments.

'Can I ask why you came here?' Lucy said, scrunching the material of her dress between her fingers.

Exhaling slowly, Charlotte wondered how candid to be with Lucy. She realised some of the young women here might have a desire to find out sensitive information that could be used against their competitors, but Lucy seemed sweet and kind, and she couldn't imagine she was trying to trap Charlotte into saying something she shouldn't.

'My father died a few years ago,' Charlotte said slowly. 'At home there's me, my mother and my two younger sisters. We have a small estate and a farm…' She paused, wondering how best to explain how she and her mother clashed over the prospect of Charlotte ever marrying. 'I want to stay and run the farm, take control of the estate, but my mother wants me to have a Season, to find a husband.'

Lucy nodded as if it were a familiar story to her.

'Although she would never say it I know my mother worries about me and what would happen if she were to pass away or fall ill. She doesn't like me shouldering all of the responsibility myself and often hints that if I were to marry a man who would look after me, and by extension the farm and everything I care for, it would be a weight off her mind.' Charlotte looked over at Lucy. 'How about you? Why are you here?'

'My father is a vicar and I am the eldest of three. Our family is respectable, but my parents do not have the funds to give me a proper Season, even though my father is keen I should marry well.' She shrugged. 'Lady Mountjoy knows my family through some of the charitable work she does with the church and she suggested I might like to come and be part of her gathering here to see if I would be suited to a London Season.' Lucy paused and Charlotte could see the young woman was weighing up saying any more.

'Is there something amiss?' Charlotte said gently.

Lucy nodded. 'I feel terrible, but I am deceiving Lady Mountjoy—I'm deceiving everyone.' It was a moment before the young woman composed herself enough to speak again. 'I am already engaged, you see.'

This wasn't what Charlotte had been expecting. 'Oh.'

'My parents do not know. No one knows, but we are terribly in love and plan to marry when he returns from the army. He was sent away before we could wed.'

'How do you know him?' Charlotte probed cautiously. Lucy seemed a sensible young woman, but she always felt suspicious of relationships where promises had been made, but not fulfilled. Every so often her mother would sit her down and tell her an awful story of some young woman who had believed a man's promises and was now ruined.

'We grew up together. He is the youngest son of Sir Thomas Weyman, who owns much of the land that is included in my father's parish. We have always been inseparable, but as we grew older we realised it was more than friendship.'

'Does his family know about your engagement?'

Lucy shook her head. 'His father would not approve. Sir Thomas has William's life mapped out for him and is planning an advantageous marriage to someone with a little more social standing and fortune than the local vicar's daughter.'

'But William is willing to go ahead and defy his father.'

'Yes.' She smiled softly. 'I know it sounds foolish, but William is a good man and I know he loves me.' She hesitated and then continued, 'I need to be patient and await his return.'

'I am sure Lady Mountjoy will understand.'

'She is a very kind lady, but I hate deceiving anyone. I do not want to deprive any of the other young ladies of the chance of a Season either, not when I will not be using the opportunities it would deliver.'

'When is William due to be home?'

'As yet we have no idea. It may be another year or it may be a few months.'

'Then keep quiet,' Charlotte urged her. 'Protect William and protect your chance of happiness. I think Lady Mountjoy will be understanding when the truth comes out and hopefully by then you will be married and settled.'

'That is what I thought, but every so often I have this little wobble, this little surge of guilt.'

'Of course you do, it's only natural, but you can't do anything to jeopardise your future. In a few years when you are Mrs William Weyman any deception on your part will be long forgotten.'

'Thank you, Charlotte, you don't know how good it is to talk. I feel as though I've been carrying this burden on my shoulders ever since we arrived here and it is lovely to actually confide in someone.'

Charlotte hesitated, wondering whether she should talk to Lucy about the kiss with Lord Overby, but quickly decided against it. Even though she couldn't stop thinking of the wonderful warmth that had jolted through her when Lord Overby's lips had met hers, she needed to put it from her mind. It had been a single occurrence, a mistake, something that was best forgotten and not shared with anyone else.

Tomorrow she would focus on getting to know the other young ladies here at Rowlings Hall and do her very best to avoid Lord Overby and by the next day it would be a thing of the past, put from both their minds.

Chapter Ten

There was a flurry of activity around her as Eliza dashed into the room armed with a box of multicoloured ribbons. It was impossible not to be swept up in the excitement of everything with the energetic young woman around.

'I wonder if any of the gentlemen will be handsome?' Eliza mused, whipping out a pale pink ribbon from the box and holding it against Charlotte's hair. 'I do hope they're interesting. I could tolerate a man with more questionable looks as long as he is engaging.'

'I can't wait to dance,' Lucy said, a dreamy look in her eyes. 'I do so love to dance. I've heard Lady Mountjoy has decided that since we are among friends she will allow the musicians to play a waltz.'

Charlotte grimaced. She wasn't a terrible dancer—her mother had taken great pains to make sure she knew all the steps to the most popular dances and she was quite graceful in her movements. Her problem was lack of practice. She hadn't attended enough dances, hadn't accepted enough invitations to have mastered the art of dancing while also interacting with someone else. She still needed to count her steps, to think about what way she needed to turn and which foot to step on to first. It meant she was absolutely fine if she was allowed to dance in silence, but as soon as someone started to talk to her she struggled.

'I heard Lord Gillingham is attending,' Lucy said as she helped Eliza pin the ribbon into Charlotte's hair.

Eliza's eyes widened a little. Lord Gillingham was thought of as one of the most eligible bachelors in England. He was young, wealthy, attractive and apparently charming as well.

'I doubt Lady Mountjoy has been able to persuade Lord Gillingham to attend her little gathering. Perhaps a grand ball in London, but I can't see he would want to spend his week helping debutantes become polished before entering London society,' Charlotte said.

'Lord Overby is here,' Eliza said quickly. 'And he is dashing and influential.'

'Lord Overby is Lady Mountjoy's nephew.'

'Lots of young men would find some excuse to stay away,' Lucy said quietly. 'I think it shows what a kind man Lord Overby is that he agreed to help his aunt, and us, like this.'

At the mention of Lord Overby Charlotte was sure her cheeks flushed, but luckily the other two young women were too busy pinning her hair to notice. Despite her best efforts to put the Marquess from her mind it felt as though everything had reminded her of him today. Even her dreams had been plagued by the man.

Charlotte shifted in her seat at the memory of the dreams. Twice she'd woken in the night, hot and bothered, writhing in the bed. She hadn't been able to recall all the details, but there had been flashes of memory, images that made her whole body tingle and feel as though it were on fire.

At least she hadn't seen him all day. Lord Overby had been absent at each meal and she hadn't even caught the slightest glimpse of him as they had strolled around the garden in the morning and played cards in the afternoon. No doubt he would be at the ball this evening but there would be plenty of other people to act as a barrier between them. She probably wouldn't even have to speak to him.

'I can't wait,' Eliza declared, 'Even though it

is only going to be small, it is the first taste of what a London Season would be like.'

The ball this evening at Rowlings Hall included the five debutantes and the five gentlemen Lady Mountjoy had invited to be part of their little gathering. It would be intimate, but there was a buzz of excitement all the same among the young ladies.

'There,' Eliza declared, standing back and looking at her work in the mirror. Charlotte moved her head from side to side, admiring the pretty way they had styled her hair, so a few loose strands curled and framed her face. She would never have been able to achieve anything near as intricate herself.

'Shall we go down?'

All three of them stood for a moment, smoothing down their dresses and checking everything was straight in the mirror before they left the room.

The house was large, but even from upstairs Charlotte could hear the music from the string quartet. It sounded delicate and enticing, as if calling them down to dance.

The ballroom was beautiful with hundreds of candles lit and placed around the room. A huge crystal chandelier hung in the middle and the light from that made the room sparkle. Fresh flowers had been placed in huge vases and at one end was a table laid out with drinks and delicious-looking food, if any of the guests became peckish after dancing.

Lord and Lady Mountjoy stood at the entrance of the ballroom, welcoming everyone in. Lord Mountjoy as usual seemed to stand a step back from his wife, allowing her to take the lead on talking to everyone as they arrived, but Charlotte could see the quiet way he took everything in, his eyes assessing each person, his head tilted ever so slightly to one side as he listened intently.

'Miss Greenacre, Miss Stanley and Miss Freeman,' Lady Mountjoy said, a smile breaking out on her face. 'Perfect, now we wait for Miss Ashworth and we have everyone. Once Miss Ashworth is here I will make the introductions.'

Charlotte's eyes darted around the room. She told herself she wanted to see who was here, to take a look at the other guests, but she knew deep down she was looking for *him*. There were two gentlemen deep in conversation over by the musicians and another two standing and talking to Miss Huntley, but nowhere was Lord Overby.

All at once she felt a rush of relief and disappointment. The nervous tension that had been building up inside her had nowhere to go, no release, and she was hoping to get this first meeting over and done with. If she could face him and not make an utter fool of herself, not throw herself into his arms and beg to be kissed again or stutter and stammer and signal to everyone exactly how she felt, that would be a success.

'Miss Ashworth,' Lady Mountjoy greeted the last of their group as she entered the ballroom, looking around nervously. 'Wonderful, now everyone is here shall I make the introductions?'

Like a duck gathering her ducklings, she shepherded the four young ladies over towards the gentlemen. The men all turned politely to their hostess, stopping their conversations as they approached.

'Gentlemen, may I present Miss Ashworth, Miss Stanley, Miss Freeman and Miss Greenacre.'

Charlotte lowered her eyes and sank into a shallow curtsy as she was introduced.

'Ladies, I have the pleasure to introduce you to Mr Hardman, Mr Willis, Mr Prentis and Mr Farthington.'

The gentlemen inclined their heads in turn as they were introduced. Two were young and fresh-faced—they looked not much older than Charlotte. Mr Prentis was older, his hair streaked

with silver and his bearing more rigid and serious. The last man, Mr Farthington, sat somewhere in the middle, age-wise, and looked as
nervous as Miss Ashworth to be included in the
festivities. He kept swallowing, making his Ad-
am's apple bob up and down, and Charlotte had
to force herself not to stare it was so hypnotic.

'Good evening, Miss Greenacre,' a low voice
said into her ear, making her shiver with the
proximity. She spun round, aware she was ignoring the gentlemen she had been introduced
to, but unable to stop herself. 'Or may I still call
you Charlotte?' He spoke quietly, as if ensuring
no one else could overhear them.

Against her better judgement she nodded.
Her name sounded dangerous coming from his
lips, dangerous and seductive.

Her eyes flicked over Lord Overby and she
felt her breath catch in her throat. There was
something compelling about him tonight. He
was dressed in a well-fitted evening jacket and
crisp white shirt that seemed to highlight his
physique. The pale blue cravat was perfectly
knotted at his neck and his whole appearance
made the rest of the gentlemen look a little dull
and dowdy.

She'd expected him to avoid her, to stay away
unless they were surrounded by others, but here

he was, seeking her out as soon as he had entered the ballroom. Charlotte tried to start listing all the reasons she should politely exchange a few words and then move on, but she knew it would be impossible.

'Have you had a pleasant day, Lord Overby?' She desperately tried to make her tone light and airy, to try to hide from him how much their kiss had affected her, but as soon as the words left her mouth she knew her pitch was at least an octave higher than usual.

'I have, thank you...' He paused and leaned in closer. She caught a hint of his scent, something warm and enticing she couldn't quite place, but made her want to bury her face in his neck all the same. 'If I am calling you Charlotte, then you must call me Robert.'

'Robert,' she murmured, testing the name out on her tongue. In all the years she'd known him she hadn't been aware of his first name. It felt deliciously illicit to be calling him by a name that only his closest companions would use.

'I'm sure my aunt will announce the dancing soon. Do you like to dance, Charlotte?'

Before she could temper her response she screwed up her nose and shook her head. Robert threw his head back and laughed, making some of the other guests turn and look.

'It's not that funny,' she muttered.

'No other young woman vying for a place to accompany my aunt for a London Season would admit she didn't like dancing. Next you'll be saying you find balls a complete bore.'

She pressed her lips together.

'You *do* find balls a complete bore.' He laughed again.

'Stop it, everyone is looking.'

'Does it matter? We're not doing anything we shouldn't.' For an instant his eyes darkened, and she knew he was remembering the kiss they'd shared the day before. 'Not at the moment anyway.'

'I don't find balls a complete bore,' she said, trying to relax her clenched jaw. 'At least I haven't been to enough to make up my mind what I think of them.'

There was something different about Lord Overby—Robert, she corrected herself—tonight. Something glittering and dangerous. A hint that he might do something outrageous in the middle of the dance floor and not care who was watching. Charlotte knew she should make her excuses and get as far away from him as possible or risk being taken down with him, but she seemed unable to take that first step.

'Would you like to dance now?' His eyes

contained a challenge that she knew she would have to accept.

'No one else is dancing.'

'Someone has to be first.'

'Everyone will stare at us.'

He shrugged. 'That doesn't bother me. Unless you are too scared?'

'Your taunts are useless on me.'

'Dance with me,' he said again, offering her his hand.

The musicians had finished the piece they were playing and, seeing Charlotte and Robert approach the dance floor, they struck up the first notes of a waltz. Charlotte tried to swallow, but her throat was too dry. It had to be a waltz, the most intimate of dances. The dance where she would be held close, forced to look into Robert's eyes. It would be impossible to ignore their proximity.

It was as though she were in a dream. Her feet moved of their own accord and even though she hated it when people stared at her she allowed Robert to manoeuvre her to the centre of the ballroom. Her pulse quickened as he placed his hand on her lower back and ever so gently pulled her towards him.

Closing her eyes for a moment, she began to

count, trying to remember when to turn, feeling her body stiffen as she started to panic.

'Charlotte,' he murmured in her ear, 'look at me.'

After a moment she obeyed, opening her eyes and looking up at him.

'Do you trust me?'

Slowly she nodded, realising it was true. She might hardly know this man, but she did trust him.

'Then let me lead you. I promise I won't let you stumble.' He looked sincere and she knew instinctively he wouldn't let anything happen to her.

Charlotte made herself relax. She let the tension flow from her muscles and allowed herself not to think, but to respond to the gentle guiding pressure of Robert's hands. He was a very good dancer. It was clear from the easy, confident way he stepped, always exactly in time with the music and his relaxed posture. At first as they began to whirl around the ballroom Charlotte felt all eyes on them, but after a minute everyone else faded into the background and it was as though it was just the two of them.

Robert smiled down at her, his eyes sparkling. Charlotte felt her heart catch in her chest and suddenly she realised what all the fuss was about. She realised why all the young ladies of her acquaintance dreamed about dancing and balls. If this was what they experienced, then she could understand why they lived for the next social event.

All too soon the last notes of the waltz swelled and then faded and Charlotte was standing in the middle of the dance floor in Robert's arms. Even though she knew she should step away, even though she knew she should be the one to break the connection, she couldn't seem to bring herself to do it. A few more seconds and people would begin to whisper, but even if her reputation depended on it she couldn't have moved.

Luckily Robert drew in a ragged breath, gave her a smile and then stepped away and bowed.

'Thank you for the dance, Miss Greenacre,' he said, offering her his arm. Briskly he walked her back to the gaggle of young ladies, depositing her firmly in their midst.

She expected him to linger, but instead he gave her a stiff bow and retreated to the other side of the ballroom to where two of the gentlemen stood.

Charlotte felt bewildered. She knew they had shared something they shouldn't have, especially not in front of all these people, but there was no need for him to abandon her quite so brusquely.

As she tried to concentrate, all she could think about was the man in her peripheral vision, stalking from group to group in the ballroom, but making sure he never got anywhere close to her again.

Chapter Eleven

'You look like you need a drink,' Lord Mountjoy said to him quietly as he tried to concentrate on something Mr Farthington was saying.

Robert had hoped no one would notice his slip in composure, but he'd known if it was going to be anyone it would be his uncle. Lord Mountjoy was a quiet man, influential in Parliament and wealthy both in monetary terms and in happiness. He loved his wife, loved his children and tried not to get involved with any of the minor squabbles between his tenants or local landowners.

'Is it that obvious?'

'My dear wife is engrossed in trying to coax Miss Ashworth out of the corner, I don't think she will notice if we slip away for a few minutes.'

Without waiting for Robert's answer, the

older man turned away and headed out of the ballroom, making his way to his private study down the hall. He closed the door firmly behind Robert once inside, shutting out all music from the ball.

'How are you, my dear boy?' Lord Mountjoy asked him as he poured out two generous glasses of brandy. His uncle seemed to forget he was no longer the lanky youth who had spent many happy summers making mischief with his cousins around the estate of Rowlings Hall. Lord Mountjoy held up a hand before Robert could answer, quieting the reply on his lips. 'How are you *really*?'

Robert let out a long, deep sigh. 'I'm fine,' he said slowly. 'Much better than last year and a hundred times better than the year before,'

'But you're not happy?'

'Life is satisfactory. I have good friends, more income than I could ever spend. A quiet life, but quiet isn't bad.'

'How long has it been now?'

Even though the question was vague Robert knew exactly what Lord Mountjoy was asking.

'Two years, three months and four days.'

'Ah. Still counting.'

'Not intentionally.' The date of his late wife's

death was imprinted on his brain and it seemed impossible to be rid of it whatever he tried to do.

'You have been out of your official mourning for some time,' Lord Mountjoy said, taking a long gulp of brandy.

'Yes.'

'But life is nowhere near approaching normal.'

Robert shook his head. Right now he couldn't imagine his life being normal ever again.

'Robert, you know Letitia and I love you like a son?'

Robert nodded his head. They'd cared for him better than his own mother in his hour of need.

'Then may I speak bluntly?'

'Of course, Uncle.'

'Amelia was awful. She was an awful wife and an awful person. She would have quite happily ruined your reputation and made you the topic of gossip and scandal for her own selfish desires.'

'I thought we weren't meant to speak ill of the dead.'

'I find I cannot bring myself to have a single charitable thought about your late wife,' Lord Mountjoy said. He was animated, lively, more so than Robert had seen him in a long time and he felt a swell of affection for the older man who had guided him through so many of life's obstacles.

'She was awful,' Robert murmured.

'She was awful and then she died.' Lord Mountjoy paused, giving Robert a sideways glance. 'I would hate for her to be successful in ruining your life from the grave, Robert.'

Robert let his head fall back on to the chair and for a moment closed his eyes. Sometimes he hated to admit how much the drama Amelia had brought into his life had shaken him, derailed him from the sure course he'd been on. He'd been doing everything right. He'd inherited the title from his father when he was young, but after university he had focused on making his mark in Parliament and ensuring everything thrived on the estate in Somerset and the two others he owned in Devon and Suffolk. After he'd become confident everything was running smoothly he'd started to look for a wife. It hadn't been all practical. Of course he had wanted an heir, but he'd also wanted a companion, someone to share his life with.

'She hasn't ruined my life.'

'You are shying away from the chance of happiness, keeping yourself remote, separated from everything.'

'That's not true. Last year I attended some of the Season's events and I am always present in Parliament for the important debates.'

Lord Mountjoy gave him an assessing look and Robert was surprised by the sudden change of tack when the next words came out of the older man's mouth.

'Miss Greenacre seems a very pleasant young woman.'

'I'm not sure pleasant is the right word to describe her. Although she certainly isn't unpleasant. Spirited, perhaps, or energetic.'

'You have spent a little time with her?'

'She lives on the neighbouring estate. I barely knew her before a few days ago. What has Miss Greenacre got to do with anything?'

'You smile when you look at her, Robert.'

'Sometimes she amuses me.'

'You don't know how rarely we've seen you smile these last couple of years.'

Letting out a loud sigh, he allowed the image of Charlotte to linger in his mind. Whenever he thought of her there was a spark of heat that ran through this body, exciting and energising him. And that kiss… Quickly he cleared his throat. His uncle didn't need to know how it felt when he had kissed her.

You're more than base instincts, he reminded himself.

It was what he'd been trying to tell himself all day, that it didn't matter if he wanted to pull Charlotte into his arms whenever he was near her; it was merely a passing attraction, something that could be controlled. He'd been trying to prove that to himself this evening, trying to prove that even if he held her close in his arms he could control the desire that flooded through him. It was why he'd asked her to dance, why he had pulled her to the dance floor even when no one else was dancing. It hadn't quite worked on this occasion, but he wasn't ready to openly admit that yet.

'One day I hope you might be ready to trust someone again,' Lord Mountjoy said.

Robert shook his head. He couldn't imagine the day he would feel comfortable enough to let someone else get close enough to share every aspect of his life with.

'I know you have a wonderful marriage, Uncle, but I truly think you are in the minority among the *ton.* There is so much focus on family connection, on duty and money and status, that I wonder how many marriages are functional, let alone happy?'

'Then go against the norm, discard the option

of marrying for a hefty dowry and instead open yourself to the possibility of marrying for love.'

This time Robert didn't shake his head. His uncle didn't need to know he was so jaded from his marriage that he didn't think it was possible to love again.

Lord Mountjoy took a long gulp of his drink, then toyed with the glass, seemingly trying to decide whether to say more.

'I don't wish to become overly sentimental, Robert,' he said slowly, 'but Letitia and I are aware of the impact your childhood had on you. We know that nothing can substitute the love of a parent even though we tried our very hardest to show you we loved you like one of our own children.'

Robert inclined his head. His childhood had been happy until his father had died. Until then it hadn't seemed to matter that his mother was distant, absent most of the time. Only when his father was gone did he realise quite how his mother struggled to care for him, even with the multitude of tutors and servants to do most things.

'You did treat me as one of your own children.' He smiled at the older man. 'You still do.'

'We think of you as one of our children.' Lord Mountjoy reached over and patted him on the hand. 'I don't want you to think that it is something to do with you, this unluckiness in your relationships. Your mother was flighty and Amelia downright terrible, but it is not your fault that neither of them stayed.'

Robert closed his eyes. He didn't really like talking about it, even though he knew his uncle made a very legitimate point. Lord Mountjoy was observant and shrewd and in a few short sentences had burrowed down to the fear that followed Robert every time he thought about moving on with his life.

He was confident in his success in Parliament, as a landowner and in his management of his estates and wealth. He had a few good friends who he regarded as close as family. The only thing he was uncertain of was his ability to form the closest of relationships. It was the one area of his life he hadn't been successful in.

'I think,' Robert said slowly, choosing his words carefully before continuing, 'I am best keeping away from any romantic complications.' He held up his hand to ward off any further protestation from his uncle. 'At least for now. I am sure my feelings will change, but two years and three months is not all that long to be a widower.'

Lord Mountjoy leaned over and clapped him

on the shoulder. 'I will leave the matter alone now,' he said with a smile. 'But if you ever need a sympathetic ear, remember that both I and your aunt are always here for you.'

'Thank you.'

Standing, Lord Mountjoy threw back the last of his drink and set down the glass on the desk. 'I had better return to the ball before Letitia notices I am gone.'

'I shall return soon.'

'Yes, those debutantes need a sympathetic dance partner.'

Left on his own, Robert closed his eyes for a minute and then let out a loud exhale of breath. He knew he was lucky to have his aunt and uncle care for him so much, but sometimes it would be easier if he was left to try to ignore his problems rather than have someone else gently point them out.

He knew he found the idea of letting someone close again difficult, knew that deep down there was this deep-rooted feeling that anyone he cared for would leave him, but that didn't mean he wanted to do anything about it. His plan was to carry on exactly as he was for the next few years and hope that at some point the pain and heartache from the last couple of years would just subside and go away.

Sitting up in his chair, he gulped down the last of his brandy, telling himself he would enjoy thirty more seconds of peace before he returned to the ballroom with a smile on his face.

'You don't sound happy,' a soft voice came from behind him, making him jump in his chair. He hadn't heard the door open and close again or any footsteps entering the room.

'You shouldn't be here,' he said without turning round.

'Because it is Lord Mountjoy's study? Or because I shouldn't risk my reputation being alone with you?'

'Both.'

'You were acting strangely. I was worried about you.'

A short, sharp laugh escaped him and he turned to see a frown on Charlotte's face.

'We barely know one another, Charlotte, how would you know if I were acting strangely?'

'All the other times we've conversed you've seemed normal in your manner—tonight you were acting differently.'

'Perhaps I do not like balls.'

'If that is it, then I wish you goodnight. I am sorry for intruding.'

He was behaving like a cad and he hated himself for it. She'd turned and walked back over to the door by the time he was up out of his seat and close enough to reach out and stop her.

'I'm sorry,' he said, placing a hand lightly on her arm. 'I'm in a foul mood and I have no right taking it out on you.'

She seemed to soften at his honesty and let her hand drop from the door handle.

'Although you really shouldn't be here alone with me.'

'I announced loudly I had stepped on my dress and was going to find some pins to mend it to anyone who would listen. I don't think anyone will come looking for me.'

'Still, you shouldn't be here.'

Her eyes flicked up to his and a spark of desire flared and danced between them. Robert found himself wishing she was someone else, someone it would be perfectly acceptable for him to engage in a passionate affair with. A jolly widow, perhaps, someone who wasn't a complete innocent.

Ever so quickly he saw her tongue flick out and wet her lips and he knew she was feeling the same turmoil inside as he was.

'I can leave,' she said, although she made no move towards the door.

'You'll have to stay now, or everyone will know you were lying about your dress. If anyone comes in, you'll have to hide behind the curtain.'

Charlotte smiled at that, relaxing a little, and allowed him to guide her to one of the chairs.

'Why are you in such a foul mood?'

The question took him by surprise. Not many people of his acquaintance were as direct as Miss Greenacre.

Before he could stop himself he answered her completely honestly, 'I wanted to kiss you when we were dancing.'

'Oh.' He saw the colour flood to her cheeks and was fascinated by the speed at which her blush reached all the way to her ears. 'And that put you in a foul mood because...?'

'I asked you to dance to prove to myself I could desire you but not act on it, not be affected by it, and then all I could think of was kissing you in front of all the other guests and damn the consequences.'

'Ah.'

Robert had to suppress a grin. It was worth laying his emotions bare to see Charlotte lost for words for once. Normally she had a sharp observation for every situation.

'I did wonder why you were glaring at me from across the ballroom.'

'I wasn't glaring,' Robert said, although he half suspected he had been.

'I thought I'd done something to upset you.'

'You have.'

'Oh.'

Robert gripped the arms on his chair. It was hard sitting so close to her, talking about kissing her and wanting to reach out and pluck her from her armchair and pull her into his lap. He thought she would fit perfectly perched on his knee and then he could take his time exploring the soft skin of her neck, her shoulders and get lost in the sweetness of her lips.

He coughed. This was ridiculous. Never before had he been so tempted by someone he so clearly could not have. She was an innocent, a debutante—even one kiss had been too much of a risk.

'I don't see what *I've* done,' she said eventually.

Quickly he stood, knowing if he sat so close to her for any longer he would act rashly and they would both be lost to the desire that was flowing between them. Striding over to the unlit fireplace, he rested his elbow on the mantelpiece and took a few deep breaths. He wasn't a green boy. He was a man of many years' experience in the world. If he told himself he couldn't have Miss Greenacre, that should be the end of the matter.

He groaned as he felt a soft hand on his shoulder. The little minx was now standing directly behind him. It was as if she were purposely trying to torment him, although he knew she was the least wily person of his acquaintance.

Slowly he spun, noting how Charlotte's hair glinted in the candlelight, begging to be touched. She looked beautiful, the pale pink of her dress shimmering and catching the light and the flush of colour in her cheeks making her look full of life. Her lips were parted slightly, her chest rising and falling quicker than it should.

The last time he had kissed her he had been in charge, initiating it and guiding her through. This time she stepped up to him, raised her hands to his face and reached up to kiss him ever so gently on the lips. It was barely more than a brush of skin against skin, but Robert felt something burst inside him and all the raw desire and pent-up attraction flooded out, threatening to consume them both. He gripped her tightly, pulling her body against his, and then tangled his hand through her hair, not caring he was messing it up. In that moment all rational thought was lost and he felt as though they were spinning out of control, just the two of them, leaving everything else behind.

Charlotte let out a low moan of pleasure as he began kissing the soft skin of her neck and over her collarbone and then she gasped as he pushed down the neckline of her dress. She pulled him backwards and together they tumbled into one of the armchairs, his body pressed against hers. He felt her dress bunch up beneath them and his hand brushed against the delicate skin of her thigh.

Robert froze, his whole body stiffening. He looked down at Charlotte and then quickly scrambled back, aghast at what they'd nearly done.

It took Charlotte a few seconds to also come to her senses, but when she did she leaped up from the chair frantically trying to pull up her dress.

Robert felt sick. If they'd gone any further, if they'd continued down the path they'd begun, he would have been forced to marry her. Charlotte was not the sort of woman you could dally with and then leave. He closed his eyes as the world spun around him, hoping she wouldn't expect a proposal now.

'I'm sorry,' he said stiffly, standing back

while she continued to tug at her dress to try to get it looking respectable again.

'Don't apologise,' Charlotte said and he could see the tears in her eyes.

'That shouldn't have happened.'

'I know.'

'It was my fault, of course. I hope you can forgive me.'

'It wasn't your fault,' she said quietly. 'Not entirely.'

Robert felt some of his anxiety ebb out of him. She hadn't immediately demanded he marry her, and she was taking responsibility for the kiss even though it was he who should know better.

He stepped towards her, pausing as she flinched a little at his touch. 'Your hair was caught,' he said as he unhooked it from underneath a lacy bit of dress.

'I need to go,' Charlotte said, her eyes wide darting from side to side in panic.

'Take a moment,' he cautioned, but before he could say any more she was out of the door and had disappeared down the hallway.

Robert sank back into one of the armchairs and put his head in his hands. Never before had he been overwhelmed by desire like that, never had he been unable to trust himself to act sensibly. He was lucky Charlotte didn't think like some other young woman, didn't immediately look at him and see a future as a marchioness; otherwise he could be in real trouble.

Chapter Twelve

Charlotte smiled absently at Mr Farthington as he proceeded to tell her all about his noble ancestors and vast family tree. It was hard to tell whether he was trying to impress her or whether it was a subject he thought would interest anyone. In truth, she was pleased to have a little time to her thoughts. Mr Farthington didn't seem to need any encouragement except the odd murmur or smile—he had been talking non-stop for fifteen minutes now and showed no sign of ceasing.

Her mind wandered to the evening before and the encounter with Robert in the study. She'd known it was foolish to follow him in there, but despite her better judgement she had found herself making an excuse to slip from the ballroom anyway. So many times she'd pondered whether she'd secretly hoped they might kiss, whether it was what her subconscious mind had wanted, but she really didn't know.

Closing her eyes for an instant, she remembered the passion of his kiss, the way he'd tumbled her back into the chair as if he couldn't resist her. She had been powerless to stop him, not because of any physical factors, but because she had been so caught up in the moment. She'd wanted more, almost screamed with frustration when he'd pushed himself off her and stepped away. Shaking her head, she wondered what that made her.

'Are you unwell, Miss Greenacre?' Mr Farthington asked and she opened her eyes to find him peering at her anxiously.

'It's the heat,' she murmured, fanning herself with her hand. It wasn't even particularly hot, but she knew it was an acceptable excuse for a young woman sitting in the sun.

'Let me fetch you a glass of water,' Mr Farthington said, springing to his feet.

'Thank you.'

Mr Farthington hurried back towards the house and Charlotte let out a little sigh. Only seconds later Eliza came and flopped down in the chair Mr Farthington had vacated.

'I thought he was never going to stop going on,' Eliza said. 'Well done on getting rid of him.'

'He seems pleasant enough, but I hope he doesn't expect me to remember anything he's spoken about.'

'I wonder why so many men think we enjoy listening to their dull interests. Or can't tell when someone is stifling a yawn.' She looked across at Charlotte quickly. 'Have you recovered from last night?'

'Oh. Yes, thank you. I'm not sure the life of a debutante is the one for me. I felt a little overwhelmed after a few dances.'

'I thought it was wonderful. The music, the candlelight, the beautiful dresses. Imagine the ball last night but with twenty times the people in attendance. It would be heavenly.'

'I hope Lady Mountjoy chooses to take you with her, Eliza, I think you would shine in the ballrooms of London.'

'I hope we can go together, Charlotte. You, I, Lucy and even quiet Jane Ashworth.'

'Good morning Miss Greenacre, Miss Stanley,' Mr Hardman said as he came on to the patio brandishing a set of Pall Mall mallets. 'I don't suppose you'd like to join Mr Willis and myself in a game of Pall Mall?'

'What a wonderful idea,' Eliza said, jumping to her feet and taking a mallet from Mr Hardman. 'Come on, Charlotte, it'll be fun.'

'I don't think I've ever played before.'

'It's easy,' Eliza said as she took an experimental swing of her mallet. 'You hit the ball through the metal hoop in the fewest number of hits.'

'I'll set out the course,' Mr Hardman said. 'We have four mallets so if anyone else would like to play perhaps we can be in teams.'

'Splendid. I'll ask Miss Freeman and Miss Ashworth.' Eliza hurried off to where Lucy and Jane were sitting, and Charlotte watched as she quickly rounded them up and herded them towards the lawn.

Charlotte picked up one of the mallets, feeling the weight of it in her hands. It was satisfyingly heavy and had a good swing to it.

'There's six of us now,' Eliza said as she returned with the two other young women. 'I think I saw Mr Prentis in the library. Let me see if I can find two more gentlemen to join us.'

'Or Miss Huntley,' Mr Hardman called after her.

A minute later Eliza returned with Mr Farthington, who was holding a glass of water in his outstretched hand, and Lord Overby. Charlotte received the water gratefully and took a great gulp, ensuring she manoeuvred herself to be as far away from Lord Overby as possible.

'Wonderful,' Eliza said, clapping her hands. 'Now we are eight.' She glanced around calculating. 'Mr Farthington, why don't you partner with Miss Ashworth? Mr Hardman with Miss Freeman, Lord Overby with Miss Greenacre and I will be with you, Mr Willis.'

Charlotte opened her mouth to protest—the last thing she needed was to spend any more time with Robert—but quickly closed it again. Eliza would want to know why and she didn't fancy explaining about their illicit kiss in the study last night.

'I've set out the course,' Mr Hardman said. 'To make it more fun I've spread out the hoops a bit. First back to the centre point wins.'

'Splendid,' Eliza said.

'Splendid,' Lord Overby muttered and Charlotte was surprised to find him quite so close behind her. He hadn't acknowledged her yet, hadn't even glanced in her direction. She felt a surge of irritation and swung the mallet more firmly backwards and forward, narrowly missing his toes.

'Perhaps I should hold that,' he said, gripping the handle and trying to take it from her.

'No, I'm fine. Why don't you choose the ball?'

'Fine.' He stepped forward and selected the

red ball, then handed it to her. 'In case you hit it into the undergrowth.'

'Why do you assume it'll be *me* who loses the ball?'

He raised an eyebrow, properly looking at her for the first time. 'You forget I spent much of my youth here. That Pall Mall set saw me and my cousins through some long summers.'

'Oh.'

They walked stiffly side by side towards the starting point.

'Ladies first,' Lord Overby said as Charlotte held out the mallet to him.

The other three couples had already taken their turns as Charlotte lined up the mallet with the ball. She swung, hitting the ball squarely with a satisfying thud, but as soon as the mallet hit the ball she knew it had been far too hard, far too powerful. The red ball looped up into the air, soaring across the lawn and landing in a large bush that separated the grass area from the formal gardens.

Lord Overby looked at her and raised an eyebrow.

'Don't say anything,' she said, pointing at him with the mallet.

He held out his hands in front of him and she could see he was trying to suppress a smile.

His first of the day if his previous scowls were anything to go by.

'The red ball wasn't such a bad idea after all,' he murmured as he led the way over to the bush.

He rummaged around in the bushes for a while with Charlotte standing right behind him.

'I think you're looking in the wrong place.'

'You're welcome to come in here and take over.'

'Surely a red ball isn't that hard to spot?'

Robert stepped back and motioned for her to take his place and she ducked under the low branches and tried to peer in through the dense foliage.

'Maybe it went all the way over the top,' he said, disappearing from behind her.

'I didn't hit it that hard.'

A minute later he reappeared, brandishing the ball in one hand, and placed it just outside the bush for their next shot.

'It's your turn, Overby,' Mr Hardman said. 'We've taken ours.'

Charlotte watched as he lined up the shot and expertly tapped it just right to send the ball sailing through the first metal hoop.

'What a shot,' Mr Willis said, clapping his hands.

Charlotte begrudgingly had to concede it was

a very good shot and had put them back on par with the other couples.

Everyone else took their turns, progressing across the lawn. This time Charlotte tapped the ball far too lightly and it travelled only a few inches.

'We're looking for a perfect level of force somewhere in between your last two hits,' Robert said after the ball rolled to a stop.

'Thank you. I think I could have worked that out by myself.'

'Just trying to be helpful.'

They were far enough away from the other couples to be afforded a degree of privacy, but Charlotte could see Robert did not wish to talk about anything other than the game.

Robert's shot took them through a second hoop despite it having to travel halfway across the lawn, but meant Charlotte was left with the challenging job of skirting the rose beds.

'My aunt loves those roses,' he murmured in her ear as she lined up to take her turn.

'You're not helping.'

'One wrong move and you could destroy hours of work carefully cultivating the rose bushes.'

'Perhaps I will do better if there is nothing distracting me,' she said through gritted teeth.

'Imagine one poorly hit ball and it could upset her enough to send you straight back home…' He paused and then stepped in even closer. 'Forget I said that. I know how much you don't want to be here and I wouldn't want to be involved in the destruction of my aunt's beloved plants.'

'Go away,' Charlotte said, tapping his toes with the mallet as she swung backwards.

Robert stepped away, but she could still feel his eyes on her back and it made her unable to concentrate properly. Normally her co-ordination wasn't bad and although she had never played a game like this before she did pick things up quickly. The only thing that could be putting her off was Robert standing behind her all the time.

'I blame you for this,' she muttered as she hit the ball.

It soared past the roses and back to a wider spot on the lawn.

'Good shot,' Robert said, taking the mallet from her. His hand brushed hers and she jumped back as if she had been shot.

She knew he had noticed her reaction, but chose to ignore it, striding off to take his turn after the other gentlemen.

'You turn, Miss Greenacre.'

There were only two more hoops to pass through now, but they were a fair distance apart. Her confidence increased by the last successful hit, Charlotte lined up for her next turn, experimentally swinging the mallet to ensure it would result in the hit she wanted. On the backswing it went a little too low and she groaned as she felt the wood make contact with the ball, sending it hurtling in the wrong direction.

'Wow,' Robert said as he peered off the lawn and into the garden. 'You like to make this difficult, don't you.' He turned to the others. 'Carry on without us. We'll join back in when we find the ball.'

He didn't wait for her as he headed into the formal garden, weaving this way around the paths, every so often stopping and crouching to look into the denser foliage.

'It wouldn't have come this far,' Charlotte muttered, hoping she was right. She didn't like being bad at things, especially something like this. She felt with all the time she spent outdoors she should be able to master hitting a ball through a series of metal hoops.

'The first time I played with my cousins I smashed one of the windows in the garden room,' Robert said as he used the mallet to gently pull back the bedding plants. 'Luckily Lord Mountjoy had it all sorted before my aunt ever found out. She loves that jungle.'

'You actually smashed a window?'

'The balls are quite hard and we were playing far too close to the house.' He shrugged. 'I practised a lot after that.' Robert smiled in remembrance. 'My cousins teased me mercilessly for months after. They still do if they see me with a mallet.'

Charlotte was surprised at the domesticity of the image that sprang to mind. Of course Robert must have had a childhood like everyone else, but she couldn't quite imagine him running wild in the grounds of Rowlings Hall.

'Ah,' he said, stopping and straightening. 'I can see where the ball is.'

'Where?' She followed his gaze and groaned as he pointed at the small pond that sat in the middle of the garden. It was a few feet in diameter with a stone wall around the edge and now in the height of summer the surface was covered in waterlilies.

Sure enough, as she peered in through the murky water she could see the flash of red among the green of the pond weed. Typically, it was right in the middle of the pond, not an easy reach from the side.

Perching on the edge of the stone wall, she leaned over, wondering if her arms were long enough to reach in and pluck the ball from the bottom.

'You'll fall in,' Robert said, already turning away.

'You don't mean to leave it there?'

'It's in the middle of the pond. As much as I would appreciate a cool dip on such a hot day, I am not about to do it in my aunt's garden pond.'

'I think I can reach it.'

'It's a Pall Mall ball, Charlotte, it isn't worth it.'

She ignored him, stretching out. If she leaned all the way back, her fingers were hovering over the ball on the top of the water. Surely it wouldn't be too hard to dip her hand in and grab it.

'Don't do it,' Robert warned.

'I think I can…' She reached back a little further and plunged her hand into the water, gasping at how cold it was on her skin.

'Charlotte,' Robert said sternly and out of the corner of her eye she saw him take a step back towards her.

'Just a little more…' Her fingers brushed against the smooth, painted surface of the ball and for an instant it was in her grasp. It was slippery and she had to scrabble to hold on to it. Charlotte felt herself begin to topple as she leaned a little too far and with a shout she lost her balance completely and plunged into the pond.

The shock of the cold water against her skin was enough to make her forget to keep her mouth closed and she inhaled a lungful of the murky water. She plunged to the bottom of the pond and scrabbled around for an instant, in complete panic, before strong hands grasped her under the arms and hauled her back up to the surface. As soon as she was out of the water she began spluttering and coughing, trying to catch her breath by taking in long gasps of air.

Robert was holding her, half-submerged in the pond, the water up to his thighs, his arms wrapped around her in support. He must have plunged in without hesitation when she'd fallen, he'd been there so quickly. Now they were both dripping wet and filthy.

'I'm sorry,' she said quietly once she had her breath back.

She didn't get to hear what he thought for at that moment the rest of the group who had been playing Pall Mall rushed around the bushes into the formal garden, all looking taken aback by the scene in front of them.

'What on earth happened?' Lucy asked, recovering first and rushing towards them.

'I fell in the pond,' Charlotte said quickly. 'Lord Overby was kind enough to fish me out.' She felt a bubble of laughter building up inside her and had to work hard to suppress it. They would think her hysterical if she suddenly started giggling.

'Perhaps we should get you out of the pond,' Lucy said as she reached the stone wall.

Charlotte glanced quickly up at Robert, who was still holding on to her. He slowly released her arms, but kept hold of one of her hands to steady her across the pond until she reached the edge. Mr Farthington and Mr Willis reached out to assist her down and within a few seconds she was back on dry land, dripping with pond water.

'Let's get you inside and cleaned up.' Lucy took charge, whisking her away from the shocked faces. As they rounded the bushes to head back across the lawn Charlotte glanced back to see Robert hopping down from the wall surrounding the pond. She couldn't tell if he was angry with her by the expression on his face, but she knew at some point they were going to have to clear the air. It wasn't healthy to ignore the intimacy they'd shared the evening before or anything that had happened since, but perhaps she would focus on that once she was warm and dry.

Chapter Thirteen

Robert had half expected Charlotte to ignore his invitation. If it had been for a stroll through the grounds or a hand of cards, she probably would have, but he hoped the temptation of riding one of Lady Mountjoy's fine horses would be enough to bring her out of where she was hiding in her bedroom.

He murmured to the horses as he waited, both bridles in his hand, having told the grooms not to wait. He enjoyed the repetitive process of saddling a horse and often did it himself before he took Washington out for a ride.

'Good afternoon,' Charlotte said as she came into the stables. She was dressed in a riding habit that fitted her snugly about the waist. It didn't look as new as the other dresses she had been wearing over the last few days, but he guessed she had chosen comfort over style when it came to riding.

'I wasn't sure you would come.'

She shrugged, not meeting his eyes, and stepped up to the horses, stroking first one, then the other. Her manner was gentle but firm and he saw the love and respect in her eyes for the animals she had only met a few moments earlier.

'This is Canute, one of my aunt's fastest horses. I thought you would like him to ride, but if you would prefer one of the others then we can saddle them for you.'

'No, Canute is perfect, thank you.'

He led the horses out into the stable yard, leading Canute to a mounting box for Charlotte to step up on to.

'I hate these things,' she muttered, pulling at the skirt of her riding habit.

'Oh?'

'At home I often wear breeches if I go out riding on our land. It means I can mount myself and ride astride—it's much more comfortable.'

Robert was struck by an image of her shapely thighs and buttocks clad in a pair of tight breeches. He coughed and tried to force the picture from his mind, but he knew it was impossible.

Reluctantly she climbed up on to the block and he helped her get settled on the saddle before handing her the reins and vaulting up on to Washington's back.

'Are you ready?'

'Yes. Where are we going?'

'I thought we could explore the parkland.'

Charlotte didn't say anything more, but allowed him to lead her out from the stable yard and along the path that led away from the gardens. After a couple of minutes they had reached the open grass. The hills were gently undulating on the land that made up the Mountjoy estate, with some steeper sections a little further away from the house.

'Are we really just out for a ride?' Charlotte said after a few minutes of sedate riding.

'No.' Robert thought it best to be direct with her. 'I think we need to talk, to discuss what has happened these last few days, and we need to do that away from the house.' A frown crossed her face, but she didn't disagree. He pressed on quickly. 'I think I need to make my position clear.'

'Fine, but I want to ride first.'

Before he had a chance to answer her she sat up straighter in the saddle, adjusted her grip on the reins and urged Canute forward into an easy canter. For a second he marvelled at how quickly she found her rhythm with a new horse and how Canute, a notoriously headstrong stallion, was responding to her.

It was refreshing to feel the wind whipping against his face after a few days of mainly indoor activities. He loved to ride, loved to be out in the open air and, even though he dreaded the conversation he needed to have with Charlotte, for a few moments he allowed him to enjoy his surroundings.

Even though she didn't know the estate well, Charlotte chose a good route, guiding Canute away from the house towards the lake a couple of miles distant. It was a beautiful spot with a folly overlooking it and surrounded by weeping willow trees. Not once did Charlotte stop or look back to check he was still following and he wondered for a moment about her independence. From the little she'd told him and snippets of gossip from the neighbours they shared he knew she didn't go out much, but preferred to spend her time on her family's farm and small estate. It was an unusual life for a woman of her social status, but it sounded like one that suited her well.

He caught up with her at the edge of the lake

as she slowed Canute to a walk, shielding her eyes from the sun as she looked out over the water.

'It's beautiful here,' she said, not turning to look at him.

'Yes, it is. It was where I would always come if I wanted a little privacy when I was young.'

'The water looks so clear, so refreshing.'

'It's cold. There's a stream that feeds it with crystal-clear water, but it means the temperatures are icy even in the heat of the summer.'

'You've been in?'

'Many times. I learnt to swim in this lake.'

She turned to look at him now and he saw the flicker of interest in her eyes.

'My cousin Tom is four years older than me and he hated being the only boy in the house with four sisters. Even a cousin four years younger than him was better than that. Every summer when I came to stay we would race from the house to the lake and the winner was the first one to make it to the other side. After a couple of years when I nearly drowned he took pity on me and taught me how to swim properly.'

'You'd run all the way from the house?'

'Yes. It never seemed that far.' He shook his head wistfully. 'It'd probably half kill me now.'

He watched as she looked over her shoulder in the direction they'd come and then assessed the distance across the lake.

'You're considering it, aren't you?'

Charlotte smiled, the first proper smile he'd seen from her all day.

'It does sound like a challenge.'

'I'm not sure my aunt would approve of me corrupting one of her debutantes by encouraging scandalous behaviour.' The truth of his words crashed down on both of them and he knew the time had come to discuss the kisses they'd shared.

'Do we have to talk about this?' Charlotte asked, closing her eyes and turning her face away.

'Yes, we do.'

'Fine. Can't we say it was a mistake, promise we'll keep away from one another and carry on?'

'I owe you an explanation, Charlotte.'

She sighed, but turned back to face him.

'Sit with me for a while.' Quickly he dismounted and looped Washington's reins over the branch of a tree. Then, holding a hand out, he helped her down.

Once they were settled on the bank of the lake, Robert tried to decide what would be the best way to phrase what he was about to say next.

'I'm aware I compromised you, Charlotte, that I put your reputation in jeopardy.'

She sat completely still beside him and everything about her screamed she didn't want to have this conversation.

'I am also aware that the gentlemanly thing to do, the right thing to do, is to ask you to marry me.'

Her eyes widened at this and Robert realised the thought hadn't even crossed her mind. She really was naive in the ways of society. It was a relief in many ways, but he knew he needed to have this conversation all the same.

Charlotte squirmed, having to force herself to stay seated. She wanted to get up, to stride around, anything but sit and listen to what Robert wanted to say to her.

The kiss had been wonderful, *in the moment*, but now she wished they could forget about it. It was clear from how Robert was acting he didn't want anything more from her and she certainly was not looking to marry anyone. Robert was attractive and her pulse quickened every time he came near her, but she was wise enough to know the difference between desire and love.

Desire could be suppressed. Love wasn't to be argued with.

'I don't want to marry you,' she said quickly, hoping that wasn't where he was headed. For an instant she pictured her life as his wife. It wasn't an altogether horrible image, but she knew if she married *anyone* her life would change beyond recognition. No longer would her main focus be the estate and farm and no husband, not even the most liberal and progressive, would allow her to ride around the farm dressed in men's clothing doing the job of the master of the estate.

'Good. You're a lovely young woman, Charlotte, and attractive, too. I took advantage of you.'

'No.' She shook her head, but she knew most wouldn't view it that way. He was the man of the world, the one with the experience. Robert was her first kiss whereas he'd probably kissed dozens of women.

'I haven't felt like that for a very long time,' he said, looking out over the lake into the distance. 'It caught me off guard and I went too far.'

Charlotte remained silent, wondering if he was thinking about his late wife or some other woman in his past. She felt the first stirrings of jealousy and quickly pushed them away. He was not hers to feel jealous over.

After a few moments of silence he turned and regarded her, his eyes flicking over her face as if trying to read something.

'I don't know if you have heard much about my marriage,' he said quietly, his expression troubled. 'For a while it was one of the favourite subjects of gossip among the *ton*, but the details may not have reached you in rural Somerset.'

She shook her head. The gossip hadn't reached her, not until this trip to Rowlings Hall.

'I married my wife, Amelia, five years ago. We were introduced by a mutual friend and within weeks I was completely besotted with her.' Robert closed his eyes and she knew he was being transported back to those first exciting weeks of courtship. 'She was from a good family fallen on hard times, although estranged from most of them. Looking back, I realise that should have been a warning sign.'

Charlotte didn't say anything. She was fascinated by this glimpse into his past life. Robert seemed so sure of himself, so confident and competent that she couldn't imagine him letting his heart rule his head.

'Within a month I'd proposed and within three we were married. Straight after the wed-

ding I began to realise what a mistake I'd made.'
He took a deep breath and then glanced over at
her. 'You don't need to know all of the horrific
details, but we were very unhappy. I felt she was
unreasonable, and she felt I was. Amelia em-
barked on an affair and announced her intention
to start a life with her lover.' He grimaced and
shook his head. 'I agreed to divorce her, despite
the difficulty it would bring me in my position
in Parliament. By this point I was glad I would
soon be rid of the constant fighting.'

She didn't have much to compare it to. Her
parents' marriage had been a little dull but contented and various aunts and uncles seemed
similarly satisfied in their choice of spouse.
Being married to someone who actively wanted
to cause you upset sounded horrific.

'A week after I agreed to the divorce she told
me she was pregnant.' He must have seen the
absolute shock on Charlotte's face as he quickly
shook his head. 'We hadn't been intimate for
months, so she was clear it was not my child.
Two weeks later I received a letter telling me
she'd had complications in the pregnancy and
had passed away.'

'That must have been such a shock.'

'At first I didn't believe it. I insisted on seeing

her…' He trailed off, his head dropping down to his hands.

'I'm so sorry, Robert.'

'It was a difficult period.' He looked at her before he spoke again, giving her time to register everything he'd said. 'I didn't tell you for sympathy—I don't think I deserve any sympathy. The situation was awful, but there were many ways I could have acted better. I told you so you would understand.'

Slowly she nodded her head. She knew he was a highly private person and wouldn't have shared this episode from his life lightly. Nor was she conceited enough to think he confided in her because he liked her so much. His story was an explanation, a gentle warning.

'I understand,' she said, wishing she could get up and run, but knowing after what he'd told her she needed to sit this out until the end.

'I like you, Charlotte, and I respect you. Even though we do not know each other well, if I were to marry anyone I think you would be a good choice.'

'But you don't want to marry anyone,' she said quietly.

'I do not plan on marrying again. Ever. I am sorry for kissing you and I am sorry I cannot do the right thing by you and marry you, but

I hoped by explaining everything you might understand.'

'I understand and I meant what I said earlier. You don't have to worry because I don't want to marry you either. I might not have as compelling a reason as you, but I am not looking for a husband.'

His eyes searched her face and eventually he nodded as if satisfied.

'Good.' He stood and held out his hand to her. Allowing him to pull her to her feet, she dropped his hand as soon as she was standing. Even though she understood why he had felt compelled to bring her out here and make his situation clear, it felt as though he was assuming she was someone she wasn't and that hurt.

'I never even thought of trapping you into marriage,' she said quietly.

'That's not what I thought, Charlotte.'

'It's what you were worried about. Not *all* women want to marry you, Robert. Not all women want to get married.' She said it softly, aware he had unburdened himself to her, but still needing to say her piece. 'Thank you for sharing your past with me, but you really don't have to worry. No one will ever know about the kisses. I will not entrap you in marriage.'

Before he could say anything more she strode

over to the horses and untied Canute, struggling up into the side saddle by herself, having to use the branch of the tree to help pull herself up.

'Charlotte, wait,' Robert called after her as she turned Canute's head and urged him forward.

She ignored him, feeling the sting of tears in her eyes. Willing herself not to cry, she cantered off, wondering why she felt quite so hopeless, quite so upset.

Chapter Fourteen

Wondering if she would respond to a note a second time, Robert checked in both directions and then slipped the piece of paper under Charlotte's door. He felt awful that he'd upset her. It hadn't been his aim, but he could see he'd been blinkered in his approach. She'd told him she wasn't going to pressure him to marry her because of the kiss and then there he was, insisting she understand his reasons for not marrying. He'd felt as though he'd needed to tell her, but now he could see it had been condescending.

Quickly he walked away, not wanting anyone to see him lingering outside Charlotte's door. Neither of them needed any gossip or speculation associated with them.

As the day wore on he wondered if she had somehow left the estate without anyone knowing. She had pleaded a headache the night before at dinner and, as far as he knew, hadn't emerged from her room today. It would be just like her to have locked the bedroom door from the inside and scrambled down from the first-floor window.

There was a gnawing guilt building inside him and as he stood on the terrace behind the house he wondered how he might properly apologise to Charlotte if she refused to see him again. The idea of their short-lived friendship being over made him feel more upset than he should be, but he quickly pushed away this thought before he was forced to analyse it.

'Something smells good,' Charlotte said as she stepped through the terrace doors.'

'Mrs Williams has a soft spot for me. When I asked her to put a basket together she rather outdid herself.' He paused, waiting for her to meet his eye. 'Thank you for coming.'

'Until a few minutes ago I hadn't decided whether I would.'

'I'm glad you did.' He offered her his arm and after a moment's hesitation she took it. Carrying the sizeable basket with his other hand, he led her through the gardens and out into the parkland.

'Where are we going?'

'There is a beautiful little spot down by the river. I thought we could head down there.'

They walked mainly in silence over the undulating hills, but Robert was pleased to find there was nothing awkward about it. He knew Charlotte could hold a grudge and he had given her something to be truly annoyed about, but she was quiet and contemplative and not overtly angry.

'Here,' he said as they reached the banks of the river. Tied up was a sturdy little rowing boat. It was watertight even though it must be twenty years old—he and his cousins had often messed about on the river in it.

'We're going in that?'

'Unless you don't want to.'

She was down the bank and scrambling into the boat before he could even hold out a hand to assist her. With a grin he placed the basket on the boat and climbed in after her. Charlotte grabbed hold of the oars and set about positioning them.

'I suppose you want to row.' She held out the oars reluctantly.

He raised an eyebrow. He hadn't even considered she might want to row the boat, but he wasn't sure why he was so surprised.

'If you would like to, I have no objection.'

'Oh, good. My mother says it's terribly unladylike to do physical things like this when there is a man around to do it for you, but where is the fun in sitting back and letting someone else do everything for you.'

Robert settled back at the front of the boat after untying the rope that held it tethered to the bank. He watched in silence for a while as Charlotte found her rhythm, pulling the oars through the water with surprising strength. All those hours working on her family's farm had made her physically fit and soon the boat was speeding through the water.

'Thank you for agreeing to come out with me,' Robert said softly as she slowed a little.

'I almost didn't, but the chatter in the house is all about our little stay in Bath and I thought I might scream if I had to talk any longer about who might be in attendance at the Assembly Rooms and what dresses everyone was going to wear.'

'Ah. So it was a case of good timing rather than my persuasive letter-writing skills?'

'Exactly. Although this is a nice surprise. I like being on the water.'

Robert traced a pattern with his finger using the little droplets of water on the side of the boat. The wood was rough and splintered in places and he tried to remember if once the boat had been painted.

'I'm sorry for yesterday,' he said quietly.

For a moment Charlotte stopped rowing, allowing the boat to drift in the current as she run her hands over the ends of the oars and then finally looked up at him.

'I had this idea in my head that I needed to explain why I couldn't marry you, that I needed to show you it wasn't because of you, it was because of me.' He shook his head. 'I'd worked out what I was going to say and then pressed on, not listening to anything you said or taking into account how you might be feeling.'

Charlotte nodded her head and then picked up the oars again.

'Once you told me you didn't expect us to marry because of a couple of kisses, that should have been enough—I can see I didn't have to keep pressing the point.'

'Thank you,' she said softly. 'Although I am glad you told me about your late wife. I know it must have been hard for you to do.'

'Some things are difficult to talk about.' He regarded her for a moment. 'So tell me—why are you so adamant you don't want to marry? Or is it just me you're against being tied to?

Which I would completely understand given my poor track record.'

'I've never imagined it as the future for myself. When I was younger I dreamed of travelling and seeing something of the world, and then, when my father passed away, all my focus was concentrated on the estate and the farm. That's where I devote all my energy.' She shrugged. 'I suppose I can't picture it really. I can't imagine meeting someone who could entice me to give up the farm and the freedom I get there to run things my way.'

'You think most men would want to take over?'

'Take over or expect me to give it all up entirely to spend my days running a household and raising children. Even the most enlightened of men that move in our circles would balk at their wives getting their hands dirty on a farm.'

'Perhaps you're right, but maybe a compromise could be made that allowed you to keep some of what you love.'

She eyed him for a moment and then sighed. 'I am well aware of what I am and what I offer, Robert. I have a pleasant enough face and good teeth, but I am no sparkling beauty. My tongue is often too sharp and I jump to conclusions far too quickly. I'm not the perfect candidate for a wife even before I start asking to have the freedom to do what I please with my time.'

'You sell yourself short,' he murmured.

Charlotte shook her head. He wanted to argue more, but was very aware they were in quite close proximity and if he started listing her virtues it might be misconstrued as flirting.

'You might not think you are the perfect candidate for a wife, but you will be *someone's* perfect.'

Charlotte laughed at this and pulled more heavily on the oars.

'Would you like me to take over?'

'Perhaps you can row us back once we've had some of that delicious picnic you've packed.'

'Is that a hint you'd like to stop for something to eat?'

'The smells are tormenting me.'

Robert pointed out a good spot to approach the bank and he found somewhere to tie the boat up once he'd hopped out. It rocked precariously as Charlotte stood, but she regained her balance quickly.

'Careful, you don't want to take a dip twice in a few days.'

Shuddering, Charlotte slowed down, allowing him to take her hand and steady her as she stepped out of the boat.

He'd also packed a blanket and laid it out a few feet from the river bank, setting the basket in the middle. As he dug in and laid out the food he realised he was smiling. It was a beautiful evening and they were in a stunning spot, with the sun starting to drop over the hills and reflecting off the river. Charlotte seemed to have accepted his apology and against all odds he was enjoying her company. For the first time in a long time he felt happy.

'That smells delicious,' Charlotte said, reaching out and helping him to unwrap some of the picnic.

They sat quietly while they ate for a few minutes, both enjoying the food too much to interrupt it with conversation, but as the edge was taken off their hunger they began to talk about the area of the country they both loved so much. It was easy conversation flowing between them and Robert felt a warm contentment spread over him as the afternoon turned into evening.

Charlotte laid back on the blanket and closed her eyes. She felt happy, much happier than she had expected to feel when she'd finally decided to accept Robert's invitation this afternoon.

'So does this mean we're friends?' she asked, not opening her eyes to look at him.

She knew he was smiling even without looking, she could hear the warmth in his voice.

'Friends with Miss Charlotte Greenacre,' he mused. 'Who would ever have thought it?'

'We don't have to be if you don't want.'

'No, I know how much you've admired me for years. I won't deny you friendship now.'

'Although we'd better keep it quiet. I don't think anyone would understand.'

'No, perhaps not. I'm not sure I really understand. Only a few days ago you attempted to climb out a stable window to avoid having to say hello to me.'

'You did let me think you'd stolen my birthright, the land of my family.'

'That was your misconception, nothing to do with me.'

'Hmm.' She fell silent. 'You didn't tell anyone we were coming here today, did you?'

'No.'

'Me neither. I pleaded tiredness and a desire to be fresh for the trip to Bath tomorrow and retired to my room. I expect you didn't have to make any excuses.' She propped herself up on her elbow and shifted so she was facing him.

'No, I informed my aunt I wouldn't be joining them for dinner.'

'It must be nice to have freedom like that, to

be able to announce something and not have it questioned or scrutinised.'

'I suppose. I've never really thought about it.'

'I expect you haven't.'

She fell silent, wondering what it would be like to be a man. Many times she had lamented the rules that governed her sex and wished she could have the freedom a man would in her situation.

'What do you hope the outcome of these few weeks is, Charlotte?'

For a long moment she considered. A couple of days ago she would have said she hoped she would be eliminated from Lady Mountjoy's selection early on and allowed to return home, but her feelings had changed a little. She was enjoying the friendship building between her and some of the other young women—especially Lucy and Eliza. The social events were actually fun when she was surrounded by friends. Then there was Robert himself.

Quickly she snatched a glance at him. He looked relaxed, happy, reclining back on one elbow, the sun glinting off his hair. Over the course of the last few days she had tried to suppress the feelings she had for him, not wanting to examine them too closely. She'd suggested a friendship and was hopeful that would be enough to quieten the clamouring of her heart every time he got close. She wasn't sure how friendships between a man and a woman normally worked, but she felt a little lingering underlying attraction was not completely out of the normal.

'I will admit I am enjoying myself more than I ever expected, although I do miss everything about home, of course.' She paused, picking absently at the blades of grass. 'When I first arrived I wanted to return home as quickly as possible, but I don't feel like that now.'

'Would you like to go to London with my aunt?'

Vehemently she shook her head. 'No, London is too far, too much. I think I would like to stay for the next week, until your aunt makes her decision, and then I can return home and know when my mother asks that I did not do anything to put my chances of being selected at risk, but I was not the right choice.'

'What if my aunt selects you?'

Charlotte pulled a face. 'I doubt she will. I do not have the beauty or grace of Miss Huntley, the attractive energy of Miss Stanley, or the sweetness of Miss Freeman. Even Miss Ashworth has her own charms with her intelligent sincerity.'

'My aunt may seem effusive and superficial at times, but underneath that bubbly exterior she is a very shrewd woman. She is well aware of the characters of all of her guests and I wouldn't worry she's been taken in by Miss Huntley's flattery.'

'Oh. Who do you think she will choose?'

Robert considered for a moment and then smiled. 'Knowing my aunt, she'll end up taking you all to London.'

'She is very generous.'

'She is. And she loves being surrounded by people. It makes her happy.'

'You spent a lot of your childhood here, didn't you?'

'Yes, especially later, after my father died. It was a wonderful place to be swept into, made to feel loved and wanted.'

She wondered if he hadn't felt that way at home. He'd alluded to his mother being flighty and she reasoned that could be the reason he was so close to Lord and Lady Mountjoy.

'I'll always be grateful that they opened up their home to me,' he said quietly.

They lapsed into silence and Charlotte had the urge to reach out and take his hand. She knew he was thinking about his family, could see it from the frown on his face. She wanted to run a finger across his brow and smooth out the furrow there, to distract him from the pain he was feeling, but she knew to do so would be to start down a path she couldn't allow herself to tread.

'We should be getting back, just in case anyone checks on you and finds you gone. While it's still light it might be assumed you've gone for a walk, but I imagine there would be panic if you were not to be found after dark.'

Sighing she nodded, knowing he was right. Together they packed the basket up, folded the blanket and made their way down towards the river. The boat was bobbing gently in the water and Robert held her hand as she stepped inside. This time she took the little bench at the front of the boat, allowing Robert to sit in the middle and be in charge of the oars.

He was quicker than her, pulling the oars on powerful strokes through the water, so even though they were going upstream they made good time. She watched as his muscles tensed under his shirtsleeves and found it hard to tear her eyes away from him.

Friends, she reminded herself. They were friends, nothing more. She needed to control herself better, to stop her thoughts running away from her.

It would be easier if she still disliked him. When she'd thought him a land-stealing thief it had been much easier to ignore the tension between them.

Biting her lip, she pulled her gaze away. This evening had showed her how pleasant it was to have a friendship with Robert. It would be silly to ruin that because she thought about kissing him all the time.

In no time at all they were back at the point where they'd started and Robert jumped out to secure the boat to a wooden post. As Charlotte took his hand to climb out of the boat, it rocked a little and she felt herself losing her balance. Before she could even stumble Robert tightened his arms around her and held her to his chest, lifting her out of the boat and carrying her up the bank, only setting her down when they were on level ground.

Charlotte felt her heart pound in her chest, knowing it wasn't from the thought that she might lose her balance and fall into the river, but the proximity of the man holding her. She could feel the warmth of his skin through his shirt and she had the urge to pull the white cotton from his waistband and slip her hands up inside.

Robert looked down at her and Charlotte held her breath. She realised that despite all her protestations over the last couple of days she wanted him to kiss her, wanted him to wrap his arms around her and lower his lips and not stop until they both forgot the reasons they were not meant to get close to one another.

He cleared his throat and Charlotte was sure he was going to step away, but he held her for a few moments more, his hands relaxing a little and tracing absent-minded circles on her shoulders.

'There,' he said eventually, stepping back, 'on solid ground again.'

For a moment Charlotte couldn't speak, the words refusing to come out. Then she gave a nervous laugh and quickly moved even further away.

'Shall we return to the house?'

Quickly she nodded, but pretended she hadn't seen his proffered arm and strode off towards Rowlings Hall.

Chapter Fifteen

Closing her eyes, Charlotte hugged the warm little body to her and stroked his soft ears.

'At least you're not complicated,' she murmured to the piglet, feeling his body relax in her arms.

'Charlotte,' Lucy exclaimed as she entered the stables. 'One of the maids said I'd find you here, but I didn't quite believe them. Is that a pig?'

Charlotte laughed at Lucy's incredulous expression.

'This is Arnold, my piglet. He's staying in the stables while we're here.'

'How…? I don't understand,' Lucy stuttered, coming to sit on the bench beside Charlotte.

'I brought him from home and Lord Overby was kind enough to arrange for him to stay in the stables after he caused havoc in my room.'

Lucy burst out laughing and tickled the little pig's head with her fingers.

'You truly are one of a kind, Charlotte Greenacre.'

'Is something wrong, Lucy? You look agitated.'

'No, although I do have news and I wanted to share it with you. You've been so kind keeping my confidences.'

Checking around her before speaking, Charlotte lowered her voice. 'Is this about your young gentleman?'

'Yes. William has written, he assures me of his love and affection in the letter and hopes to be home soon on leave so we might marry.'

'That's wonderful, Lucy.'

Charlotte saw the happiness in her friend's eyes and wondered what it would feel like to be so close to marrying the man you loved. Although there was still a lot of risk involved for Lucy, Charlotte admired the way her friend was forging on ahead and following her heart. She doubted she would ever be brave enough to do the same.

'I had to share the news with someone. I'm so excited, I hope it will not be too long until he can come home and then we will marry and no one will be able to keep us apart.'

Charlotte squeezed Lucy's hand, hoping it was as easy as that for her friend. She knew getting married would be difficult enough even without the wider family in opposition.

'The carriages are almost ready to leave,' Lucy said as Charlotte stood and gave Arnold a little squeeze.

'I'll see you in a few days,' she promised the piglet and then brushed a few stray bits of straw from her dress.

They were soon to depart for Bath, with Lady Mountjoy deciding they should experience the delights of staying in town. There was a ball planned at the Assembly Rooms tonight and to-morrow they were going to take tea with some of Lady Mountjoy's friends.

Lady Mountjoy's town house was large, but not big enough to fit all the young ladies and the gentlemen she had invited for the week to Rowlings Hall, so the gentlemen were going to stay in the country and Lord Mountjoy was organising a hunt to keep them occupied. Charlotte had no doubt they would appreciate a reprieve from all the socialising expected of them.

'I don't wish to speak out of turn,' Lucy said quietly as she fell into step beside Charlotte for the walk back to Rowlings Hall. 'But I saw you walking through the garden yesterday afternoon with Lord Overby.'

Charlotte felt the heat flood to her cheeks and cursed her pale skin for always showing a blush and betraying her emotions.

'Yes, we went for a stroll together,' she said, trying to make it sound like the most natural thing in the world. 'Do you think anyone else saw?'

'No, it was when I had returned to my room to get a shawl for the evening, but everyone else was downstairs and I think unlikely to have seen you.'

'Not that there is a reason for me not to want to be seen with Lord Overby.'

'Of course,' Lucy said quickly.

Falling quiet, Charlotte had the urge to confide in Lucy about the kisses she had shared with Robert and how she was feeling torn between how she should behave and how she wanted to.

'You care for him, don't you?'

Faced with such a direct question Charlotte nodded her head. 'I don't know if "care" is the right word. Can you care for someone you've only known a few days?'

'I think you can.'

'We kissed,' she said, bending her head in to

Lucy's so there was no chance of anyone else overhearing.

'Oh, Charlotte, how wonderful.'

'I'm not sure it is. The kiss was wonderful, of course, but he then went to great pains to make it clear he could not marry me. We have decided to become friends.'

'Oh.' Lucy was frowning. 'Is that what you want?'

'Yes. At least it should be.'

'Should be?'

'Well, I don't wish to marry, I don't wish to lose my freedom to a man. I want to go back home and continue running the farm as I was before. I want to be allowed to make my own decisions and not have to defer to a husband.'

Lucy regarded her for a moment. 'That all sounds very good and noble in theory, but is it what you really want?'

'Yes, of course.'

'You don't worry about how you will feel in fifteen years' time when your sisters are married and living lives of their own? When it is just you left on that farm of yours?'

'I hadn't really thought about it.'

'I don't wish to presume, Charlotte, but I do wonder if it is a way of protecting yourself, this need to focus on the work of the farm.'

Lucy glanced at her and saw Charlotte wasn't too offended by her forwardness before continuing. 'There might be someone out there for you who would allow you to continue to have a hand in running the farm and the estate with your mother even after you were married. Not everyone is looking for a wife who fits into a particular mould.'

Charlotte shook her head, even though she knew in some ways Lucy was right. She had felt so safe, so secure until her father had died, and then after his death she'd been paralysed by fear that everything could change in an instant, everything could be taken away from her so quickly. She knew that was where this need to be in control with matters on the farm and wider estate came from. If she were in control, then she could ensure nothing went wrong to jeopardise their security.

'Sometimes we have to take a risk to find true happiness.'

'I *am* happy,' Charlotte said, but the treacherous thought crept into her head, questioning her, making her wonder if she truly was.

'Good, I will lecture you no longer. I'm sure it is the last thing you want. Now, tell me how was the kiss? Was it completely and utterly wonderful?'

A warmth swept through her as she remembered Robert's lips on hers, the possessive way he'd pulled her to him. She'd felt powerful, attractive, while being lost in the heady desire that had overwhelmed her.

'I never knew a kiss could make you feel so much,' she whispered to Lucy, glad to have someone to share this with.

'It's marvellous, isn't it? When William kisses me I feel as though I am floating a full two feet off the ground.'

'That's exactly how it feels. I never wanted it to end.'

'Do you think he might kiss you again?'

'No, he made it *very* clear it was a mistake. A pleasant mistake, but a mistake all the same.'

'I suppose he was very badly affected by the circumstances that surrounded his first marriage.'

'Mmm…' Charlotte said, not wanting to impart anything Robert had told her in confidence.

'Still, how thrilling for you. Away from home barely a few days and already you have a very eligible gentleman paying you attention.'

They were nearly back at Rowlings Hall now and Charlotte led the way around to the front of the house where Lady Mountjoy was ushering the group of young ladies into the carriages. She had organised a second so they would have plenty of room for the trip to Bath without someone having to ride in the curricle with Robert. The luggage was strapped to the top already and Charlotte could see Miss Ashworth and Miss Huntley were already seated in one carriage.

'Ah there you are, Miss Greenacre and Miss Freeman—why don't you come with me in the second carriage? Miss Stanley can join either group when she appears.' Lady Mountjoy motioned for them to climb up into the carriage while she stood peering at the front door as if she could make Eliza appear by simply wishing her there.

As Charlotte settled herself on to the seat of the carriage with Lucy next to her, she turned to look out of the window, her breath catching as Robert walked into view. He was dressed informally in dark trousers and a white shirt with the sleeves rolled up to his elbows. She liked how relaxed he was at Rowlings Hall, how he seemed to be able to treat it like his home even though he was a guest of his aunt and uncle.

He said a few words to his aunt, making the older woman smile, and then caught Charlotte's eye and made his way over to the carriage.

'Miss Greenacre, Miss Freeman, I trust you will have an enjoyable stay in Bath.'

'Will you be attending the Assembly Rooms' ball tonight, Lord Overby?' Lucy asked the question, but Charlotte was glad her friend had. She found herself inching forward to hear the answer.

'I hope to, Miss Freeman, but it does depend on the other guests. My uncle tires more easily than he used to and I have promised my aunt to take some of the burden of the host's responsibilities. I am unsure whether the gentlemen will want to stay here after the hunt or make the trip to Bath.'

Lucy nodded in understanding and Charlotte felt a thrum of energy as Robert turned to her.

'I wanted to assure you that I will look after Arnold while you are away, Miss Greenacre.'

'Thank you, that's very kind.'

Robert smiled at her, more restrained than usual as there was someone else present, but with warmth all the same.

'Perhaps you would both save a dance for me if I am able to join you in the Assembly Rooms tonight.'

'That would be lovely, Lord Overby,' Lucy said, although her expression hinted that she knew the request was directed more at Charlotte than herself.

He jumped down from the carriage and moved away, waving them off as Lady Mountjoy settled into her seat with Eliza in tow and instructed the carriages to depart.

Chapter Sixteen

Despite what he had told Charlotte and Miss Freeman earlier in the day, Robert would have been quite happy to miss the ball at the Assembly Rooms. Not because of the company, but because of the memories that assailed him when he walked through the wide doors into the high-ceilinged rooms.

Much of his courtship of Amelia had played out in the ballrooms and parks of London, but it had been here in Bath he'd first met her. It was at a similar ball at the Assembly Rooms that he'd first laid eyes on his future wife, where they'd had their first dance, where she'd first started to bewitch him. She might have been out of his life for well over two years, but he still felt the need to avoid the places that brought up too many memories of her.

He was good at hiding his emotions, though,

and he doubted that anyone would see through the smile on his lips or the bland expression on his face. Gossip had followed him in the weeks and months after Amelia's death, but he had soon realised if he didn't react to people, didn't give them any more juicy titbits to dissect over their morning cup of tea, soon some other scandal would take their attention.

As he entered the Assembly Rooms he allowed the other gentlemen to move on ahead, glad to be rid of their company for a while. They were not men he knew well. He might converse with them at the card tables or make polite conversation while passing at his gentlemen's club, but a few days spent in their company was by far enough.

'You're getting old and grumpy,' he muttered to himself. It was true, there were only a select few people he would actively seek out to spend his time with. His eyes flitting over the room, he didn't want to admit there was only one person he was interested in spending time with tonight.

Even though she was turned away from him he recognised her immediately. She was dressed in an ivory dress with a gold thread detail. It was simple but elegant and dipped at the back to reveal the creamy smoothness of her skin.

He had the urge to stride over and place a kiss on the nape of her neck, to feel her shudder as he knew she would under his touch.

'Friends,' he said to himself. 'Just friends.'

It was a ridiculous prospect when he thought about it. Charlotte consumed his thoughts every waking minute and for the past two nights had been plaguing his dreams, too. The idea he could ever fall into an easy friendship with her, be content strolling arm in arm across the landscape they both loved in contented companionship, felt a little ridiculous, but he was a firm believer in needing to work at things to make them happen. If he told himself a thousand times they were only friends, at some point he might start believing it.

For a few minutes he skirted the edge of the room, allowing his eyes to flit back to Charlotte every now and then. She was arm in arm with one of the other young ladies, Miss Freeman, heads bowed together as if they were sharing confidences. He wondered if she were saying anything about him and the idea made him pause for a moment, but he realised she would have to choose who she shared her secrets with carefully—her reputation was much more precious than his.

Every so often a fleeting smile would cross

her face and Robert felt himself smiling in response as he watched her.

He was about to approach, to make some small talk with all the ladies in his aunt's little group and claim a dance from each as was expected of him, when he overheard Charlotte's name mentioned in a conversation between two young women. They were not women he knew well, although both looked vaguely familiar, and he suspected he'd been introduced at some local event in the last couple of years. Edging closer he listened, wondering what these two young women had to say about Charlotte.

'She's quite respectable looking when she makes an effort.'

'I'm surprised she knew to wear a dress rather than those awful trousers she insists on wearing around the estate.'

'I would be mortified if anyone saw me in such attire.'

'Her dress tonight is passable, I suppose, although I doubt many of the gentlemen will ask her to dance. Who would want to get entangled with a young lady who is more comfortable with the pigs and sheep than polite company?'

Robert felt a swell of anger, but quickly squashed it down. Charlotte wouldn't thank him for making a scene. In all likelihood she would shrug off the other women's hurtful comments and pretend they didn't cut her. Or laugh and say they weren't wrong, that she would rather spend her time with the farm animals.

With a decisiveness about his step he strode through the room, his sense of purpose meaning people stepped out of his way. He didn't stop until he was at Charlotte's side.

'You must excuse me for interrupting, Miss Freeman, but Miss Greenacre promised me the honour of the first dance and I think it is almost time.'

Miss Freeman graciously stepped back, leaving Charlotte staring at him as though he had two heads.

'I did—' she said, but he whisked her off before she could finish the sentence. As she fell in beside him she tried again. 'I did nothing of the sort. You never asked.'

He wasn't about to tell her what he'd overheard. Although she might shrug it off, he had a feeling deep down it would affect her. It would make her shy away from further social situations and dent her newfound confidence.

'I know. I am sorry for interrupting the talk between you and Miss Freeman.'

The music that had been playing gently in the background paused for a moment as the musicians shifted and then started a lively tune for the first dance. It was a quadrille, a dance he'd danced a hundred times before, but for a moment he felt sick to his stomach.

It was the same dance, the same music even, as the first time he'd danced with Amelia here at the Assembly Rooms.

'Is something amiss?' Charlotte whispered and he realised he'd frozen to the spot halfway to the middle of the dance floor.

'No,' he said, his voice betraying the lie.

'We do not need to dance if you do not wish it.'

He shook his head. The whole reason he'd whisked Charlotte away was to show the gossips that Charlotte was in demand, was desired and popular. He couldn't escort her halfway to the dance floor and then abandon her—that would be worse than not asking her to dance at all.

Taking a shaky breath, he pushed all thoughts of Amelia aside and focused on Charlotte, the woman in front of him. With her looking on in concern he took up his starting position for the dance and soon they were stepping and spinning in time to the music. It took all of Robert's concentration to focus and he hated the worried look on Charlotte's face which showed she wasn't really enjoying the dance, but slowly he was able to make his posture and bearing a little less stiff, his expression a little less serious.

'You look very severe,' Charlotte whispered to him as the dance came to a close. 'Everyone will think I've done something to upset you.'

Robert tried to relax his frown. 'I'm sorry, this hasn't worked out how I hoped.'

'What are you talking about?'

'I asked you to dance because I overheard two horrible young women saying something disparaging about you. I knew if I asked you to dance other gentlemen would follow and it would put a stop to the gossip about you.'

'Let me guess,' Charlotte mused. 'They said something horrible about the clothes I usually favour, or the fact no man will ever want a woman who insists on mucking out her own horses.'

'That's very accurate.'

Charlotte smiled and there was only a hint of sadness to it.

'I've been listening to the same comments for years. Don't feel you have to defend me from the likes of the Westmore sisters.'

She nodded in the direction of the two young women who had been so unnecessarily cruel in their remarks.

'You don't care what people say about you?'

Charlotte shrugged. 'Of course I do. A little. Normally I avoid it by not coming to any of this type of event. Then the petty jibes don't even reach my ears.' She smiled at him. 'The Westmore sisters will be all in a flutter to see you, though, and not too happy you chose me to dance with first.'

'Perhaps we should make sure they have noticed.'

'You're the most eligible man in the room—' she shook her head with a wry smile '—actually, you're the most eligible man in the county. There is no way they'd have failed to spot you or the attention you pay me.'

'Surely to be eligible you have to be in the market for a wife.'

'Your aloofness, your conviction that you will not marry again, makes you more of a challenge, but that excites some women. They think the prize will be bigger, the admiration more. After all, if they are the one to tempt the aloof Lord Overby into marriage again, then they must be completely irresistible.'

'No one will tempt me into marriage again.'

'*I* know that, but a lot of young ladies would think of it as another little obstacle to overcome.'

'For someone who doesn't frequent ball-rooms too often you seem to know a lot about the mind of the debutante.'

'It's fascinating when you think about it—all these young ladies from good families scrambling to find a husband with a decent income and hopefully at least some of his own teeth.'

'But that competition shouldn't make us forget basic human decency. I understand the Westmore sisters are your rivals in the business of securing a suitor, but surely they don't need to disparage you to elevate themselves.'

Charlotte laughed. 'I don't think that's why they're doing it. I think they're spiteful. No one really sees me as a threat to their marriage prospects.'

'Most men I know would rather be married to you than someone so spiteful and petty.'

Shaking her head Charlotte dropped her voice a little. 'That's not true, you know it as well as I. The Westmore sisters are what most men want in a wife. Docile, content to stay at home and see to their husbands every need, pretty and compliant.'

'Then most men are fools.'

'They're coming over.'

Ushered over by their mother, a tall, thin,

severe-looking woman whose expression only softened as she caught Robert's attention.

'Miss Greenacre, I thought that was you. We don't often see you at the Assembly Rooms, so it took me a moment to place you. How lovely to see you again.'

She looked expectantly between Charlotte and Robert as if waiting for the introduction.

'Good evening, Mrs Westmore, I trust you are well. Miss Westmore, Miss Lydia,' she greeted the two young ladies who were trying their utmost to look sweet and appealing. 'Have you been introduced to Lord Overby?'

'A pleasure,' Robert murmured, bowing in turn to each of the ladies in front of him.

'It is an honour to have as distinguished a man as yourself at the ball tonight,' Miss Westmore said, fluttering her eyelashes.

'We have often said it is a shame more gentlemen do not attend these little balls. There is always a lack of partners,' Miss Lydia said, looking up at Robert expectantly.

'Quite,' he said, but made no offer to dance with either young lady. 'If you would excuse us, I think my aunt, Lady Mountjoy, is trying to catch my eye.'

With a perfunctory bow he firmly led Charlotte away from the shocked Westmores.

'That was rude,' Charlotte said. 'And incredible.'

'They were rude to you. I don't see why I should have to be polite to them.'

She half turned and glanced over her shoulder. 'They're still standing there in shock. You know I'll get the blame for this.'

'How does that work?'

'The wonderful Lord Overby cannot be blamed. He must have been influenced by that horrible little Greenacre girl.'

Robert smiled. 'The perils of being close to the most eligible bachelor in the county.'

As they weaved their way back through the room Robert realised all his earlier preoccupation about Amelia had disappeared. A few minutes in Charlotte's company and she had made him stop dwelling on the painful memories. Now here he was, laughing and smiling in a place where he thought all he would ever be able to think about was his late wife.

With some reluctance he deposited Charlotte back with the other young debutantes, requesting a dance from each of them and spending the next couple of hours dutifully escorting one after the other to the dance floor.

'I don't care what anyone else says,' Lady Mountjoy said as the ballroom was starting to empty a little, 'I couldn't ask for a better nephew.'

'I have been on my best behaviour tonight.'

'Look how the young ladies glow from your attention.'

'It has been a successful evening.'

As his aunt had predicted where he had first stepped other gentlemen had followed and her five debutantes had danced every dance, their dance cards filling up quickly after he'd stepped out on the dance floor with them.

'Have you enjoyed yourself, Robert?'

He patted his aunt on her hand. 'Do you know… I have.'

'Good. You've looked happy tonight.'

'So have you, Aunt.'

She smiled happily. 'I do love the buzz and excitement of the social Season.'

'And the matchmaking?'

Lady Mountjoy didn't even pretend to protest, giving him a contented little nod acknowledging she did love trying to find exactly the right partner for the people that surrounded her. He'd always supposed it came from being so happily married herself and wanting the same for the people she cared for.

She yawned and he saw the signs of fatigue in her eyes.

'Shall I arrange for your carriage?'

'Thank you, Robert dear, that would be perfect.'

It took a few minutes to round up the debutantes and usher them towards the carriage waiting outside. Robert had hoped he might have a few seconds with Charlotte, but she looked as exhausted as the rest of them, so he steadied her as she climbed up to the carriage and then waved everyone off, watching until the vehicle rolled around a corner and out of view.

Chapter Seventeen

It was unbearably hot and everyone was low on energy after the ball at the Assembly Rooms the night before. They'd returned to Rowlings Hall from Bath just after lunch and most people had drifted away to rest for an hour or two. Lady Mountjoy had arranged for an informal afternoon tea to be served in the drawing room and now all the guests were gathered either in here or on the terrace outside.

Charlotte fanned her face with her hand, wondering if she looked as sticky as she felt. She longed for a refreshing dip in a cool lake or river, or even a paddle in an icy stream. Anything to combat this intolerable heat.

'We need something to distract us,' Lady Mountjoy said, with considerably less energy than she normally had.

'I could play,' Miss Huntley suggested, although she made no move to stand or make her way to the piano.

All of a sudden there was an uncharacteristic sigh from Miss Jane Ashworth. Miss Huntley bristled, but it soon became apparent that Miss Ashworth was in a world of her own and not passing judgement on Miss Huntley's musical skill. She was sitting with her feet tucked underneath her on one of the beautifully upholstered armchairs, a book of poetry open to about halfway through and her eyes focused on the words in the book.

'What are you reading, Miss Ashworth?' Lady Mountjoy enquired.

'Oh.' Miss Ashworth looked up as if only just remembering there were other people in the room. '*The Odyssey.* A translation, of course, it is far too hot to be struggling through the original.'

'You read Latin?' Miss Huntley said, raising a perfectly shaped brow.

'Ancient Greek. Yes.' She gave a little shrug and looked as though she wished people would stop looking at her. 'I find something gets a little lost in the translation, but sometimes my brain is too tired to translate as I read.'

'You young ladies today are so accomplished,' Lady Mountjoy said with a beaming smile. 'You've given me a wonderful idea for a little afternoon activity, Miss Ashworth.'

Charlotte shifted in her seat. She wasn't sure she was up to any organised activities this afternoon. Surely it was too hot for anything but lounging around and complaining about the heat.

'Miss Stanley, would you be a dear and gather all the gentlemen? I think they are in the library playing cards.'

Eliza stood and ambled out, returning a few minutes later with all the gentlemen.

'Thank you, Eliza. Gentlemen, please have a seat. I thought we might choose a gentle activity for this afternoon given it is unbearably hot.'

'Swimming?' Robert suggested with a twinkle of mischief in his eye.

'Don't be absurd, Robert. I thought we might write some poetry.' She paused for a moment and looked around the room, gauging the reaction.

'Poetry?' Robert said with a raised eyebrow.

'Yes, poetry. We shall split you into pairs and you will have an hour to write a few verses of poetry. Perhaps we could have the poems read before dinner.'

'There will be a winner?' Miss Huntley said,

perking up and sitting up a little straighter in her chair.

'There will be a winner,' Lady Mountjoy confirmed.

'How will the partners be chosen? And what should be the subject for the poetry?'

'I will choose your partners. The subject—' She stopped to think for a moment. 'How about what all the best poems are about—love?'

Miss Huntley nodded in satisfaction, her eyes darting from one gentleman to the next.

'Miss Stanley, you will be with Mr Hardman. Miss Huntley, why don't you partner with Mr Willis? Miss Ashworth, you go with Mr Farthington. Miss Freeman, you can go with Mr Prentis.'

Charlotte swallowed and looked up, her eyes meeting Robert's.

'And, Miss Greenacre, you can partner with Lord Overby.'

As she watched, Robert leaned in towards his aunt and murmured something in her ear. Lady Mountjoy swatted him away good naturedly.

'Let us reconvene at four o'clock. Paper and pens are in the library.'

Slowly everyone trickled out of the room, the gentlemen finding their partners and leading them to the library to pick up the supplies they would need.

'Miss Greenacre,' Robert said, motioning for her to step out of the room ahead of him. 'I have the perfect shady spot for us to retreat to.'

'What did you say to your aunt just now?'

'I told her to stop trying to interfere. To stop matchmaking.'

Charlotte gasped. 'She's trying to make a match between us?'

Robert's hand flew to his chest. 'I'm wounded that the idea horrifies you so.'

She gave him a playful push. 'Stop it. Does your aunt know...?' She trailed off, not wanting anyone to overhear her admitting she had been indiscreet with Robert.

'Of course not. She's relentless in her efforts. Every time she sees me even glance at an unmarried young woman she's ready to invite them into the family.'

'Ah.'

'She was instrumental in helping her daughters find their husbands and is always on the lookout for her next project,' he said as they entered the library and picked up some sheets of paper and a pen. 'How are your poetry skills?'

'I don't think I've ever written a poem.' She glanced at him. 'I'm sure you have written a verse or two when trying to impress a young lady?'

He grinned. 'I've never needed it.'

A laugh burst from her lips at the satisfied look on his face and she had to cover her mouth as Miss Huntley and Mr Willis turned to look at them.

'Come, as I said, I've got the perfect spot. Somewhere we won't be overheard.' He led her out of the library door on to the terrace and then down into the gardens. Charlotte had spent a lot of time over the last week wandering around the gardens at Rowlings Hall and thought she knew the formal gardens quite well, so she was surprised when they turned down a little path and came into a secluded hedge-lined clearing with a wrought-iron table in the middle and a bench behind it.

'This is lovely,' Charlotte said, looking around her.

'Enough to inspire some romance?'

For a moment she thought he meant something else and her heart fluttered in her chest. She glanced up at him and saw the serene look on his face and realised he was not talking about seduction. Swallowing hard, she sat down and laid out the sheets of paper on the table.

'What should be included in a poem about

love?' Robert mused, oblivious to her moment of discomfort.

'I hardly think I am the best person to answer that.'

He regarded her seriously for a while. 'You have seen love, between your parents, between others. And you have experienced love, even if it is not of the romantic kind.'

She thought of the wrenching pain she'd experienced when her father had died and the way her mother had held on to her as if she were drowning. Shaking her head, she pushed away the painful memories—she knew there was more to love than pain. She thought of how her mother had looked at her father when he played the piano and the time her mother had carried her home when Charlotte had been thrown from a horse even though she was almost fully grown and a whole head taller than her very petite mother. She smiled as she remembered the stories her father would tell her every night without fail as he tucked her into bed, no matter how tired he was or what difficulties his day had held.

'You're right, I've known a lot of love.'

'More than me,' he murmured so quietly she was sure she wasn't meant to hear.

Tentatively she reached out and rested her

fingers on the back of his hand. He'd spoken a little about his family. Of course she knew his father had died when he was young and that his mother was still alive, but she had sensed some tension whenever he spoke of his mother.

'Do not look at me with pity in your eyes, Miss Charlotte Greenacre,' he said sternly.

'I sometimes think that I assume that people have the same general family background, the same childhood experiences, that I did,' she said slowly. 'But of course that is not true.'

'No.'

'It is something that shapes so much of our lives, how we were loved as children.'

She looked down and saw her thumb moving backwards and forward across the skin of his hand. She hadn't realised she was doing it. With a jolt of surprise she looked up and her eyes met his. For an instant it felt as though everything else faded into the background. The noise from the garden stilled and the rest of the world dimmed. It was just her and Robert sitting on the bench side by side with their whole lives stretching out before them.

Charlotte flicked her tongue out across her lips, knowing she should move her fingers, but somehow not being able to.

'So what does love mean to you, Charlotte?'

His voice was so low and deep Charlotte shivered at the sound of it. There was an invisible force pulling her towards him and she felt her body inch ever closer. She couldn't resist, couldn't even blink to break the connection between them, and all she could think of was how his lips would feel on hers.

After far too long she managed to sit up straighter and force her hand to move from his, instead clutching at the pen they had brought from the library. It was a welcome distraction and meant she couldn't use her hand to touch Robert.

'Love…' she murmured, frantically trying to make some sort of coherent sentence about love.

Taking a few deep breaths, she tried to settle herself, but Robert chose that moment to edge closer and lean over her shoulder. She felt his breath on her neck and suddenly she was useless for anything but spinning fantasies again.

'Love…' she said again, but still nothing would come.

Gently Robert reached over and took the pen from her hand, sliding the piece of paper closer to him and then with barely a moment's pause he began to write. Line after line flowed out of him on to the paper as she looked on incredulously.

His writing was neat and his words well-spaced, meaning Charlotte could read as he wrote, but it wasn't until he had come to a stop and she could appreciate the whole verse in its entirety that she truly understood how lovely the poem was.

'It's something to start with, we can change it, add to it, edit it.'

'Robert, it's beautiful. Where did you learn to write like that?'

'Writing isn't something that you learn,' he said with a soft smile. 'It is something that has to come from in here.' He touched his chest and she marvelled at how honest he was with her when they had only really known each other well for a short period of time.

His eyes flicked over her face and she wondered what he saw when he looked at her. Slowly he reached out, tucking a strand of hair behind her ear and then letting his fingers linger before falling back to his lap.

'What would you change?'

'I know it is meant to be a collaboration, but I'm not sure I can change anything,' Charlotte said, forcing her eyes back to the poem.

'There must be something. Look, this line doesn't flow well, it is longer than the rest and disrupts the rhythm.' He paused and then read the line he wasn't quite satisfied with out loud. 'Unable to resist risking everything for one kiss.'

'But it is so heartfelt, so true. We can't cut it.'

He smiled at her. 'Perhaps we can change it then, alter the words, the rhythm.'

She nodded, conceding. For a time they worked on the poem, taking each line in turn and discussing whether one word could be substituted for another or whether to leave it as it was.

'I like this line,' Charlotte said, pointing to one on the paper, her fingers lingering next to Robert's as their eyes met.

'Never do I want to contemplate a day spent without you.'

Charlotte swallowed, her mouth suddenly dry. As he said the words, she felt they were written for her and her alone. It was a heady feeling, one she knew she should dismiss, but her heart wouldn't let go.

'Our hour is almost up,' Robert said eventually and she didn't think she imagined the hint of regret in his voice.

'Do we have to go?' The words were out of

her mouth before she could stop them. She bit her lip, feeling a flush of embarrassment.

'Perhaps we have one more minute,' Robert said, his voice low with a hint of danger. 'Shall I read the poem out loud to you?'

She nodded, not realising at first that she was holding her breath until there was an unbearable ache in her chest.

He started to read and Charlotte couldn't tear her eyes away. She knew if they stayed here in the seclusion of this part of the garden for much longer she was at risk of doing something she shouldn't. Every part of her ached to be touched. She wanted to reach out and pull Robert towards her, so his body was pressed against hers, so he had no option but to kiss her.

'Ah, there you are.' Eliza's voice came from around the hedge. 'Lady Mountjoy sent me to find you. Time's up.'

Even though they hadn't been touching they sprang apart guiltily. Charlotte stood far too quickly and banged her knees on the table, letting out a strangled cry.

'Careful,' Robert said, steadying the table.

'I'll tell her you'll be along in a minute,' Eliza said, barely able to keep the smile from her face.

Charlotte closed her eyes, telling herself it was for the best.

* * *

'What wonderful poems,' Lady Mountjoy enthused. 'You all worked so hard.'

Robert sat back, observing his aunt and her guests. She was in her element, surrounded by people, holding court. His aunt was never happier than when she had a full house of happy people.

'Who is the winner?' Miss Huntley asked sweetly, fluttering her eyelashes.

Robert looked at her. Objectively he could see she was a good-looking young woman, but there was something too sharp, too cut-throat about her. As always his eyes wandered over to Charlotte, where she was sitting demurely, hands folded in her lap. Charlotte might not have the high cheekbones or tumbling golden hair, but there was no question that she was more attractive. Her smile was genuine and warm and her eyes sparkled with humour.

'That is a hard decision,' Lady Mountjoy said. 'Perhaps you have an opinion, Lord Mountjoy?'

'I do have a favourite,' the Earl said quietly. 'I thought it captured the essence of what love is.'

'Which was your favourite?'

'Miss Greenacre and Lord Overby's.' He

gave Charlotte a warm smile as he spoke and Charlotte returned it.

'Congratulations,' Mr Farthington said loudly, nudging Robert as if worried he might not have realised he had won.

Charlotte grinned, catching his eye. She might not want to be the one chosen by his aunt to go to London, but she couldn't hide her competitive spirit. It was clear she liked to win.

Chapter Eighteen

'Come on, Charlotte, it's starting in a minute and we don't want to be late.' Eliza grabbed her by the hand and dragged her out of the bedroom while Charlotte was still jabbing pins into her hair. They'd returned to Rowlings Hall the day before and today was the penultimate day of the house party. Lady Mountjoy had announced there would be a grand set of games to be played this afternoon and there had been speculation from some that she would be looking to see who embraced the event with the most enthusiasm to help make her choice as to who would go to London with her.

They raced down the stairs and into the sunshine to find everyone else already assembled.

'Oh, wonderful, now we're all here I will explain what we are doing this afternoon,' Lady Mountjoy said, holding a parasol above her head to shield her from the sun. 'I have arranged a little competition and the winners will be crowned king and queen for the day.' She looked around, beaming. 'You will be in teams—one lady and one gentleman—and you will race to complete a series of challenges. The first pair to successfully complete them all and make it back here to me and Lord Mountjoy will be the winners.'

Charlotte glanced around her to see the varying expressions. Miss Ashworth looked horrified, a couple of the gentlemen had slightly bored expressions on their faces, but Eliza and Miss Huntley looked as keen as could be.

'First you will both need to shoot three arrows into a target. You can have as many goes as you like, but you each will need to hit the target three times. Then when this is done you will have your leg tied to your partner and will race as one to the stables. From there it is a ride across the fields to the lake where we have some rowing boats. Each couple will need to row to the middle of the lake where there is a small island. On the island we have placed five ribbons—pick one up and row back to shore. You then ride back to the stables and then race on foot back to the start.' She beamed at everyone and clapped her hands in excitement.

'Now I will ask the ladies to step forward

and choose a slip of paper with a gentleman's name on it.'

Miss Huntley went first, picking a piece of paper with Mr Willis's name on. She looked him up and down appraisingly, clearly disappointed not to be with Lord Overby, but conceding hers was not the weakest of partners.

Jane went next, picking out Mr Hardman's name, and then Lucy stepped up and picked out Mr Prentis. Charlotte had to suppress a smile as Eliza looked between the two remaining gentlemen. Mr Farthington was not the finest partner one could ask for and Lord Overby was clearly superior physically.

She dipped her hand in and selected a piece of paper and Charlotte found herself holding her breath. She could see the writing on it as Eliza unfolded it and felt her heart sink when she saw Lord Overby's name. For an instant Eliza hesitated and then treated Mr Farthington with her sunniest smile.

'Mr Farthington, it seems you and I are partnered.'

Charlotte blinked, glancing down at the piece of paper in her friend's hand again. It clearly said Lord Overby's name. Eliza caught her looking and screwed up the paper, leaning in to Charlotte before she went to join Mr Farthington.

'He clearly doesn't have eyes for me. Why waste such an opportunity?' Eliza murmured.

Trying to suppress a smile, Charlotte went to stand next to Robert.

'I hope you're better at archery than Pall Mall,' he murmured in her ear.

'Careful you're nice to me or I might see to it you fall in the lake.'

'And jeopardise our chance of winning?'

Charlotte screwed up her face. 'I have something to tell you,' she said quietly, so no one else could hear. 'I'm fiercely competitive and if we don't win this I might not ever forgive you.' For an instant when Lady Mountjoy had been running through the rules of the competition Charlotte had thought about hanging back, perhaps not giving it her best effort. If she won, then it might draw the Countess's attention and that was the last thing she wanted, but Charlotte knew she couldn't fight her nature and it was her nature to want to win. She would have to allow her competitive side out and deal with the consequences later.

'Duly noted.'

Lady Mountjoy gestured for them to take up their starting spots and they moved to a point in front of the targets that had been set up for archery.

'I can talk you through a few tips,' Robert said, picking up the bow. 'You hold the bow like this with an outstretched arm, up so it is level with your eyeline and the target. Notch an arrow like this and then pull the bowstring back firmly, making sure you keep your elbow up.'

'Let the competition begin,' Lady Mount-joy called and there was a clatter of bows and arrows.

'Shall I demonstrate?' Robert asked.

Raising an eyebrow, Charlotte said nothing, but took the bow from him, notched an arrow and let it fly, watching critically as it hit the target about five inches off centre. Quickly she let loose two further arrows that hit the target easily before handing him the bow.

'Perhaps you don't need a demonstration,' he said with a smile. This was one of the things she loved about Robert. He was a confident man and that meant he wasn't intimidated by the success of others. He was certain of his own abilities and knew his place in the world so didn't mind if someone was better than him at something.

Quickly he let three arrows fly, all hitting the target close to Charlotte's. He grabbed her hand and together they ran to the next stage. Charlotte glanced at the other couples, all still struggling to hit the targets.

Robert picked up one of the ribbons that had been placed for them to tie together their ankles and offered it to Charlotte.

'Would you like to do the honours or shall I?'

She shrugged, feeling a shiver of anticipation run through her as his fingers brushed ever so lightly against her ankle. Even though there were people a few feet away she couldn't help imagining him running his hands up her leg, caressing the soft skin.

'Ready to run?' He straightened up and broke into her totally inappropriate thoughts. She managed to nod and linked her arm through Robert's and they started off at an awkward run. He was so much taller than she that it felt very uneven and unbalanced and they stumbled a few times before getting into their stride. She saw Robert make an effort to shorten the length of each step to better match hers.

It felt a long way to the stables through the garden and Charlotte was finding it hard to control her giggles. The whole situation was completely absurd and she wondered what anyone outside their little group would make of it if they came upon them.

'Thank goodness that's nearly over,' Robert said as the stables came into view. They were both breathing heavily from the exertion and Charlotte felt as though she needed to sit down and compose herself.

The grooms and stable boys were waiting with five horses lined up in a row.

'There's only five,' Charlotte said as Robert bent to unlace the ribbon from around their legs.

'It's one horse per couple, miss,' a helpful stable boy piped up.

Robert looked at her appraisingly for a moment. 'How likely is it you're going to sit docilely in behind me?'

'In the interest of winning I suppose I could try.'

Robert selected his own horse and quickly mounted and then steadied Charlotte as she climbed up on a mounting block and swung her leg over behind him. It was difficult sitting astride in a dress, even more so when she had to balance behind Robert off the saddle, but as she wrapped her arms around his waist and felt the firm muscles under her hands she lost some of her uncertainty.

'Hold on tight. Are you ready?'

As Robert urged the horse forward into a

trot Miss Huntley and Mr Willis came stumbling into the stable yard. By the sound of it Mr Willis was being firmly berated with a list of shortcomings by Miss Huntley and looked thoroughly miserable.

Charlotte shifted her weight and held on a little tighter. 'You can go faster. I promise I won't fall off.'

'The way you promised you wouldn't fall in the pond?'

'That's unfair. I'm very comfortable on horseback. You're more likely to be thrown than me.'

She felt him chuckle and the movement made her realise quite how close they were sitting. A slight movement of her hands and she would be near his waistband. As it was, she could feel the taut abdominal muscles under his cotton shirt.

Despite his teasing, Robert did urge Washington to pick up the pace and soon they were speeding towards the lake. As they slowed near the banks Charlotte slipped from Washington's back even before he had come to a complete stop and raced towards the rowing boats as Robert tied the reins to a nearby tree.

'Hurry up,' Charlotte shouted, wobbling on to the rowing boat and taking up position by the oars. Robert pushed them off from the side and she started rowing, making good progress to the middle of the lake. 'Get ready to jump,' she said, positioning the boat so he would have an easy bit of bank to jump up to.

'Do you want me to row back?' He threw the question over his shoulder at her as he raced for the ribbon.

'Maybe,' she shouted, eyeing up the forms of Miss Huntley and Mr Willis dismounting on the far side of the lake. None of the other couples was in sight, but it wouldn't take long for Miss Huntley and Mr Willis to overtake them. She knew it was only a game, a little bit of fun, but she was having a tremendous time with Robert and, as she'd confessed, she'd always had a competitive streak in her.

Holding on to the edges to steady herself, she scuttled to the end of the boat and took up a position on the bench there.

Robert grabbed a ribbon and sprinted back to the little rowing boat. He grinned at the sight of Charlotte urging him to run faster. He'd caught glimpses before of how competitive she was now she was determined to beat the opposition. Even though the whole contest was a little ridiculous, he found he was enjoying himself. He had an unfair advantage in that his aunt had often set up little races such as these when he came to stay as a child. Over the years he'd loved racing against his cousins to win the title of champion.

Still, he hadn't expected as an adult to enjoy this so much. Over the last couple of years he'd struggled to enjoy much at all. When the mess with Amelia had first consumed his life he had wondered if he could ever be happy again. Slowly, needing privacy and solitude to heal, he had started to take pleasure in the small things in life.

Now he was careful to appreciate little things that brought him pleasure. Over time he knew that those little things would build up to a wider happiness. At first it was appreciating the beauty of a sparkling lake in the sunshine, but as time went on he found he could marvel at the perfection of the natural world.

What he hadn't ever expected again was to feel such happiness doing something like this, something with someone else.

He studied Charlotte as he clambered back into the boat, pushing off with the oars and pulling with strong strokes through the water. Her expression was so alive, her face so animated. He loved how much she felt everything, how she allowed herself to truly enjoy the things that caught her interest. There was no holding back with Charlotte, she had decided to embrace this game and so was throwing herself into it completely. She didn't care what anyone else thought of her and wasn't preoccupied with how she looked while she was racing across the estate.

'What?' She caught him studying her and suddenly looked self-conscious.

'I'm admiring your competitive spirit.'

'Hah. Most do not think it something to be admired in a young lady. I'm sure I should be demurely following your lead and acting a little more helpless and incapable.'

'That would go against your character.'

'True.' She grinned. 'I'd start by trying to act demure and docile and get annoyed halfway through. I wouldn't be able to help myself.'

They were nearing the bank and Charlotte stood, looking as though she were going to jump on to the bank as he had done on the other side. Her balance wasn't quite as good as his as the boat wobbled and she stumbled, rocking it even more. He thought it had stabilised in time for the front of the boat to knock against the bank.

Time seemed to slow as he saw her lose the battle for her balance and start to fall from the boat. Robert lunged forward, hoping to be in time to catch her, but her wrist slipped through his fingers as he grabbed at it.

Charlotte fell with a splash into the lake. It was shallow here, with the bank sloping down and if she had managed to keep her footing and stepped into the water only the bottom few inches of her dress would be wet. Unfortunately the way she fell meant she tipped from the boat, landing on her hands and knees in the murky water.

Robert was there immediately, stepping into the shallows and pulling her up before she was completely soaked through. For a long moment she looked down at her sopping wet dress, covered in mud at the knees and splattered from the waist up, then she raised her eyes to his and he felt a bubble of laughter rising up inside him.

She laughed first, the sound bursting from her as if she couldn't control it. As she clutched at his arm, struggling to take a deep breath, he couldn't contain his laughter any longer and joined her. They were still standing in the water, both laughing, when Miss Huntley and Mr Willis's boat bumped into the bank.

'Oh, dear,' Mr Willis said, eyeing them with a hint of disdain. 'Do you need some help?'

'No, thank you,' Charlotte managed to gasp.

Robert saw the barely disguised disgust in Miss Huntley's gaze as she pulled Mr Willis away from the pair.

'Charlotte,' Robert said, leaning down to whisper in her ear. 'I know you're sopping wet and covered in mud, but what do you say to wiping that look from Miss Huntley's face and stealing the win from them?'

For a second she must have forgotten where they were and their promise to keep their distance from one another and she flung her arms around his neck. He felt every curve of her body pressed against him and felt the urge to carry her off into the woods and do everything he had been imagining over the last few days to her until the sun went down.

Her eyes met his and he could see the same desire, the same urge to do away with caution and follow what both their bodies craved.

'What happened, Charlotte?' Miss Freeman's concerned voice broke into the moment and Charlotte hastily stepped away.

'I took a little tumble, that is all. My dress is ruined, but I am fine otherwise.'

'If we want to have a chance at winning, we'd better get going,' Robert murmured, looking behind him to see Miss Huntley and Mr Willis disappearing into the trees.

Charlotte gripped his hand and together they ran for Washington. It was a little harder mounting without a block for Charlotte, but Robert watched as she used the tree branch to lever herself up behind him.

'Go,' she shouted before she was fully settled, and he urged Washington first into a trot and then, when he was sure she was holding him tightly, into a canter. The water from Charlotte's clothes was seeping into the back of his shirt, but he didn't mind. It was rather refreshing in the heat of the afternoon.

By the time they'd reached the stables they had caught up with Miss Huntley and Mr Willis and Charlotte was much quicker down from a horse than either of the other couple.

'Ready to run?'

She picked up her sodden skirts in one hand, giving him and the grooms a glimpse of her ankles, took his proffered hand with her other and together they started to run as fast as they could through the gardens.

They reached Lord and Lady Mountjoy ten seconds ahead of Miss Huntley and Mr Willis and collapsed on to one of the benches on the terrace.

'What have you done to poor Miss Green-acre?' Lady Mountjoy bustled over and looked Charlotte up and down. 'You look completely bedraggled, my dear.'

'You say it as if you expect me to have pushed her in the lake.'

'She is soaked.'

'She took a little tumble.'

'Robert, I expected you to take better care of Miss Greenacre.'

Robert grinned, first at Charlotte and then his aunt. 'Ah, but we won, that's the important thing.'

They sat dripping on the bench as the other couples made their way back, having to wait for a good ten minutes for Miss Stanley and Mr Farthington to come hurrying through the gardens.

Robert allowed himself to relax. He felt happy, truly happy, and it was an emotion he hadn't felt for a long time. Rowlings Hall always had exerted a calming influence on him, like his aunt and uncle, but this was more than that. Robert didn't just feel content, he felt happy.

Glancing at Charlotte he wondered how

much of that was due to the woman sitting next to him. She had a different way of looking at the world which was therapeutic. Where she wasn't trying to impress all the time, wasn't trying to fit in, he'd seen how happy she was in her own skin.

'You're nothing like Amelia,' he murmured, too quiet for Charlotte to hear.

It was true, her personality couldn't be more different from his late wife's. Charlotte was happy and carefree whereas with Amelia it had all been about appearance. She wouldn't have derived pleasure from racing on horseback over the fields or taking control of a curricle for the first time. Amelia had been all about how things looked. She'd reeled him in with this impression of being in love with him and then turned his world upside down.

'You're smiling at me,' Charlotte said to him as Eliza and Mr Farthington flopped down on to one of the free benches.

'Am I not allowed to?'

'What's making you smile?'

He thought about telling her the truth, that he was smiling because of how unlike his late wife she was, but he knew it would sound strange saying those words out loud.

She might even take offence if she realised

one of the reasons he liked her so much was because she didn't remind him of his first wife in any way whatsoever.

'I enjoyed this afternoon,' he said, coming in closer so only she could hear him. 'Thank you.'

Chapter Nineteen

'I'm glad I caught you, Robert,' Lady Mountjoy said as she hurried into the study and closed the door behind her. 'I wanted to get your opinion on the young ladies.' She held up her hands to ward off his protestations. 'I know you said you did not want to help me judge, but I'm asking for a few opinions.'

'I may not be the best judge, Aunt.'

'Nonsense. Just because that horrible wife of yours deceived you doesn't make you a bad judge of character. She deceived everyone.'

'Still, perhaps you should trust your own judgement. Or Lord Mountjoy's.'

'Miss Greenacre is a sweet young thing,' his aunt said, ignoring his protestations. She shot him a sly, side look and he had to stop himself from laughing. *This* was what his aunt had really come to talk to him about. 'Remind me how you know her.'

'She thought I'd tricked her mother into selling some of their family land after her father's death.'

'I assume you've corrected her now given the way she looks at you.'

'And how do you think she looks at me?'

'The young lady is obviously in love with you, Robert. I think you know that.'

He considered for a moment, closing his eyes and leaning back so his head rested on the edge of sofa. Charlotte had certainly thawed in her feelings for him and he knew there was an attraction that throbbed and pulsed between them, but he wasn't convinced she was in love with him.

'We are friends, Aunt—unlikely friends, I grant you, but friends all the same.'

'This was what I was afraid of,' Lady Mountjoy said, sighing dramatically and motioning for him to move over so she could sit beside him. She took a moment to settle herself, arranging her skirts around her and then patting him in a motherly way on the hand. 'Now, I know you have had your trials in life, Robert, and not everything has run as smoothly as you would have wished, but that doesn't mean you should hide yourself away from the opportunity to be happy. *Especially* when it is right in front of you.'

Robert thought of his happiness earlier in the day when Charlotte had flung her arms around him, or how contented he'd felt as they'd collapsed on to the bench at the end of the race.

'I know your parents weren't the best example of a happy marriage and your own was quite frankly a disaster, but that doesn't mean you should give up.'

'It's not giving up, Aunt, it is not wanting to experience something quite so terrible again.'

'It wouldn't be so terrible a second time.'

'Perhaps not, but I am not willing to risk the hard-won contentment I now feel with the world for "perhaps" or "maybe".'

Lady Mountjoy sighed a heartfelt sigh.

'I know it is uncharitable, but sometimes I curse my silly sister for not being a better mother to you, not giving you a better example of unconditional love.'

Robert closed his eyes for a moment. He was sure his mother loved him, in her own way. When he was a child, a little after his father had died, he had longed for a tight hug, a kind word, or a simple acknowledgement that it was the two of them against the world, but it had never come. It had been a long time since he had accepted his mother for what she was: shallow and selfish. It didn't mean she didn't love him, just that she loved herself more.

'I've never begrudged my mother the life she made for herself after my father died.'

Not content with the quiet life of a dowager marchioness, his mother had soon left him in the care of Lord and Lady Mountjoy to travel for a few years and then when she returned had paid him less attention than her string of lovers. She'd never remarried, but enjoyed her notoriety, not caring what anyone else thought of her as she aged.

'I have always been happier on my own,' he said quietly. It wasn't quite the truth, but it was easier than trying to explain the complex mess of panic, dread and anticipation at the thought of ever letting anyone into his life again.

'Oh, Robert.'

He saw Lady Mountjoy had tears in her eyes and he patted her hand.

'I'm quite content as I am, Aunt. I have you and my uncle, all my wonderful cousins who are more like siblings to me and I have some good friends.'

'We only have one life, Robert, and I do not wish for yours to pass you by. I would hate for you to get to your sixth or seventh decade and realise what you've missed out on.'

'Come,' he said softly, 'please don't worry about me. I am much happier than I was two years ago. Back then I'm sure you despaired I would ever socialise again—and look at me now.'

Lady Mountjoy nodded, but still looked a little morose.

'You asked me what I thought of the debutantes,' he said more to distract her than anything. 'Of course I hold Miss Greenacre in high regard. Miss Freeman also seems sweet and sincere. Miss Ashworth is very quiet and I wonder how well she would do in the ballrooms of London, but she is kind and charitable and if she wants a chance of a Season then I think she deserves it. Miss Stanley is sharper, but she would sparkle in London and from the kindness she shows the other young ladies I feel she has a good heart.'

'And Miss Huntley?'

'I do not feel I have got to know Miss Huntley well and do not wish to speak unfavourably about someone I perhaps have not spent enough time with.'

'But you do not wish to get to know her more.'

'There's something cold about her, something calculating.'

'I did notice she hasn't made friends with the other young ladies. Although some of the gentlemen do seem to be taken with her.'

'Aunt Letitia, are you matchmaking again?' he teased her.

'Nonsense. I wouldn't think to interfere.'

'Perhaps we should ask Clara if that is true, or Catherine.'

Lady Mountjoy smiled at the mention of two of her daughters, the two she had played an instrumental part in pushing them towards their respective husbands. Husbands they were currently sharing very happy marriages with.

'There's no harm in showing two young people they would be well suited and, if they aren't quite ready to see it, sometimes situations can be orchestrated to allow them the time to realise it for themselves.'

'You are one of a kind, Aunt Letitia. When will you make your decision with regards to the debutantes?'

'I think I should tell the young ladies before they go home in a couple of days. Making them wait any longer would be unfair.'

Robert nodded, realising the implications of what his aunt had said. In a couple of days

Charlotte would return to her farm. She would go back to her mother and sisters and resume her job of trying to make the farm and estate as profitable as possible. They would no longer enjoy afternoon strolls and stolen moments. He wouldn't have an excuse to seek her out and any visit would have to be formally arranged and properly chaperoned.

'I fear I have set myself up with an impossible task,' his aunt said, smiling at him softly. 'I arranged this party thinking I was giving one or two young ladies an opportunity they wouldn't otherwise have, but in selecting a couple to take with me to London I will also have to disappoint some of them as well.'

'I'm sure they will understand. You did make it very clear they wouldn't all be accompanying you to London.'

'Yes, I suppose I did,' Lady Mountjoy said with a sigh. She stood and laid a hand on Robert's shoulder, lingering for a second. 'Remember we love you, Robert, whatever you decide for your future.'

Left alone with his thoughts, he found all he could think about was Charlotte. Over the last few days it had struck him over and over again how different she was from his late wife. In her manner and temperament, in her likes and dislikes, even in the way she spoke and dressed, everything was different from Amelia. Perhaps that was one of the reasons he liked Charlotte so much.

With a wry smile he shook his head. That wasn't the reason, the reason was *her*, but it was why he was sitting here and for the first time in years contemplating whether there was a small possibility he might want to take a chance on someone.

Standing, he started to pace the room. The idea was ridiculous. For so long he had built this cocoon around himself to keep the rest of the world out. Surely it should take someone more than a few days to break it down to find their way inside.

He felt excited, agitated, suddenly with the desire to see Charlotte. He wasn't about to do anything outrageous, like declare his feelings, but he had this urge to find her, to walk with her and talk with her and try to work out exactly what it was he wanted.

It was still an hour before dinner and he knew most of the young ladies would be in their rooms, changing and having their hair dressed by the maids who ran frantically from one room to the next at this time of the evening. He knew Charlotte didn't entirely eschew these preparations, since being at Rowlings Hall she had always been well turned out with her hair neatly pinned and a dress appropriate for the occasion. He also knew she didn't spend as long primping and preening as the other young ladies, often rushing back to her room with just twenty minutes to spare before dinner.

'Arnold,' he murmured to himself with a smile. She'd be in the stables.

Charlotte swept some of the hay to one side, adding a fresh layer on top. The stable boy Robert had paid to look after Arnold during his stay was doing a good job. Every day when she came to see the little piglet the stall was clean and Arnold's water topped up. The piglet was well fed and seemed happy, nuzzling around in the hay.

'I had a feeling I would find you here.'

A wide smile spread across her face and Charlotte had to take a second to get it under control before turning round. She had the urge to throw her arms around Robert's neck even though it would be completely inappropriate.

You're falling for him, the little voice inside her head said.

As much as she tried to deny it she knew it was true. One more smile, one more stroll among the roses, and she might lose herself completely to this man.

For a few moments she watched as he hopped over into the stall and made a fuss of Arnold.

'Everyone else is getting ready for dinner so I knew where you would be.'

'I still have time, don't I?' She had a sudden panic that time had flown past faster than she had expected and now she would have to go to dinner without getting changed, with bits of hay clinging to her dress.

'A few minutes still.'

'Rose, the maid who comes to help me every evening, always gives the loudest sigh when I come rushing in late. I don't think I'm her favourite person to help dress for dinner.'

Robert hopped out of the stall and offered her his arm. 'I won't keep you too long, then. I had the urge to see you before dinner.'

She blinked, surprised at his directness. Even over the last few days Robert had been careful not to appear too enthusiastic each time he'd seen her. His reactions were measured and deliberate much of the time as if conscious that he was always being watched. She supposed that was what came of being so eligible and attractive to the young women in society. He would have perfected his mannerisms and expressions so as not to inadvertently make a young debutante think he favoured her over any other.

'Will you take a stroll with me around the garden?'

She nodded, her heart thumping in her chest. As she climbed out of the stall she had to stop her mind from racing from one impossible thought to another. This was nothing special, nothing irregular, just a man wanting to walk through the gardens with a friend.

Still, Charlotte's heart was thumping in her chest as they left the stables and Robert offered her his arm. She wasn't sure what her subconscious mind thought might be happening, but her reaction to even the hint of something between them showed her that despite all her protestations she wanted a future with this man.

Friendship was all well and good, but she secretly was yearning for more. Desire pulsed through her body whenever he was near and she craved his touch, his kiss. More than that she wanted intimacy. She wanted to know his deepest thoughts and feelings, she wanted to share his hopes and dreams.

Stifling a laugh, she tried to push all these thoughts away. Only a few of days ago she'd been assuring him in no uncertain terms that she didn't want to marry him, that he had nothing to fear from her in that department. Now all she could think of was him wrapping his arms around her and asking her to be his.

'Was there something you wanted to talk to me about?' She forced herself to act as normally as possible.

'No, I wanted to see you, that's all.'

They strolled across the lawn and towards the formal garden. Robert seemed at ease, relaxed, but wasn't in a hurry to tell her what was on his mind.

'I enjoyed the race today,' Charlotte said.

'I did, too. I haven't laughed like that in a long time.' He shook his head ruefully, 'I'm never sure about my aunt's ideas, but everyone seemed to be having fun.' He paused. 'Perhaps not Miss Stanley.'

'No, she was rather hampered by her partner.' She glanced sideways at Robert, wondering whether to say more. 'She picked your name out first.'

Robert turned to her with surprise in his eyes. 'She read out Mr Farthington's name.'

'I know.'

'Does she like him?'

Charlotte laughed and then felt bad for being so uncharitable. 'No, she finds him dull and a little trying.'

'Does she dislike me so much, then?'

Charlotte shook her head. 'Who could dislike you?'

'I can be surly.'

'It's just with me you're on your best behaviour...' She paused. 'No, she knew of our friendship and thought it would make me happy to be partnered with you.'

'Perceptive young woman. And generous, too, to take on a partnership with Farthington.' Robert fell quiet. 'She does not know about our...kiss.'

'No.' She was sure Eliza didn't know, although of course Lucy did, but she was confident Lucy would keep her secrets and therefore Robert didn't need to know there was one more person out there who knew of their indiscretion.

Glancing at his face, she saw he had grown serious. 'It is important, Charlotte, that we tell no one of our moment of intimacy. Even someone trustworthy could inadvertently let something slip. Sometimes it is the smallest comment that starts a rumour, that rumour becomes gossip and the gossip becomes scandal.'

She bit her lip, wondering if she should tell him that Lucy was aware of their kiss. She'd never set out to betray Robert, but Lucy had guessed there was something between them and it had been nice to confide in someone sympathetic. She was confident Lucy would not tell anyone, Charlotte was a keeper of her secret, after all, but she knew Robert would not like someone he didn't really know having knowledge of their kiss.

Sighing, she knew she should tell Robert. It was only fair. He might be a little annoyed for a moment or two, but he was reasonable and she was certain he would see there wasn't anything to be concerned about once she had explained things.

As she opened her mouth to say something there was a shout from the direction of the stables. Together they both turned, having to raise their hands to shield their eyes from the bright sun.

'The pig's on the loose!' a red-faced stable boy shouted as he came running towards them. Sure enough, moving fast just in front of him was the blurred form of Arnold. He was squealing in excitement and Charlotte wondered for a second if he was afraid or thought this a game. She'd often had to chase him over the last few weeks, and he had always seemed to enjoy it, but she was aware he was in unfamiliar surroundings being chased by someone he didn't really know.

'Don't let him out of your sight,' she called, springing into action immediately. The last thing she wanted was for Arnold to escape into the parkland. If that happened, they had no chance of catching him and he would likely end up some predator's dinner.

The piglet ran towards her and for an instant she thought he would run right into her arms, but at the last minute he squealed and darted off into the rose garden.

'This pig is surely more trouble than he's worth,' Robert muttered, but Charlotte was pleased to see he darted after the little creature, weaving through the rose beds.

She hoped no one was watching them from the house. Anyone looking out of the windows that overlooked the garden would see her, a stable boy and a marquess chasing a pig around the garden. She doubted if this got out she would ever live it down. For ever more she would be the young lady who, instead of flirting with the Marquess, made him chase a farmyard animal through a rose garden.

Seeing Arnold dodge left, she split off from the main path and circled round, hoping they might be able to trap Arnold between them. At first the little piglet seemed to be pulling further away, but after a few twists and turns finally he was in the middle of Robert coming up behind and Charlotte approaching from in front.

'Be ready to grab him if he slips past,' Robert said to the stable boy, not taking his eyes off the piglet.

'Yes, my lord.'

Robert stepped forward calmly, his movements slow and steady in an effort not to scare the pig into darting again.

'I think I've got him,' Robert said as he launched himself forward. Charlotte could see as soon as he dived that he was a second too late. Arnold wriggled left and Charlotte launched herself at the pig but misjudged as well. Rolling awkwardly on the ground and into Robert's firm body, Charlotte saw the stable boy jump as well and manage to grab hold of the piglet.

'I've got him,' the boy said, triumphant.

Charlotte smiled weakly up at him, all the air knocked from her lungs by the way she had fallen.

'Take him back to the stables and make sure he can't get out,' Robert said gruffly.

'Yes, my lord.'

'Thank you.'

Charlotte watched as the young lad hurried

away, holding Arnold in his arms with a grin on his face.

Slowly she turned to Robert, pushing herself up on her elbows.

'You really committed to that jump,' Robert said, groaning as he sat up as well.

'So did you.'

'Couldn't have Arnold loose on the estate. Who knows what mischief he might cause?'

'I think I've bruised my ribs,' Charlotte said, tentatively touching the bottom of her ribcage. She'd fallen heavily and knew she would be sore in the morning.

'Here.' Robert got to his feet and pulled Charlotte carefully up. She took a few short sharp breaths and then the pain began to subside a little. 'Let me see.'

Slowly, gently, his fingers began to probe her ribs over her dress, pressing over the area and checking her face to see when she winced.

'It's tender there.'

They were standing close, his hands still lingering on her body and Charlotte felt everything go still around them. She couldn't quite tell when his touch went from concern to something more, but all of a sudden his hands were around her waist and he pulled her body towards his. For a long moment they stood like that, lips inches apart, their bodies swaying together in harmony.

'Someone will see,' Charlotte said, glancing in the direction of the house.

'No, we're hidden.' He was right, they were hidden by a hedge that shielded them from the line of sight from even the upstairs windows of the house.

'We shouldn't…'

'No, we shouldn't.'

Despite their protestations, Charlotte knew they would kiss. She could see the desire in Robert's eyes, desire and something more. It was as though for the first time he was allowing himself to enjoy this, to enjoy her, as though it wasn't something completely illicit, something to fight himself over.

As his lips brushed against hers Charlotte lost all power of conscious thought. Her whole body felt weak as if she couldn't hold herself up and a wonderful warmth spread from her lips all the way down to her core. She wanted more, wanted to feel his hands on her, to feel his lips on her, and she realised in an instant that she loved this man.

If he asked her to marry him, she would say yes in an instant, even though she had always vowed she would stay unmarried and independent. This one kiss seemed to hold so much promise, so much hope and her head was filled with images of their future together. It was a future she had not even known she'd wanted, a future she had been too scared to imagine when it had seemed an impossibility.

'I love kissing you,' Robert murmured, pulling away a little to kiss her ear, her jaw, her neck.

She laced her fingers together behind his neck and felt her whole body suffuse with warmth. At first she had thought he was going to say *I love you* and she found she was holding her breath, but she wasn't even that disappointed when he had said he loved kissing her. It was a step in the right direction. Maybe they could both stop denying the strength of feeling between them, maybe this was the start of something wonderful.

'I love kissing you, too.'

'I know I shouldn't, I know I should feel bad about this, but I find it hard to resist you.'

Charlotte smiled. It was impossible not to when he was saying things like that to her.

He bent his head low, looking as if he were about to kiss her again, and Charlotte closed her eyes ready to be swept away in the bliss of it all, but suddenly there was a noise to their left and they jumped apart guiltily.

'I've put the pig back in the stables, my lord. I've checked he can't get out this time and I've given him some food.'

'Thank you...'

The stable boy grinned and then started to saunter away, but neither Charlotte nor Robert saw the knowing smile on the young lad's face.

'We should go in,' Robert said, making no effort to move.

He was looking into her eyes, searching her face. She wanted to find out what he was thinking, what was going through his mind, but she knew he would need time to work out what it was he wanted from her now there seemed to have been a shift in how he was with her.

'We should.' She reached up on tiptoes and brushed her lips ever so gently against his for a second, then turned away to walk back to the house, her heart pounding in her chest.

Chapter Twenty

Charlotte was humming to herself as the ladies got up from the dinner table and made their way into the drawing room. Miss Huntley headed for the piano and sat down, rifling through the sheets of music before settling on a song.

'Charlotte, would you take a walk along the terrace with me? I am a little warm and would like some fresh air.'

Charlotte turned to see Lucy standing there, a look of excitement in her eyes.

'Of course.'

She walked side by side with her friend and together they stepped out into the evening air. It was slightly cooler than in the house, but not all that much. The sun had dropped below the horizon while they were having dinner and now it was almost completely dark, but still the heavy heat of the midsummer day lingered.

Charlotte wished she had a fan to cool her a little, but she'd not brought one with her to Rowlings Hall, never thinking to dig it out from the drawer at home where it was kept.

'I have to tell you I saw you in the garden earlier,' Lucy said, dropping her voice low as they strolled away from the house.

Immediately Charlotte felt the heat in her cheeks and she was glad it was dark to hide her blushes. 'Oh?'

'It looked as though there was a commotion with that piglet running around.'

'Arnold escaped.'

'Ah. Lord Overby seemed very diligent in helping you catch him.'

'He was very kind. He knows how much Arnold means to me.'

'Charlotte, I don't wish to embarrass you, or force a confidence you don't want to make, but I also saw you two together after the incident.'

Pausing, Charlotte took a moment to compose herself. Lucy was kind and trustworthy and wouldn't tell anyone what she had seen. She already knew Charlotte and Robert had shared a kiss before, so it wasn't a complete disaster that she had seen another between them. What Charlotte was really worried about was how it had happened. Both she and Robert had thought they were safe, that they were completely shielded from view of the house by the dense hedge that separated that part of the rose garden from the lawn.

'How did you see us, Lucy?'

'My room is at the end of the house. I have a view into the rose garden from there,' Lucy said quietly.

'Is anyone else's room down there?'

Lucy thought for a moment. 'Miss Huntley's is next to mine, but I know she was downstairs with Lady Mountjoy at the time. I don't think anyone else could have seen.'

Charlotte let out the breath she had been holding and sank down on to one of the benches at the other end of the terrace.

'Thank you for telling me. Hopefully no one else saw.'

Lucy perched down beside her and seemed to want to say something more, but hesitated.

'I know it was foolish,' Charlotte said quietly, still not able to regret the kiss she had shared with Robert in the gardens earlier. It had seemed like the start of something, the promise that there could be something more between them.

'I do not wish to interfere in a matter that does not concern me,' Lucy said slowly, 'but

I feel as though as your friend I have to say something.'

Charlotte nodded, waiting. She could sense Lucy's unease at the situation.

'Be careful. I know better than to listen to the rumours, but Lord Overby is a man who has been surrounded by scandal these last few years. It may not seem much to him to become embroiled in another, whereas it would be devastating for you.'

Charlotte closed her eyes. She shouldn't be talking about this with Lucy, not after Robert asked her to keep things secret, but what was the harm? Lucy already knew about the kiss—a few minutes discussing how Charlotte felt wouldn't do any more damage.

'I don't think he flirts with scandal,' Charlotte said. 'He is keen to avoid any hint of it, given what happened with his late wife.'

'You care for him, don't you?'

Silently Charlotte nodded. She was still adjusting to the realisation that she loved Robert. She loved the gentle way he teased her, the way he allowed her to be herself and express herself with no judgement. She loved the affection in his eyes when he looked at her and the burning passion she felt when he kissed her.

'I do. I think I might love him.'

'Does he share your feelings?'

'I don't think he wants to.'

'Ah.'

'I don't know what to do. If I was being a good friend, I would step away as this is what he thinks he needs, but if I am following my own heart I would tell him how I feel.'

'I don't feel I can give you much advice, Charlotte. Lord Overby is a difficult man to read.'

Charlotte closed her eyes and tipped her head back so it rested against the wall, conscious the rough stone would pull some of her hair from its pins, but not able to find it in herself to care enough to move her head.

'I have always been a staunch believer in following your heart,' Lucy said after a moment. 'But I don't know Lord Overby well enough to know how he would react to you declaring what you felt.'

'I think the problem is I still can't quite believe how I feel, Lucy. All these years I've been quietly scornful of the women who follow the same path, marrying the most wealthy or well-connected man they can find and giving up the things they have previously declared all important to them.' She shook her head.

'You're allowed to change, Charlotte. We

can't expect people to be fully formed by the time they reached sixteen. Or have fixed ideas about what they want from life before they have actually experienced it.'

Charlotte fell silent as she contemplated Lucy's words. 'I suppose.'

Lucy gave her hand a squeeze and then stood. 'Come, I've probably said too much. Let's return to the drawing room and forget about gentlemen and their kisses for one evening.

Robert recoiled in shock, unable to quite believe what he'd heard, unable to believe that, despite him asking her not to, Charlotte had clearly been discussing their relationship, their kisses, with someone else. He'd sat with the other gentlemen and his uncle for a few minutes, waving away the cigars Mr Willis and Mr Prentis had offered around. When the smoke had started to become thick and cloying he'd excused himself, never having been able to stand cigar smoke. As a younger man he'd used to sit there with the smoke curling round him, pretending it didn't bother him. Now he didn't care if anyone thought he was strange or rude and normally excused himself as soon as anyone started smoking.

After escaping the dining room, he had toyed

with joining his aunt and the ladies in the drawing room, but had decided against the idea. It had been nearly two weeks of dancing and talking and playing cards and he decided an hour or so on his own was what he needed.

That was why he had slipped out through the door from the study on to the terrace, planning to have a moonlit stroll around the gardens.

For a moment he felt as though he couldn't breathe, as though he had been punched in the gut and all the air knocked out of him. Since that afternoon he had been in turmoil, wondering what to do with this new realisation that he cared for Charlotte. There had been part of him that wanted to suppress the knowledge, push it away and try to continue with his normal life. The other part of him was cautiously reminding him she was nothing like Amelia, nothing like his mother even. She was kind and loyal and wouldn't betray him.

Staggering to a bench, he sat down and tried to think rationally. He was aware in matters of trust he could sometimes exaggerate and he needed to make sure he wasn't being too harsh.

Robert took a few deep breaths and closed his eyes, running over what he had heard. It was clear Charlotte had told Miss Freeman about their relationship, about their kisses and intimacy, even though he had specifically asked her not to. She had agreed, giving him her promise only a few hours earlier, and already she had broken that promise.

'You can't trust her,' he told himself. He couldn't trust anyone.

He felt like a fool. He'd been just about ready to open his heart, to take a chance, and think about letting someone get close, even though he knew he shouldn't.

Standing, he strode out into the darkness of the garden. Even though it was getting late he felt the need to be away from the house, away from people. If he saw Charlotte now he wouldn't be able to stop himself from showing how much her betrayal had hurt him and the last thing he wanted was to make a scene.

Tomorrow, with a little space and time, he would be able to face her, to see her with other people and not let on how close he had come to letting her in to his heart.

Chapter Twenty-One

Charlotte was glowing as she came down to breakfast. Even though she'd tossed and turned most of the night, too giddy with excitement to sleep properly she still felt refreshed and energised. Just admitting the night before to Lucy that she wanted something more with Robert was freeing, as if a weight had been lifted from her. It felt absurd now she thought about it that she had worried about being fickle, about realising she wanted something she had always said she didn't.

Now that she could admit she wanted a relationship with Robert, that she wanted marriage and a family, it was as if she had been released from her expectations of herself. It wasn't as though she had given up on her other passions, but perhaps there was a way she could still be involved in running her family estate and farm while building a relationship with the man she loved.

You're getting ahead of yourself.

It was true. Although they'd kissed again in the gardens yesterday, Robert hadn't said anything to her about marriage. He hadn't made her any promises. A few days earlier he'd made it clear exactly how he felt about marriage. Still, she sensed something had changed in him and she hoped it might be a willingness to let her in, to give her a chance to show him she was nothing like his late wife.

She was almost humming by the time she sat down at the breakfast table. There was only Miss Huntley and Mr Willis present so far. Lady Mountjoy always took her breakfast in her room, so the meal was often informal with no set time. The guests rose when they wanted and trickled in to the dining room when they were dressed and ready for the day.

Pleased to see Mr Willis and Miss Huntley deep in conversation, Eliza sat down a few places away along the table. She would be glad to have her thoughts to herself for a few minutes while she sipped a hot cup of tea and ate some buttery toast.

She was buttering her second slice when Robert appeared at the door, his expression blank and impossible to read. She smiled at him warmly and felt a wave of confusion hit her as he gave her a formal and impersonal nod in greeting.

For a moment she watched him as he stiffly chose a seat and sat down, thanking the footman as he set a plate in front of him. Apart from a fraction of a second when he had first walked into the room he hadn't even tried to meet her eye. He sat a few places away, meaning any private conversation would be impossible.

Charlotte swallowed, wondering if she had imagined the warmth from him yesterday, but then quickly dismissed the idea. They'd *kissed*. You couldn't get much more intimate than that.

For a few minutes she focused on her breakfast, chewing her toast slowly, every so often flicking sideways glances in Robert's direction. He was resolutely stony-faced. At first she panicked, wondering what she had done wrong, then she felt a flicker of irritation. Surely it would have been easier to sit down next to her so they could bend their heads together and discuss whatever it was that had annoyed him.

'Good morning, Lord Overby,' she said pointedly.

'Good morning.' He barely looked up from his cup of tea as he spoke to her. It was an acknowledgement, but only the bare minimum to be polite.

'Did you sleep well?' she continued, determined to make him look up at her.

'No, not really.'

'Oh, dear. Did something disturb you?' She could hear her voice becoming harder with each question and tried to force a sunny smile on her face. She was aware she didn't respond well to people's moods and she didn't want to start berating Robert if he was feeling morose because of some bad news or something similar.

'No.'

'Is something the matter?' She dropped her voice so only he could hear, wishing he would look up at her.

He swallowed his mouthful of tea before answering and even though it was a delay of only a couple of seconds Charlotte felt as though time was stretching out while she waited for his answer.

'Perhaps now is not the time to discuss it...' He paused. 'And here is not the place.'

At his serious tone Charlotte's heart sank. There was something wrong and by the way he was refusing to meet her eye for more than a second it was something that involved her. She thought back over the past twenty-four hours and the only thing she could settle on was the kiss they'd shared, but that didn't make any sense. Yesterday he'd been warm and caring even after they'd kissed. It was the whole reason Charlotte had allowed herself to hope and dream all evening that there might be the chance of something more than friendship between them.

'Oh. Perhaps later, then,' she managed to say. For a long minute she looked down at her cup of tea, needing some time to compose herself before she looked up again.

'Are you back to London after tomorrow, Overby, or staying in the country?' Mr Willis said as Miss Huntley fell quiet at the other end of the table.

'I haven't decided yet. I prefer the country in the summer. London can be unbearable in the heat, but there are a few things that need my attention in the coming weeks.'

Charlotte blinked. She had been putting off thinking about what would happen after they all bade farewell to Lady Mountjoy. She was under no illusion that the older woman would choose her to accompany her for a London Season, not when there were others who would take to it so much better. That meant she would be returning to the estate, to the farm. For a moment

Charlotte allowed herself to bask in the joy that thought brought her. She would see all the animals again, ensure everything was on schedule for the harvest later in the summer and be able to spend time chasing her younger sisters around the farm. It would be good to be home.

She had assumed Robert would be close by. She couldn't imagine suddenly losing the closeness they shared. In her mind she had imagined him popping by the farm or taking a ride along the boundary wall they shared to meet her for an afternoon in the sunshine.

'You're going back to London?' She couldn't help it; the words just slipped out.

He levelled her with an emotionless gaze. 'I haven't decided yet what my plans will be.'

'London can be tedious in the summer months,' Mr Willis said, seemingly not picking up on the tension between them. 'I've had an invitation to stay with a friend up north in the Lake District and I think I will accept. Bound to be cooler up there.'

'Indeed.'

'Do you know when Lady Mountjoy is making her announcement?' Miss Huntley said, as always focused on the prize. In the two weeks they had spent at Rowlings Hall, Charlotte had only conversed with Miss Huntley half a dozen times. The beautiful young woman was not interested in making friends, focusing all her energy on the reason they were here: the coveted trip to London for the Season.

'I think she wants to tell everyone before they leave tomorrow. I don't know if she will do it at the ball tonight or tomorrow morning.' He gave a tight-lipped smile to the room in general. 'Please excuse me, I have some correspondence to write this morning.' He stood, taking his half-drunk cup of tea with him, and quickly left the room. Charlotte couldn't help but feel it was she he was fleeing from.

She finished her breakfast in silence, glad when Mr Willis and Miss Huntley resumed their conversation, and left quickly before anyone else could enter the dining room and expect her to make conversation.

For the rest of the morning she moped around the house, hating the way she lingered in doorways, hoping Robert would appear and she could challenge him about how he'd been earlier. By midday she was regretting her decision not to walk in to the village with the other young ladies. It was the final night at Rowlings Hall and Lady Mountjoy had organised a grand ball to celebrate their two weeks together. She had invited dozens of people from the local area, some even coming from Bath for the evening. It was going to be quite an event.

After breakfast Eliza had announced she needed some new ribbons for her hair to match her dress for the evening. Lucy and Jane had been keen to get some fresh air and even Miss Huntley had agreed to accompany them to the village. Charlotte had pleaded fatigue, saying she wanted to rest so she could fully enjoy the evening, but now after a third hour on her own she wished she had gone. It would at least have stopped her wasting the morning lost in her thoughts.

Picking up a book for the fourth time, having read and re-read the same page again and again without anything going in, Charlotte sighed. She wasn't the most patient person at the best of times and now it felt as though her whole future hung in the balance and here she was, having to sit around and read a novel.

Knowing it was not how she should be handling things, Charlotte pushed away her reservations and stood decisively. If Robert wouldn't come to her, then she would go to him.

The house was quiet, especially upstairs

where the maids had finished cleaning and tidying in the bedrooms and were now tackling the downstairs areas in preparation for the ball. It meant it was easy for her to slip along the corridor towards Robert's room and tap lightly on the door. She listened as she waited, wondering if he had gone elsewhere to deal with the correspondence he had mentioned.

After half a minute the door opened and Robert looked out, his face clouding as he saw it was her.

'What are you doing here, Charlotte?'

'Something is wrong and I have spent the whole morning worrying about it and waiting to speak to you. I couldn't bear it any longer.'

'You can't come to my room. It isn't done.'

'I don't care. I needed to see you.'

He grimaced, looked behind him as if deciding whether to pull her into the room or step out of it. In the end his need for privacy won over his caution about being seen with her and he stepped back to let her enter his bedroom.

It was tidy, meticulously so, and had little signs of his occupation around the room, which made her think Lord and Lady Mountjoy kept this room for their nephew even though he had his own residence not far away. There was a small painting on the wall of a couple—the family resemblance made Charlotte think it must be his parents—and the desk had a pile of books on it that looked well thumbed and well loved.

'Two minutes,' he said. 'Then you need to leave.'

'Fine. What has happened? Yesterday afternoon and at dinner you were happy, then this morning you can barely look at me.'

'Good Lord, Charlotte, you are direct, aren't you?'

She shrugged. 'You said I had two minutes. There is no point wasting them on niceties.'

'Then perhaps I will take my lead from you. I will do you the courtesy of being direct as well.'

Charlotte hated the formal way he was speaking to her and she felt as though she had swallowed a rock that was now sitting heavily in the bottom of her stomach.

'Yesterday after our kiss I asked you quite explicitly not to mention our intimacy to anyone else. Not to be tempted to confide in a friend or let slip what had happened.'

Charlotte nodded. 'You did.' She frowned, knowing she hadn't broken his confidence and then suddenly remembering her conversation with Lucy the night before.

'Imagine my surprise then when I came out from the dining room to find you discussing the intricacies of our relationship with Miss Freeman.'

'No,' Charlotte said, shaking her head. He had it all wrong.

'I know what I heard, Charlotte,' he said, his voice cold.

'It wasn't like that.'

'Are you saying Miss Freeman doesn't know about the closeness we have shared?'

'No, I'm not saying that. She does. But—' Charlotte started to try to explain, but Robert cut her off.

'Perhaps you can see why I was surprised. Only hours earlier you made a promise to me and then I find you breaking it without a care in the world as to what it might mean for me.'

Charlotte blinked. She felt as if she had been ambushed. That wasn't what had happened, but she could see he had already made up his mind from the snippets he had heard. She wanted to make him understand that Lucy had already known about them, that she had seen them kiss. Opening her mouth to say this, she saw the bleakness on his face, the look of total and utter betrayal in his eyes. She remembered the things he'd confided in her about his late wife and realised this was a culmination of all his fears coming true. He had finally allowed himself to open up, to trust a little, to perhaps even think that one day he might have a different future and then the person he had put his trust in had seemingly walked all over it without a care for his feelings.

'That's not what happened,' she said quietly.

'I heard it with my own ears, Charlotte. There is no use denying it.'

'I'm not denying it. I'm saying there is more to it than that.'

'What more can there be?'

'Will you at least do me the courtesy of listening?'

It was a long few seconds while she waited for his response. Charlotte could see in his mind he had already decided she had betrayed him, had gone and done exactly the thing he had asked her not to. If only he would listen, though, he would see it wasn't malicious or even she who had broken his trust.

Eventually he nodded and Charlotte took a deep breath, knowing she would only have one chance to make him see he was making a mistake. She wanted to reach up and place her hand on his cheek, but she didn't dare. If he pushed her away it would devastate her and she needed to be as composed as possible to tell her side of the story in a convincing manner.

As she was about to speak there was a sharp knock on the door. They both froze, their muscles tensing and their eyes darting towards one another.

'Hide,' Robert said to her.

'Don't answer it,' she whispered.

'What if it is someone who saw you come in?'

Charlotte's heart began pounding as her eyes darted around the room looking for somewhere to hide. She started to move towards the heavy curtains, but realised she would then be visible from outside. Anyone looking up at the house would see her hiding in the window. Quickly she changed direction and hurried over to the wardrobe, pulling the door and wincing as it creaked before clambering inside.

It was dark and hot in the wardrobe, even with the door left open a crack so she could breathe as well as see and hear what was happening in the room beyond.

'Farthington,' Robert said as he opened the door. He sounded surprisingly composed, as if he wasn't hiding a young woman in his bedroom wardrobe.

Farthington's voice was muffled, but Charlotte could just about make out the words. 'I hope I'm not disturbing you, Lord Overby. I hope you might be able to offer me some advice.'

Conscious not to make a sound, Charlotte exhaled the breath she had been holding. It seemed Robert's fears she might have been seen entering his room were not going to be realised.

'Of course. Shall we head downstairs to the library where we can talk properly?'

'Would you mind if we spoke here? It is a delicate matter and I do not wish to be overheard.'

Charlotte stiffened again, wondering if perhaps Farthington had seen her, or perhaps observed their kiss the day before. Lucy had seen it, so it wasn't completely ridiculous to think someone else might have witnessed it.

Robert must have been thinking the same for he capitulated easily, inviting Farthington to sit in one of the chairs that looked out of the grand window with views over the lawn and garden beyond.

'I hope I am not overstepping,' Farthington said nervously. 'I know we do not know one another well, but over the last few days I have come to respect your serious and measured opinions when you weigh in on a subject.'

'What is it I can help you with?'

Charlotte was grateful Robert was trying to move the man on, trying to make him get to the point.

'I wanted to ask your advice about a matter of the heart. There is a young lady—' he cleared his throat twice before continuing '—and I have the utmost respect for her, but I cannot fathom how she feels about me.'

'Ah…' Robert threw a surreptitious glance at the wardrobe and Charlotte could tell he was as relieved as she to be discussing something that didn't involve an explanation of why Charlotte had crept into his bedroom.

'I want to propose to her, ask her to be my wife.' Farthington was becoming animated now, the most animated Charlotte had ever seen him. 'But I admit we barely know one another.'

'I'm not sure I'm the best person to advise you?'

'Oh?'

'I hardly had the most successful marriage.'

'Well, perhaps you could give me some of that wisdom to stop me from making the same mistakes.'

Robert seemed to contemplate this request for a few seconds and then nodded.

'I find I think better when I walk. Come and join me for a stroll about the gardens. No one will overhear us there.' This time Robert was insistent and Charlotte felt her body begin to relax as he guided the other man towards the door.

'It's so cruel,' Farthington said, wheeling round, caught up in his own dilemma.

Robert clapped him on the shoulder and turned the younger man back round, finally getting him out of the door and into the hall beyond.

Charlotte waited completely still for a couple of minutes, listening to her own breathing in the darkness. She was eager to get out of the wardrobe, eager to be out of Robert's room, but she realised there would be no talking to Robert as she had planned, not right now anyway. Who knew how long he would be caught up with Mr Farthington?

'Later,' she muttered to herself, wondering how much later it would be. Soon she would have to start preparing for the ball and after that it would be only a few hours until the cart came to take her home.

Chapter Twenty-Two

It felt as though she had spent her entire day waiting around, trying to catch a moment in private with Robert and now there would be no more privacy, not with all the eyes of the other guests on them for the duration of the ball.

Straightening up, she summoned a smile, even though it didn't reach her eyes. Tonight she would enjoy herself. She would thank Lady Mountjoy for a wonderful couple of weeks and she would spend some time with the women who were fast becoming like sisters to her. Charlotte smoothed down her dress. It was her favourite, made of cream satin with gold detail subtly threaded through so it glinted in the candlelight. When she had seen the material in the dressmaker's she had thought it perfect even though her mother had said it was too plain, too basic.

After tonight it would probably sit in her wardrobe unworn for who knew how long. Silently she reprimanded herself for such maudlin thoughts. These couple of weeks at Rowlings Hall, with the balls and the trips to Bath, had resulted in her gaining confidence in situations she hadn't experienced much before. Now if she was invited to spend an evening at the Assembly Rooms she might accept, even though it would not be the same without Lucy and Eliza by her side.

Charlotte was finding it hard to keep still, craning her neck this way and that every few seconds to see if she could spot Robert. Even if she was not able to explain the conversation he must have overheard between her and Lucy fully, she would be able to whisper a quick word or two in his ear. Perhaps it would be enough for him to stop looking at her as though she had betrayed him so completely and broken his trust in mankind once again.

'Ladies and gentlemen...' Lady Mountjoy's voice rang out clearly when there was a lull in the music. Her guests all quietened quickly, heads turning in her direction. The older woman was dressed in the most magnificent silver and midnight-blue dress with a trio of matching feathers pinned into her hair. She was beaming, seemingly loving the hubbub of the ball all around her. 'If I could impose on a moment of your time, I have something very important to announce. Where are my five beautiful debutantes?'

Charlotte felt eyes on her as everyone began to look around the room. She saw Eliza step to Lady Mountjoy's side, her face set in a mask of elegance and patience even though Charlotte knew it would mean everything to her friend to be chosen to go to London for the Season. Miss Huntley was next, taking a spot directly next to Lady Mountjoy.

She watched as Jane joined the little group and then felt Lucy's arm through hers as together they went to join Lady Mountjoy and the rest of the debutantes.

'I have had the pleasure of getting to know these five wonderful young women these last few weeks. We have talked and danced, played cards and dined, laughed and cried together. I knew when I first had the idea for this little gathering that I would enjoy myself, but I never knew how much I would come to love and respect the young ladies who have taken the time to come and stay here at Rowlings Hall.' She made eye contact with each of them in turn, smiling warmly. Charlotte was struck by how generous and how kind their hostess was and hoped whoever she chose repaid her kindness in London.

She now spoke in a softer tone, as if ignoring the rest of the guests and addressing the five debutantes. 'When I first invited you to Rowlings Hall I never imagined what a wonderful few weeks we would have and how I would come to the realisation that you all deserve every chance in the world to find happiness. For some of you that might not be achieved with a London Season, some of you may have other plans. I am aware that I originally said I would be taking just one of you to London, but after speaking to Lord Mountjoy we have agreed that it would be impossible to choose between you. We would like to invite all of you to spend the Season with us in London.'

There was a gasp from all the debutantes, Charlotte included. It had never been her aim to be the one chosen to go to London and it was still not what she wanted now, but she could still appreciate the kindness and generosity Lord and Lady Mountjoy were displaying here in deciding to help not one, but five young ladies on their way to the next stage of their lives.

There was a murmur of gratitude which peaked into a swell of chatter as everyone surrounded Lady Mountjoy to thank her and share in the excitement. Charlotte glanced to one side as she was swept towards the circle of young ladies and saw Robert watching her. His expression was serious, his face unsmiling, and even surrounded by the happiness of her friends she felt her stomach drop a little. She needed to speak to him, to make him understand.

As she was about to slip away Lady Mountjoy took her gently by the arm, guiding her a few steps to one side.

'I know you are not sure what you want from your future, my dear,' the older woman said with a warm smile, 'but if you decide to join us in London for the Season we would be very happy to have you.'

'Thank you,' Charlotte murmured, wondering if she would be expected to make the decision now.

'Take a few days to think about it. There is no rush. The preparations will take a few weeks.'

Nodding weakly, Charlotte was glad when Lady Mountjoy turned away, returning to the rest of the debutantes.

It was easy to slip through the crowds while everyone was busy discussing the announcement and within a few seconds she was in the spot where she'd last seen Robert standing. Desperately she looked around, wondering where he could have disappeared to so quickly.

She caught a flash of black moving rapidly at the edge of the ballroom and, without stopping to check if it was Robert, weaved her way through the press of bodies. She managed to catch the man's arm as he was about to leave.

'Robert.' She said his name quietly, but even so she shouldn't be using anything but a formal mode of address. He turned quickly, his eyes meeting hers, and she felt a thrum of energy pass between them. Even in his anger and upset with her there was still that strong pull of desire.

'Go back to the ball,' he said.

'I need to talk to you.'

'There's nothing to discuss.'

'Stop being so stubborn and listen to me for a minute. If you want to go back to hating me after that then, fine.'

'I don't hate you.'

'Disliking, then, or being disappointed with me.'

Robert glanced around as if checking to see if anyone was watching and then took her by the elbow, escorting her out of the ball and on to the terrace. There weren't any other couples out here yet, although the ballroom was already hot from the press of bodies and the warm summer's heat. The doors of the ballroom were flung open, so they didn't need to worry about being out here unchaperoned.

'There's so much I want to say to you, Robert,' she said, hating how closed his expression was, how he wasn't meeting her eyes. She had listened to him tell her about his first wife's betrayal, but she hadn't realised quite how much it still was affecting his ability to trust again, his ability to see something and rationalise it rather than jumping to all the wrong conclusions. 'I would never intentionally break a direct promise,' she said simply.

'Except you did.'

She shook her head. 'You are letting your panic and your past experiences cloud your judgement. What did you hear? What did you see? It can't have been the whole conversation or you would have known how it started.'

He shifted and looked at her properly for the first time, his eyes searching hers. Charlotte exhaled loudly. It was taking all of her self-control to speak so calmly. Normally if someone wronged her or came to an incorrect conclusion about her she would be hot headed and not want to bother explaining why they were wrong, but today, with Robert, it really mattered.

'Tell me.'

They were standing a few feet apart, now facing one another and Charlotte had to stop herself from reaching out across the gap to touch him. She wanted to lay a hand on his arm, pull him closer, make sure he was truly listening to what she had to say.

'Lucy saw us kiss.'

'She can't have.'

'She did. Her bedroom is on the end and she said she had a partial view behind the hedge, enough to see us kiss.'

Robert's shoulders sagged and he looked up at the house in concern.

'She doesn't think anyone else would have seen. Miss Huntley's room is next to hers and Miss Huntley was downstairs at the time so un-likely to have seen anything.'

She watched as Robert ran a hand over his brow, conflicting emotions showing on his face.

'Lucy is a good friend. She assures me she will not say anything to anyone.'

'I am grateful for that.' He stepped forward and then seemed to remember where they were. 'I'm sorry for assuming the worst, for thinking you had done exactly the thing I had asked you not to.'

Charlotte closed her eyes and nodded. Right now Robert thought he was in the wrong, but she couldn't leave it without him knowing the whole truth. It might mean they wouldn't get back to the place they had been before with their relationship, but she wouldn't be able to meet his eye with no residue of guilt unless she told him the rest.

'It isn't quite as simple as that,' she said, having to raise her voice as the musicians struck up inside the ballroom and the chatter swelled with the music. 'Lucy knew we kissed once before even before she saw us.'

'How…?'

'I confided to her about my feelings for you a few days ago and it slipped out that we had kissed.'

He frowned, as if trying to work out how he felt about this.

'It was before you asked me not to talk to anyone about it, but I do see that it still is a breach of the unspoken confidence we should have shared.'

She searched his face as he remained silent and she could see he was trying to work through everything.

Sighing, Robert stepped away and rested his arms on the stone balustrade, looking out over the garden.

'I would have preferred it if no one else knew about our…intimacy…but I can understand why you wanted to talk to someone about it when it is far from a normal situation.'

'I do trust Lucy not to say anything.'

He nodded. 'Good, then it shouldn't matter.'

Charlotte wanted nothing more than to put a hand on his shoulder, to take some of the tension she could feel pulsing from his body and help him to relax a little. It wasn't the easiest of situations, but his past experiences were meaning he was on edge even when there wasn't all that much to be worrying about.

She'd hoped that they would be able to clear up any misunderstanding between them and then perhaps return to the happiness, the sense of hope, that had been there after they had kissed in the gardens. Then she had allowed herself to dream, to wonder if a future with Robert might be possible.

Looking at his stiff posture and serious expression, she felt as though it were hopeless. Even though he could now acknowledge she hadn't betrayed him it was as if the whole thing had reminded him how vulnerable he was if he opened himself up to another person. In response he'd closed in on himself, deciding that the risk wasn't worth the potential heartbreak.

'I am sorry I thought the worst,' he said, turning to meet her eye. 'I should have come to you. Let you explain rather than shutting you out.'

She smiled weakly at him, wondering what she could say to remind him how happy they'd been, show him they still could have that. He seemed so distant from her and she didn't know how to recover the closeness they'd shared.

'It doesn't matter,' she said. 'I didn't want you thinking that of me.'

'I shouldn't have assumed.'

'I understand why you did.'

They stood in silence for a few minutes, Charlotte having to work hard to fight the urge not to cry. She might have explained, corrected his misconception, but it hadn't done what she had hoped. There was still an insurmountable distance between them. She felt foolish for hoping for more, foolish for wishing and wanting and fantasising.

'I should get back to the ball,' Charlotte said, biting her lip. She hated how she hesitated, hated how much she wanted him to spin around and take her in his arms and kiss her there on the terrace, not caring who saw.

He nodded, but didn't even look around. Charlotte inhaled deeply and then plastered a smile on her face, ready to pretend her heart wasn't breaking inside her chest.

Chapter Twenty-Three

Robert knew he must look menacing—even the mothers with daughters of a marriageable age kept away from him as he prowled around the ballroom.

'What has happened?' his aunt asked as she hurried over to him. 'You're scaring the other guests.'

He tried to relax his frown, but saw his aunt recoil at his new expression.

'Stop it, Robert, or someone will be injured in the stampede for the door. Now tell me what has happened.'

'Nothing has happened.'

'Nonsense. I am well versed in your expressions and right now you look as though someone chopped the head off your favourite horse.'

'I'm fine.'

Lady Mountjoy sighed a long-suffering sigh

that showed her years of experience raising her own children.

'You are not fit for polite company, Robert. Now I know you think it is your duty to be here to support me this evening, but I would rather you worked through whatever it is that is going on. Take half an hour, go for a walk, then perhaps you can return to the ball without making the good people of Somerset think you are about to murder them.'

He grunted. His aunt probably did have a point. He wasn't much use while he was feeling like this.

Bidding his aunt farewell, he strode out on to the terrace and without looking back escaped into the darkness of the gardens. The night was warm, so warm he needed to shrug off his jacket as he weaved his way through the formal gardens to the parkland beyond.

As he walked he tried to clear his mind, tried to give himself some respite from all the thoughts that were swirling inside his head. It was hard to do, but as the twinkling lights of the house receded behind him he felt some modicum of peace settle over him.

He walked for fifteen minutes, far enough so that the music and noise of conversation from the house had long since faded away and he knew he was completely alone and unobserved. The lake was a few hundred feet in front of him and he decided to make for that, settling down underneath a weeping willow tree when he reached the banks. As he leaned back against the trunk of the ancient tree he exhaled deeply and closed his eyes.

Everything was a mess. Two and a half years ago, when Amelia was in the process of making him the most notorious man in England, he'd promised himself he would never open himself up to heartbreak again. He would never put himself in a position where anyone else could hurt him. It would give him a lonely life, but that was a hundred times better than what Amelia had put him through.

For two years he'd stuck by this promise to himself. He'd kept everyone at a distance, eschewed social occasions, made it clear he was a man who preferred his own company. It had allowed him to heal, to discover his old self was still there under all the pain and bitterness from his disastrous marriage.

Then Charlotte had come along. Charlotte who at first had chosen to climb out of the stable window rather than acknowledge him. He smiled at the memory. She had exploded into his life, bringing her passion and her joy and made it impossible for him not to see her. Over the last couple of weeks he had found himself wanting to spend every second of every day with her.

That was even before the kisses. He closed his eyes, remembering the first time his lips had brushed hers and the mixture of desire and happiness that had consumed him. It had been unsettling for a man who had been determined never to feel that way again.

He knew he was teetering on the edge. The safest thing for him, the best thing for him, would be to walk away and try to forget Charlotte Greenacre ever existed.

Quietly he scoffed. *That* would be impossible. She was seared into his mind permanently. Even his dreams were haunted by her—when he closed his eyes he saw her smile, the sparkle that was in her eyes.

The safest thing to do would be to forget Charlotte, but would it make him happy?

Shaking his head, he knew he had to forget about happiness. Happiness was a secondary consideration. This latest development in their relationship had shown him that. When he thought she had betrayed him, when he thought she had told Miss Freeman about their kiss after she had agreed it would be best to keep it secret, his heart had felt as though it were being ripped in two.

It was much safer not to risk his heart at all.

Groaning, he let his head fall back on to the rough bark of the tree trunk, knowing it might well be too late for that. He did feel something for Charlotte, something strong and undeniable, but that didn't mean he had to act on it.

Charlotte had watched as Lady Mountjoy approached Robert and whispered a few quiet words in his ear. She'd watched as he'd purposefully strode from the ballroom and disappeared into the darkness. At that point she'd known she would follow him, even though it took a few more minutes for her to acknowledge it.

'You look forlorn,' Eliza said as she hurried up to Charlotte, her eyes dancing with excitement. 'Whatever is the matter? Has it got anything to do with the very dashing Marquess leaving the ballroom with a frown on his face?'

Charlotte shook her head.

'Do you know,' Eliza said, linking her arm through Charlotte's, 'it is such a crush in here that I don't think anyone would notice if you disappeared for a few minutes. I haven't seen Lucy for at least half an hour, but it's not as though I would think she isn't actually in the room.'

'You think I should creep away?'

'Whatever has happened between you and the delectable Marquess I am sure can be sorted with a few minutes alone together. No one ever needs to know.'

'If someone sees me, then there will be a scandal.'

'Come on,' Eliza said, linking her arm through Charlotte's. 'We will go together.'

Eliza pulled her through the ballroom until they were on the terrace. Now there were other couples enjoying the coolness of the air compared to the heat of the ballroom, strolling up and down or seated on one of the few benches dotted along its length.

Eliza made a great show of fanning herself and then lead Charlotte down the steps into the garden, heading for a couple of painted metal garden chairs situated close enough to the ballroom to still be considered appropriate to use, but not so close anyone would be observing them directly.

'Sit here with me for a few minutes and then as I go back up on to the terrace you slip into the garden. No one will know.'

Charlotte opened her mouth to protest, but

then realised it was exactly what she wanted. She wanted to try to put things right with Robert. She owed it to herself to try one more time to get through to him, to try to explore exactly what it was they felt for one another and whether that was worth taking a risk on.

'Go, now,' Eliza whispered, glancing up at the terrace. The couples who had been near the edge, looking into the garden, had turned away and Eliza was already standing ready to make her way back into the ballroom. Charlotte didn't hesitate. With a pounding heart she hurried into the garden, hoping the bushes would shield her from any interested eyes.

She had seen the general direction Robert had headed in a few minutes earlier, but it was darker in the garden than she had imagined it would be the further she ventured from the house and she wasn't sure whether to keep going straight or whether he might have veered elsewhere to find a hidden spot in which to take a few moments' peace. For all she knew he could have even circled round to the stables, asked for his horse to be saddled and ridden off into the village to find the nearest inn for a stiff drink.

As she came to the edge of the formal garden she paused, glancing back at the house. There was no movement from the terrace, no one calling out to make her think anyone had seen her slipping away. As she looked back she realised she knew exactly where Robert would have headed if he wanted to be on his own for a while. He'd talked of going to the lake when he was younger to think and spend a little time when Rowlings Hall was overrun with his boisterous cousins.

She hesitated for a moment and then quickly made her decision, swinging her leg over the low fence and heading out into the parkland.

It was much darker out here and she stumbled a few times before her eyes adjusted to the level of light and her feet became used to the uneven terrain. Luckily the ground was completely dry—she didn't fancy trying to explain to her mother why another of her dresses was ruined. It would already be hard enough to explain the one that had been soaked when she fell in the garden pond and then one that had been muddied on the banks of the lake.

The lady's maid Lady Mountjoy had assigned to help her and the other debutantes dress and get ready in the evening had worked tirelessly in trying to make the dresses look presentable again, but both still showed signs of the accidents that had befallen Charlotte while wearing them.

It took about fifteen minutes before the lake came into view and she was down by the edge of it, listening to the gentle lap of water before she first considered she might be wrong. There were hundreds of other places Robert could be. She shivered, looking around and realising what a vulnerable position she had put herself in. Out here, alone in the darkness, she was too far from the house or anyone else to draw attention if someone with nefarious motives came upon her.

Quickly she turned, not wanting to abandon her search, but knowing she must.

'Charlotte,' she heard the voice from the darkness.

Squinting, she tried to see where it had come from and it was only when she saw the swaying of the leaves on the giant weeping willow she realised Robert was under there.

Picking her way around the edge of the lake, she pushed aside the hanging leaves and entered the privacy the weeping willow afforded. Robert was sitting with his back against the trunk and motioned for her to come and sit next to him.

'You shouldn't be here,' he said softly.

'I know.'

'Someone could have followed you.'

'No one saw me.'

'I don't mean it is dangerous for your privacy, Charlotte, it is dangerous for your safety. You have to take care when walking alone after dark.'

'I know.,' She sighed. 'It seemed a good idea at the time.'

Looking down at her hands, she shook her head and wondered where all her iron resolve had disappeared to. When she had left the garden she had known what she had wanted to say to Robert, what she had wanted to make him understand. Now she didn't know how to start.

'I don't want to leave with things like they are between us,' she said quietly. 'Would it sound too dramatic if I said I couldn't bear it?'

'Not dramatic, no.'

'After tomorrow I know things will change. I will go back home and return to my normal life and these past few weeks will seem like nothing more than a dream. Perhaps our paths might cross every so often, but we will not have this…proximity.'

'It has been on my mind a lot, too, Charlotte,' he said sombrely.

She took a deep breath, steadying herself for

what was to come, her declaration. Never before had she done anything so bold, so brave, and she felt a wave of unease roll through her as she opened her mouth to speak.

Before she could choose the words she was surprised by a sudden movement from Robert. He leaned forward, grabbed her firmly by the waist and pulled her towards him, kissing her as their bodies came together.

Charlotte felt the heady mix of pleasure and anticipation explode inside her. She'd been craving this moment every second of every day since their last kiss. Giving in to her desire fully, she ran her hands through Robert's hair, all rational thought fleeing from her mind and being replaced with pure longing.

She knew she should stop him and, if she were thinking clearly, she would pull away and tell him how she felt, but this was what she wanted. She wanted *him*. She wanted him right here and now and she wanted him for the months and years and decades to come.

With a sigh she sank down into the grass, not caring that she would get grass stains on her cream dress, and gave in to desire.

Robert couldn't think straight. As soon as Charlotte had come to sit next to him he'd caught a hint of her scent, a delicate note of lavender that he imagined her using to soap her body, and he was lost. He was consumed by the overwhelming need to kiss her, to wrap his arms around her and cover her body and make love to her until they were both too far gone with pleasure to care about what came after.

'Charlotte,' he murmured as he pulled away slightly so he could look at her, 'you're driving me mad.'

For an instant she looked a little indignant, but quickly he kissed her again, feeling her relax under his touch.

Somewhere in the far recesses of his conscious mind he knew this was a bad idea, he knew it was worse than bad—it was forbidden. But right now he couldn't do the right thing and stop himself. He'd been craving this for so long, wanting *her* for so long, that now he had her in his arms, responding to his kisses, it would be so difficult to stop.

Underneath them the grass was dry and long and they were far enough away from the house or any other dwelling that he knew no one would come across them. In many ways it was the perfect spot.

Pushing away all thoughts of consequences, he lay Charlotte back on the grass and started to trail kisses down her neck, stopping at the little hollow in between her collarbones. Her skin was soft and warm and he lingered, savouring the sweetness and the velvety softness on his lips.

Charlotte arched up, pushing herself into him and he gripped her hips through the thick layers of skirts. He wanted it all, but he knew not to rush. This was something special, something they had both been craving for so long.

'Turn over,' he said, his voice coming out as a rasp, but Charlotte didn't seem to notice. He wanted to see her, all of her, and pushing her dress up or down wasn't going to be enough. After a second she complied and he set to work unfastening her dress, pulling it up over her head once it was loosened.

'I have never understood why there are so many layers,' he muttered, running his hands over the brilliant white cotton of her chemise and stays. She giggled under him and he kissed her again, all the time his fingers pulling at the ties that laced everything together.

After a minute she'd wriggled out of her stays and petticoats and it was just the loose material of the chemise left, thin and billowing with the alluring outline of her body underneath.

'Robert,' she whispered, her voice hoarse

with desire. He knew it was the invitation he had been hoping for and he couldn't hold back any longer.

Charlotte gasped as Robert laid a hand on her inner thigh and pushed up the material of the chemise. It was what she wanted, what she had secretly hoped would happen ever since she had slipped off into the darkness of the garden, but still she felt the illicit thrill rip through her.

She lay back on her elbows and closed her eyes, letting out a low moan as she felt him dip his head down and kiss the soft skin above her knee. Sparks of pleasure fired through her body, making her feel as though she were ablaze, and the sensation only intensified as his lips trailed up her leg.

Robert was pushing her chemise up higher and higher until it was bunched around her waist.

'Will you be too cold if I take this off?'

She shook her head. It might be late, but the night was hot with no chill in the air yet.

He pulled it up over her head and Charlotte suddenly felt completely exposed. It was thrilling, but she couldn't help checking around to make sure no one else was nearby.

'What about you?'

Robert smiled at her and with practised ease loosened his cravat and pulled it off, shedding his jacket at the same time. He paused for a second and Charlotte leaned forward, feeling bold, pulling up the shirt over his head. For a moment she looked at him, her eyes raking over the muscles of his chest, then she tentatively reached out and touched him.

Robert responded with a groan and manoeuvred himself over her, dipping his head to kiss her hard on the lips.

'What about your trousers?'

'All in good time.'

Charlotte was about to ask when there would be a better time than now, but she was rendered speechless as Robert caught one of her nipples in his mouth, raking his teeth against the hard nub.

'You taste so sweet,' he murmured, trailing his lips over to her other breast and proceeding to tease her until she was writhing underneath him.

'I want...' she said, hardly recognising the sound of her own voice. 'I want...'

'What do you want?'

She felt herself blush at the thought of asking for what she wanted from him, even though it wasn't any more scandalous than what they were doing now.

'What do you want, Charlotte?' he asked, pulling away a little.

'I want you to touch me,' she said quietly.

'Do you want me to touch you here?' He stroked a finger across her cheek. 'Or perhaps here?' He ran his hand down the valley between her breasts. She shook her head. 'Or perhaps you want me to touch you here?' This time his fingers brushed against her abdomen.

'Lower,' she said, loving the desire she saw reflected back in his eyes.

'Lower? You must want me to touch you here?' He ran his whole hand up her inner thigh, stopping a fraction of an inch away from where she was craving his touch.

'Higher.'

'Higher?' She felt his fingers edge upwards and felt her lungs begin to burn as she realised she was holding her breath, waiting for his touch. As his fingertips brushed ever so gently against her most private place she felt like screaming out in frustration and relief. He smiled at her, a rather mischievous smile, and for a second she thought he was about to tease her further by pulling his hand away, but slowly he began to stroke, moving his fingers rhythmically as her hips arched up to meet his touch.

Charlotte felt a wonderful warmth spreading through her body, a feeling that made her want to tense every single muscle at the same time. Her fingers were clutching at the long grass on either side of her and she let her back arch and her head fall back. It felt wonderful to abandon herself to Robert's touch, to not care about anything in the world except how his fingers felt on her body.

Suddenly she felt him shift and manoeuvre himself so he was between her legs. She tensed a little, thinking this was the moment he would fully make love to her, then gasped as instead he dipped his head and intimately kissed her.

'Robert,' she managed to utter before she was overwhelmed by the little jolts of pleasure every time his mouth touched her.

Her breathing was coming hard and fast and she felt a tension building deep inside her as his mouth brought her to a peak of tension and then with one final flick of his tongue she cried out as wave after wave of pleasure flooded through her body.

For half a minute afterwards she was unable to move, unable to do anything but appreciate the totally new sensations that had ripped through her body. As she opened her eyes she felt Robert above her, watching her with a smile on his face. Looping her arms around his neck, she pulled him in for a kiss and as he lowered himself down she felt his hardness against her.

With fumbling fingers she unfastened the waistband of his trousers and hastily pushed them down, hesitating for a second before she took his hardness in her hand. He groaned and she felt a surge of power over him as she realised how much he wanted her.

Robert kissed her again and slowly pushed into her, stopping when he saw her wince.

'Don't stop,' she whispered and he started to move slowly backwards and forward. Charlotte felt an initial ache, but gradually, as he pushed gently into her, she grew accustomed to him and the ache was replaced by a heat that started to build deep inside. She cried out as his hand came between them and he circled again and again, until she thought she could bear it no longer. With a shout she climaxed again, feeling him stiffen inside her as she was overcome with pulse after pulse of pleasure.

For a long moment neither of them moved. Robert's body was pressed against hers and she enjoyed the closeness. Slowly her breathing returned to normal and she could no longer feel her heart pounding in her chest. She was conscious that she was lying out here in the middle of the countryside completely naked, but she couldn't find it in herself to care. She felt happy, contented, and if she had her way she would lie here in Robert's arms, naked and blissful, until the sun started to rise in the morning.

For a few minutes she felt Robert's body as relaxed as hers, his breathing deep and even, but gradually as the night air cooled both their skins he began to tense next to her. The warm glow inside started to dim as she wondered if he regretted what they had done.

'Robert,' she whispered, but his name caught in her throat and it came out as a barely audible whisper.

He shifted, extricating his arm from under her body, gently but with finality. Charlotte stayed where she was for a moment and then turned over, seeking out his face in the moonlight.

Robert looked harried, stressed, not as though he had just had one of the most amazing experiences of his life. Self-consciously Charlotte grabbed at her chemise, pulling it quickly over her head.

'I'm sorry,' Robert said, his expression softening. 'I was lost in my own thoughts. How do you feel? Does it hurt?'

She shook her head. Although his words were kind there was a formality to them that shouldn't have been there considering a few minutes earlier they had been as close as anyone could be. He finished pulling on his shirt and straightening his clothes and Charlotte marvelled at how quickly he could go from looking handsomely dishevelled to looking as if he had been dressed by his valet.

Charlotte followed suit, trying to dress quickly, but struggling as her fingers fumbled with her dress. He hadn't said anything, but this all felt wrong. Five minutes ago she had been imagining them entwined in each other's arms for ever—now he was struggling to look at her.

Robert came around behind her and laid his hands on her shoulders, momentarily making her catch her breath and fall still, and then helped her to straighten and fasten her dress.

Only when she was fully dressed did she dare to look up into his eyes.

Robert was standing close, his face clouded, a furrow between his brows as he frowned. It was not the face of a man happily contemplating his future with the woman he loved.

He cleared his throat, reaching out to her,

but then letting his arms drop back to his side. Charlotte wanted to shake him, to make him tell her what was going on in his head, but she also felt as though maybe she was better not knowing.

Chapter Twenty-Four

Robert cleared his throat, knowing every moment of silence was like a knife to Charlotte's heart. He could see the love in her eyes, but also the fear, fear that he would abandon her now he had taken her honour.

He needed to reassure her. He wasn't that sort of man, but he felt the words stick in his throat. Of course he would marry her—there wasn't any other option now he had been so reckless, had allowed himself to follow his heart and not his head—but he couldn't pretend to be happy about it. In one moment of weakness he had brought himself to a place he had never wanted to be again.

She's not like Amelia, he told himself.

If he really thought about it, a life with Charlotte could be very pleasant, but it was opening himself up to more heartache he didn't know if he could withstand. He felt backed into a corner and it was all his own doing.

'I'll walk you back to the house, I'm sure you will be able to slip in unseen,' he said, knowing he needed to reassure her, to tell her he wouldn't abandon her. The promise was sticking in his throat and he felt as if his cravat was trying to strangle him.

Charlotte turned and began walking away, her shoulders hunched.

'Wait,' he called, knowing he could not let her go back to the ball like this, even if it made him feel nauseous to make promises he had told himself he would never make again. He ran a hand through his hair, wondering how to start. 'I'm sorry, I'm not handling this well.'

'What is there to handle?'

'I shouldn't have allowed this to happen,' he said quietly, seeing the flare of emotion in her eyes. 'I'm sorry.'

'Don't apologise,' she said sharply. 'I don't want your apology.'

'You might not want it, but I am sorry. I shouldn't have allowed myself to lose control.'

Charlotte's eyes widened and he felt like a cad for his words. He was going about this all wrong, but he couldn't seem to find the words to make it right.

'You lost control?'

'Yes. Of course I lost control. These past two weeks I've desired you more than I've ever desired anyone in my life. Tonight I gave in to that desire. I shouldn't have.'

'It wasn't just you,' she said sharply. 'I was there as well.'

She started to stride away, ducking under the hanging branches of the willow tree. He caught up with her in a few paces.

'That was all this was?' Charlotte asked, spinning back round to face him. 'You giving in to your desire?'

He wasn't sure how she wanted him to answer. It seemed whatever he said it wouldn't be right.

She didn't wait for him to say anything, just set off across the field. Robert cursed under his breath.

'I will handle the arrangements,' he called out after her. This wasn't how he had ever expected to propose to someone, but he needed her to realise he wouldn't leave her to her fate now.

'What arrangements?' She spun around and marched back towards him, so much pent-up energy brimming below the surface it looked as though she were about to explode.

'For the wedding.'

'What wedding?'

'Our wedding.'

For a moment she looked confused and then she shook her head. The dismissal hurt more than he thought it would.

'I'm not marrying you,' she said and he could see her furiously trying to blink away the tears from her eyes.

'Of course we will marry.'

'There is no *of course* about it. I am not marrying you.'

'Charlotte, don't be foolish.'

'Why do you want to marry me?' she said sharply, making him recoil a step.

'It is the right thing to do.'

'So not because you like me? Or respect me? Or, God forbid, even love me?' She let out a low chuckle. 'No? None of those? The only thing that could ever get you to say your marriage vows again is a misguided sense of chivalry.'

He remained silent, trying to wade through everything she had said. Of course it would be nicer for both of them if they were marrying for love, but it wasn't the case. He did like Charlotte, he enjoyed her company, wanted to be with her all the time and desired her more than he'd ever desired anyone in the world, but that was not why he was asking her to marry him.

'No,' she said again, slowly and clearly. 'I will not marry you, Robert.'

He was stunned. It hadn't crossed his mind that she might refuse him.

'What if someone finds out?'

'How would they do that? We have hardly been observed this far away from the house and neither of us is likely to tell anyone. I think our secret is safe.'

He felt as though she were slipping away from him and he wasn't ready to let go.

'You may be pregnant.'

This made her pause and he wondered if this might be enough of a reason for her. For a moment he felt a wash of relief and then she shook her head.

'Unlikely. Not from just one time.'

'But it is possible.' He knew this wasn't the right way to persuade her. She was right—a marriage based on this wasn't how either of them would want to live, but perhaps if he could get her to agree to marry him they could work out their emotions later.

Charlotte bit her lip and started to pace up and down. He stayed silent, wondering at how much he wanted her to say yes. He was proposing out of a sense of what was right, so if she refused him that should mean he could continue with his life with a clear conscience. He should feel relieved she was fighting against this so hard, but he didn't. Instead he was desperate for her to say yes, to agree to be his wife.

Robert felt something rip inside him as she shook her head again.

'No, I will not ruin my life, tie myself to a man who is only marrying me out of a sense of duty, for something that may never come about.'

'Charlotte, please think about this.'

'I have. Tomorrow I am going home. If my courses do not come when they are supposed to I will send word. If I am pregnant, then I will marry you. If I am not, then we can both get on with our lives and forget each other.' The last words caught in her throat and Robert stepped forward, wanting to reach out and hold her in his arms.

She spun away and started back towards the house at a run.

Cursing, he knew he had to go with her. They might be in the middle of the estate, but it still wasn't safe for her to be out here by herself in the middle of the night.

He didn't try to catch up with her, know-ing it would be better for both of them to have some time, to think about what they wanted and needed and revisit this afresh in the morning.

Pausing when they were back in the gardens, he watched as Charlotte slipped in to the house, making her way through an unlocked door into the library and avoiding the ball and the now-crowded terrace. He sank down on to a bench. There was no getting away from it—he had handled this badly. From start to finish.

Closing his eyes, he had a vision of Charlotte's body underneath his. She was so perfect, so beautiful, and whenever he was with her he was able to smile again, to forget his worries and his reservations about the world. He'd known it was a bad idea allowing himself to give in to the desire that had been building for days, but when she had let her body brush against his he'd known he couldn't resist her.

'She'll come round,' he told himself. Marriage might not be what he had planned for his life, but if he was going to be married to anyone then Charlotte would be the one he chose every time.

Overnight Charlotte's resolve had hardened. Nothing had changed. Today she was still returning home, back to her family and the farm and the life she had carved out for herself since her father's death. Last night had been a lapse in judgement, that was all.

She swallowed hard, trying to ignore the lump in her throat and the burn as fresh tears came to her eyes. Blinking them away, she refused to let any more fall on to her cheeks. Yesterday anything had seemed possible—today she needed to be pragmatic and stick to her resolve.

For an instant she remembered the bliss as Robert's body had entwined with hers. Then it had seemed as though everything in her life was blessed, that she was the luckiest young woman in the world—about to start on her adventure with the man she loved.

Shaking her head, she checked her appearance in the mirror, grimacing. The sallow skin of her face and dark rings under her eyes showed the lack of sleep and the time she had spent crying instead of resting. Hopefully she would be able to slip away without anyone noticing.

'We missed you at breakfast,' Eliza said as she breezed into Charlotte's room, barely even knocking before she flung open the door and rushed inside. 'Oh, dear, whatever has happened?'

The kindness from her friend was almost too much and Charlotte had to turn away so Eliza wouldn't see the pain in her eyes.

'Charlotte, what's wrong?'

'Nothing, I'm just upset to be leaving you all, that is all.'

Eliza eyed her suspiciously, then shook her head. 'I don't believe you.'

Charlotte opened her mouth to protest, but before she could say anything Lucy came into the room.

'Oh, Charlotte, what has happened?'

'Nothing. Nothing has happened. I didn't sleep well, that is all, and am sad to be leaving.'

Lucy looked at her as suspiciously as Eliza had.

'I don't believe it,' Eliza said to Lucy. 'Something has happened.' She narrowed her eyes. 'Has Lord Overby done something?'

'No,' she said a little too quickly. 'No, nothing like that.'

'Perhaps he hasn't done something you were hoping he might?' Lucy ventured, her probing a little more delicate than Eliza's.

Charlotte tried to shake her head again, but a sob escaped her lips before she could stop it.

Immediately the two other young women were at her side, pressing her to sit down.

'You don't have to tell us anything you don't want to,' Lucy said, a look of concern in her eyes.

Charlotte caught the incredulous look that Eliza gave Lucy and it was almost enough to bring a smile to her lips.

'Or,' Eliza said, stretching out the word, 'you could tell us everything and we can see how best to sort things out.'

'There's nothing to tell.' She sniffed. 'I was foolish and thought there was something more than there was, that is all.'

'You spoke to Lord Overby about your feelings?'

'In a way. He made it clear how he feels about me,' she exhaled loudly before continuing.

'I really thought there was something special between you,' Lucy murmured. 'Is there really no way through this?'

Charlotte shook her head.

'Then he isn't worth your tears,' Eliza said, wiping at Charlotte's cheek with her thumb. 'Come, don't hide away. You haven't done anything wrong. If he cannot see what he is giving up, what he is missing out on then, he does not deserve your upset.'

'I want to go home.'

'Then we will make that happen,' Lucy said with a smile. 'What needs to be done?'

'I need to finish packing my trunk and I need to get Arnold from the stables. The cart is coming at eleven to take me home.'

Lucy quickly hugged her and then rose, bustling round the room to help with the packing.

'We'll finish here. You go and get that piglet of yours and say your farewells.'

Charlotte nodded, thanking her friends before hurrying out of the bedroom. She walked quickly through the house, not wanting to be forced into small talk with anyone she didn't wish to be. She doubted all of the gentlemen would be up after the late night of the ball, but even so she was pleased when she escaped into the garden without meeting anyone.

As she entered the stables she felt some of her unhappiness melt away. She greeted each of the horses in turn and then reached over into the small stall allocated to Arnold and picked him up. In the two weeks they had been at Rowlings Hall he had grown considerably and she didn't think he would have any problems fitting in with the other piglets now at home.

He wriggled in her arms and she was looking round for some sort of open box or crate to put him in for the journey back home when she heard Robert's familiar voice outside. She grabbed a wooden slatted box with an open top and gently lowered the piglet in.

Frantically she looked around, her eyes alighting on the window where two weeks earlier she had tried to climb out to avoid having to talk to him. Now here she was a fortnight later and once again wondering if she should attempt the climb, but this time wanting to avoid him for different reasons.

'Don't even think about it,' Robert said as he entered the stables, seeing her and the direction of her gaze.

'Good morning,' she said stiffly, securing her grip on the crate and walking out past Robert with her head held high.

'Charlotte, wait,' he said, catching her arm. She shook him off, but did turn, her expression icy.

It hurt to look at him like this, to pretend she didn't care for him, but it made things easier. She didn't want him to see the pain in her eyes, to know quite how much he had injured her.

'I will send word in a month,' she said, then spun on her heel and walked as fast as she could across the stable yard and back into the gardens.

* * *

Robert watched her walk away, too stunned by the blankness in her eyes to follow immediately. Even when she had thought he had pressured her mother into selling their land she hadn't looked at him like this. All night he'd prowled round the gardens and then later when the ball was over the house, trying to work out what it was he was feeling. He couldn't shake the look of hurt and betrayal Charlotte had given him before she'd run off through the fields last night.

Today he was no closer to working out what he wanted. If he looked at things objectively he should be celebrating the fact that Charlotte didn't want to marry him. By telling him she would only accept his proposal if pregnant she had given him the freedom he had told himself he craved, but instead of feeling relief he felt empty inside.

Time and time again he had started to examine his deeper thoughts and feelings only to find it was too painful and his mind blocked him from going any further. Now he had seen Charlotte, one thing was clear: she wasn't going to want to sit down with him and discuss things to help him clarify his thoughts.

Aimlessly he wandered through the gardens,

wanting to avoid the bustle of activity at the house as all the guests got ready to leave. The debutantes were all returning home for a few weeks before joining his aunt on the journey to London at the start of the Season. All except Charlotte. Even though she hadn't said it he knew she would choose to stay behind in Somerset.

It was only when he heard hooves at the front of the house that he roused himself from his thoughts. His aunt and uncle would not expect him to be there to bid their guests goodbye, but he needed to see Charlotte one last time. Perhaps they might share a few words, something that would put an end to the torment he was feeling.

As he rounded the front of the house he paused for a moment as he caught a glimpse of Charlotte coming out of the front door. She hugged each of the young women in turn and then was embraced by his aunt. He saw her face was pale and drawn as she pulled away, hopping up next to the driver of the cart and placing the box with the little piglet in behind her. A footman hauled her trunk up into the back and Robert realised if he didn't move quickly she would be gone before he could say anything.

With long strides he hurried towards the cart

and he knew Charlotte must have seen him approach, but she didn't look at him directly. Instead she leaned in and said something in the ear of the boy holding the reins so that he gave a serious nod and urged the horse forward.

There were too many people watching for Robert to break out into a run and catch up with the cart, but as he watched her disappear down the drive he felt as if all the air had been driven from him and his heart was going to explode through his chest. He struggled to maintain his composure, aware of the other guests nearby, wondering if he would ever recover from the hollow emptiness that consumed him at the thought of never being close to Charlotte again.

Chapter Twenty-Five

'I'm sure she won't be long,' Mrs Greenacre said as she gave Robert her friendliest smile. Charlotte's two younger sisters were playing happily in the corner of the room and Mrs Greenacre reached over to pour him another cup of tea.

He wasn't so convinced. He knew Charlotte worked hard on the farm and, if engrossed in a task, wouldn't be likely to come home until it was completed to her satisfaction. Leaning back in his chair, he gave a grim smile. This time he wasn't going to give up.

It had been two weeks since the end of the house party at Rowlings Hall. Two weeks where he had been unable to do anything but think of Charlotte. He'd taken to riding along the boundary between his land and her family's in the hope that he might catch a glimpse of her. Suspiciously she had never been in that area when he was out and about, although he sometimes fancied he'd seen a flash of colour as she'd fled to a safer part of the farm.

'How is the harvest going this year?' Robert asked, sticking to safe subjects. It was well into August now with many of the fields a beautiful golden brown and the farm workers were busy from morning until night bringing in the harvest.

'It is looking to be a good year,' Mrs Greenacre said, not showing her surprise at the question. He marvelled at how well she had adapted to her change in circumstance since her husband's death a few years earlier. From all accounts after a difficult couple of years things were slowly starting to prosper on the farm here and he could see a reflection of that in the manor house. He wondered how much of that was due to Charlotte's influence on the running of the farm.

'My estate manager and tenant farmers tell me the same thing.'

'Hopefully we are due a good few years.'

He supposed she could have sold the farm and the manor house after Mr Greenacre had died and in the hard years that followed the decision to stay, to hold on and try to forge a life for themselves here, must have weighed heavily on her.

The door to the small drawing room opened and Charlotte entered, her cheeks flushed and her eyes sparkling. She stopped abruptly when she saw Robert, surprise apparent on her face. He'd decided not to ride over, instead thinking he would be able to slip in more unobtrusively if he walked the short distance between their houses. His ploy had worked, it would seem, for she hadn't known to avoid the house while he was here.

'There you are, Charlotte. Lord Overby has come to call, but unfortunately he has been waiting for a long time.'

'Your mother has been very gracious in keeping me company,' he said, standing and bowing formally to Charlotte.

She recovered quickly, sending a fleeting glance to her mother as if to wonder what they had been talking about.

'Would you excuse me for a minute?' Mrs Greenacre said, giving them her best bland smile. 'I need to check on something. I will be back shortly.'

She hurried out, leaving them together in the room with Charlotte's younger sisters, who were now looking up at them with interest. They waited until the young girls went back to their game, moving around their rag dolls in a solemn procession.

'It is too early to know yet,' Charlotte said, crossing her arms in front of her body defensively.

'That's not why I'm here.'

'Of course it is.'

'I think I'm the one to know why I'm here, Charlotte.'

'Then why?'

'Will you sit down with me?'

She shook her head, staying where she was. They were drawing some interest from her sisters now and he very deliberately sat back in the chair he had been occupying before she had entered the room. Charlotte glared at him.

'Just say what you have come to say and then leave.'

'Sit down with me.'

'No.'

'Fine, but I doubt your mother will leave us all that long on our own. If you want to risk her coming back halfway through what I have to say, then that is on you.'

Letting out a frustrated sigh, she sat on the furthest chair away from him and angled her body so it was clear she didn't want to be here.

Her eyes wouldn't meet his and swung between her lap and a point over his shoulder.

'Why are you here, Robert?'

'I missed you.'

She scoffed, only meeting his eye when he didn't say anything more.

'Tell me you haven't missed me.'

'I haven't missed you.'

'I don't believe you.'

'What does it matter?' she said, her fingers bunching in the material of her dress.

'I haven't been able to stop thinking about you since I saw you driven away from Rowlings Hall.' It was the truth. Every moment of every day he had been consumed by thoughts of her. He hadn't been able to sleep, hadn't wanted to eat. He had wandered across his estate wondering if this was what his life was destined to be now. This morning he had resolved to do something about it, which was why he was sitting here with her.

'You do not need to feel any obligation towards me.'

'It is not obligation that I feel.'

He saw a flicker of emotion in her eyes and hated that he was the reason she so quickly suppressed it.

Over the last few days he had pushed away

what he was rapidly realising to be the truth. Only with Charlotte sitting here in front of him could he finally admit what he truly felt for her.

He rose and moved closer to Charlotte, but she also stood, turning her back to him.

'I don't think I can hear this, Robert. I don't think I can take having my heart broken again.'

'I never want to hurt you again.'

At that moment Mrs Greenacre came breezing back into the room, seemingly oblivious to the atmosphere between her daughter and their guest.

'It's such a lovely day. Why don't you take Lord Overby on a little walk around the farm?' Mrs Greenacre suggested.

Charlotte looked as though she were about to protest, but eventually nodded mutely.

Only once they were outside did she round on him. 'You need to go. I don't want you here.'

'Charlotte, I know I hurt you, it is unforgivable, but I am asking for a few minutes of your time. I need to explain. Please.' He knew with her fiery temper she might still refuse him, but eventually she nodded and strode out away from the manor house.

They walked in silence for some time until they were far enough away from the house not to need to worry about lowering their voices.

Charlotte wanted to run, to get as far away as possible from this conversation. No doubt he was feeling guilty for so bluntly rejecting her a few weeks earlier and wanted to assuage his guilt. The problem was it was painful for her to be near him. She still loved him, even though it was quite clear he didn't share her feelings.

'A month ago I barely knew you,' Robert said with a rueful smile. 'And you thought I was some sort of villain, preying on your mother to steal your father's land.'

'Perhaps it would be better if we were still like that.'

'You don't mean that, Charlotte. Those couple of weeks we spent together at Rowlings Hall were some of the happiest of my life.'

She looked at him in surprise. She hadn't expected him to admit this.

'I've been in turmoil for the last fortnight, devastated that I might not ever spend time with you again, but too stubborn to admit it to myself,' he said quietly.

She didn't say that she'd missed him, too, although it was the truth. Her pain had been made double, not only hurting from his rejection, but also by the knowledge that she had lost the company of the man she loved.

'This morning I decided I needed to see you,

but it was only when I got here, when I saw you again that I realised quite what a fool I have been. I wonder if you will ever be able to forgive me.' He led her over to a spot that overlooked the rolling countryside. There was a tree with sturdy low branches and together they found one to lean on before he continued.

'I have been so caught up in trying to protect myself from allowing an awful situation like what happened with Amelia to ever occur again I told myself I didn't need to be happy, I needed to be safe.' He shook his head, 'But I am fast realising that miserable and safe is no way to live.'

She looked up at him, wondering at the turmoil she could see behind his eyes. She wanted to trust him, wanted to pull the words from him he was having such a hard time in saying, but she didn't know if she could risk hoping again.

'I am miserable without you, Charlotte. We may have only spent a short time together, but in that time you showed me everything I was missing out on. For so long I have been erecting walls around myself, around my heart, thinking it was the best way to live, and within a few days you came through and knocked down each and every one of those walls. I am ashamed to say it scared me.'

'I scared you?'

'The feelings you inspired in me scared me. Deep down I think I realised I was falling for you very soon after we properly started to spend time together, but I couldn't admit it because it would mean letting go of the fear I had of allowing someone else to get close.'

She felt her heart soar inside her chest with his words even though she told herself to be cautious.

'After we made love I felt as though I had trapped myself. I was still desperately trying to hold on to this notion that I was better off alone and I knew that by my actions that wasn't possible any more. It scared me and I reacted badly, lashing out at you.' He shook his head and turned to her. 'When I proposed to you I really thought you would say yes and then we would have all the time in the world to work out what we felt for one another.'

'I never wanted to trap you, that was never my intention,' she said quietly.

'I know. I'm sorry if I made you feel as though that was what I thought. The desire we felt for one another was irresistible. I know you couldn't have acted any differently just as I am now realising I couldn't.'

He reached out and took her hand, waiting for her to look at him.

'I can see now what I want and why I want it.'

Charlotte felt her heart pounding in her chest as she waited for his next words.

'I want you, Charlotte. Not for one evening or two weeks. I want you in my life, by my side for the rest of our lives. I want you to be my wife, not because it is what should happen because we succumbed to our desire, but because I love you.'

It was everything she had hoped for, everything in a declaration she could wish for. He loved her. She could forgive his reaction after they had made love, she could forgive his initial insistence they marry because it was the right thing to do—she could even forgive the last two weeks of turmoil. Still she hesitated, though. It was wonderful that he had admitted he loved her, but she wasn't sure if this was enough. He had been so emotionally damaged, so hurt by his late wife's betrayal, she didn't want to throw her arms around him and accept his proposal without working out if this was what was best for them both.

'I love you, too,' she said quietly.

Robert smiled, but his smile faltered as he saw her serious expression.

'I cannot deny I am a little wary though, Robert. It is a big change of heart to have in a short period of time.'

'I think the change itself has been gradual. I have been healing these last couple of years and then, when you barrelled into my life, you showed me what I was giving up by denying myself even the chance of happiness.'

'Life isn't without risks and I can't promise I will never hurt you.'

'I know. Look how I have hurt you and I am madly, passionately in love with you.'

She fell silent and he smiled at her.

'I love you, Charlotte, and I know you love me. If you're not sure, don't give me your final answer yet. I'm very happy to spend the next few weeks and months showing you how much I care for you.'

'How are you going to do that?'

He smiled at her. 'I can think of many, many ways.' There was a mischievous glint in his eye.

'Such as?'

'I could show you how much I worship you,' he said, kissing her neck. 'Or I could shower you with lavish gifts, all practical items for the modern farmer, of course. Or I could list all the things I love about you each and every day.'

She hesitated. She loved this man and he

loved her and deep down she knew that was all they needed.

'We could start now,' he murmured in her ear as he caught her earlobe between his teeth.

Charlotte gasped in pleasure as she felt his lips on her skin. She had been about to give him her answer, but decided letting him persuade her for a few minutes wouldn't be a bad thing.

Sliding off the tree branch to the ground, entwined in each other's arms, Robert kissed her, his hands stroking the back of her neck and tangling in her hair.

'I'm not sure this is fair,' Charlotte murmured.

'How's that?'

'I think you could get me to say anything while I'm in the throes of pleasure.'

Robert grinned. 'Anything? That sounds like a challenge.'

They kissed again, Robert wasting no time in laying her back on the soft grass and covering her body with his own. She felt his hardness through their layers of clothes and brought her hand up between them, eliciting a groan from Robert as she touched him.

'I can see you want to challenge me,' he whispered in her ear, 'but I warn you, Charlotte, there is too much at stake here for me to play fair.'

Before she knew what was happening Robert pushed up her skirts and began to trace his fingers up her legs. It felt incredible as he caressed her soft skin, taking his time in climbing higher, making her rock her hips forward as she silently begged him for more. Her skirts were bunched around her waist and her head back against the grass, so she didn't notice as he bent his head down and kissed her in her most private place. She let out a gasp of surprise and tried to sit up, but Robert gently lay a hand on her abdomen and urged her to relax.

Charlotte felt her skin grow hot and her muscles tighten as the tension built with every dip of his fingers or flick of his tongue.

'Please,' she begged, not really knowing what it was she was begging for. 'Please, Robert.'

'Will you marry me?' he asked, not pausing as he posed the question.

Before she could answer an orgasm ripped through her, wave upon wave of pleasure making her feel as though she were floating off the ground.

Robert took her in his arms as she slowly floated back down into reality, holding her tightly.

'I love you, Charlotte.'

'I love you, too.'

'Will you marry me?'

'Yes.'

He kissed her long and hard, wrapping her in his arms. 'Do you know I was prepared for a long campaign to persuade you?'

'Did you really think I would need that much persuasion?'

'I know how much I hurt you, Charlotte. You would have been completely justified in refusing me completely.'

Charlotte took his face in her hands and kissed him again, only pulling away to look into his eyes.

'I love you and you love me.' She shrugged. 'We all make mistakes, but why prolong our unhappiness by holding a grudge about it?'

'That is a very pragmatic way to look at things.'

'It means we can get on with the rest of our lives sooner,' she said.

'I'm not arguing with the benefits of that.'

As she sank back into his arms she felt the smile on her face and knew not much could make her happier than she was right now.

'I've also made provision for Arnold,' he said after a moment's silence.

'Oh?'

'I've built him his very own pen, in case he wants to make the journey with you to Wandlebury Manor.'

Charlotte felt her heart swell. She knew this was Robert's way of showing her he wouldn't expect her to give up any of what she loved for him. He had listened when she had talked about her love for Willow Tree Farm and how important it was to her. The place she associated with all the memories of her father would be allowed to live on and thrive.

'Thank you, Robert, I'm sure Arnold will be very happy with his new lodgings.'

'But you have to promise me one thing.'

'What's that?'

'No more climbing out of windows to avoid me.'

She tilted her head to one side, pretending to think for a minute. 'I promise.'

Epilogue

Robert smiled as he came into the stables to find his wife-to-be looking delightfully dishevelled with hay in her hair.

'Your mother is looking for you, she was rather harried.'

'What time is it?' Charlotte straightened up with a panicked look in her eyes.

'Half an hour until the guests start arriving, one hour until the wedding.'

She groaned. 'I thought I'd only been gone a few minutes.'

Robert moved towards her, smiling at the rosy glow on her cheeks and the sparkle in her eyes. She'd promised it would only be a short ride to settle her nerves before the wedding, but as usual she had lost track of time when out in the countryside she loved.

'I wouldn't let her see you in those breeches

either.' He stepped towards her and looped an arm around her waist. 'Although I rather like them. They don't leave much to the imagination, do they?'

'Stop it,' she said, but without any real conviction in her voice. 'If you get me all hot and bothered, I really will be late for my own wedding.'

'Or you'll have to walk down the aisle in a shirt and breeches.'

'My mother would never forgive me.'

He kissed her, marvelling at how even after two months of stolen kisses and secret liaisons it still felt as wonderful as it had when he'd kissed her for the first time.

'I have a wedding present for you,' he said as they turned towards the house and walked arm in arm away from the stables.

'That's exciting,' she said, 'but I haven't got one for you.'

'You agreeing to marry me is enough.'

'When do I get the gift?'

'Here.' He held out the rolled-up piece of paper he had been carrying and handed it over to her.

'What is it?'

Leading her over to the low stone wall that ran around the formal garden, he motioned for her to unroll it. The paper was thick, good quality, and covered in a series of lines and markings.

For a moment Charlotte scrutinised it with her brows furrowed and then she broke out into a grin.

'You're building me a road.'

'I thought it would help you travel between Willow Tree Farm and Wandlebury Manor, and if you need equipment or livestock moving from one to the other it will save quite a long trip going round by the country lanes.'

'This is the best present ever.'

He leaned in and kissed her again, not caring they were out in the open. Even if any of the guests arrived early they were hardly likely to be in this area of the grounds and if they did catch a sight of him kissing his soon-to-be wife where was the scandal?

'Now, go,' he said, rolling up the piece of paper, 'or your mother will expire from the stress.'

Charlotte stood outside the doors to the church, breathing deeply. She wasn't nervous about marrying Robert—these last few weeks had confirmed to her that he was the man she wanted to spend the rest of her life with. He was attentive and thoughtful, as his wonderful wedding present had demonstrated, and fun to be with. The attraction between them had also increased every day they were together and she was looking forward to not having to sneak kisses when they thought they were hidden from other people.

After today they were planning on spending another few weeks briefing Robert's estate manager on the ins and outs of Willow Tree Farm before they left for their travels. Robert had gently suggested Mr Blackstone could keep an eye on things and offer assistance to Charlotte's mother should she need it while they were away on honeymoon. It had been a thoughtful gesture and one that meant she was really looking forward to the months they were planning to spend travelling across Europe, rather than secretly worrying about the farm and her mother while she was away.

She smoothed down her dress and checked her hair was in place, ready to walk through the doors, when she was surprised by someone slipping out the other way.

'Are you ready?' Lucy asked.

'You look wonderful,' Eliza said as she appeared next to Lucy. The two young women beamed at her, taking in the beautiful cream-coloured dress that was simple yet elegant. Charlotte had talked her mother out of a number of fancier dresses and she was pleased she had persevered in advocating for the one she really liked. Eliza took some of the material in her hand, exclaiming over the silky softness of the skirt and Lucy circled around, checking her hair as if they were back at Rowlings Hall preparing for a ball.

'How is London?' Charlotte couldn't wait to hear all that had been happening.

'Incredible.' Eliza's eyes shone and Charlotte could see her friend was thriving in the capital. 'I have so much to tell you, Charlotte, so much has happened. There is this gentleman...' Eliza paused, trailing off and then smiling. 'But now is not the time. Go and get married and I will tell you everything later.'

'I can't wait to hear all about it.' She realised how much she had missed her new friends and how pleased she was they had managed to come for the wedding.

'And you, Lucy, how are things with you?'

'I'm well, Charlotte, and so happy to be here today. This is like a dream come true, I cannot tell you how thrilled I am that you've got your happy ending.'

'Hardly an ending,' Eliza said with a smile on

her face. 'More like a happy beginning. The beginning of the rest of your life as Lady Overby.'

'We should let you get married. I'm sure we
will have plenty of time to catch up after the
wedding.'

'I've missed you,' Charlotte said as they
turned to go.

Lucy squeezed her hand and Eliza kissed
her on the cheek before the two young women
slipped back into the church.

With one last moment to herself Charlotte
marvelled at the change in her circumstances
and the change in her life over the last few
months. Three months earlier she had thought
she was content with a life hiding away from
society and pouring her energy into the estate
and farm. Now she was marrying the man she
loved and looking at ways she could make both
her old family home and her new one thrive.
She would still spend some of her days worrying if the harvest would fail and if the livestock
would breed, but now she had someone to share
her hopes and dreams and fears with.

She pushed open the door to the church,
feeling a little thrum of nervous energy as
she stepped into the cool interior. There were
about twenty people seated near the front. Lord
and Lady Mountjoy were there, both beaming

proudly, as were Robert's cousins and their spouses. There were a couple of young children, too, but she didn't know his family sufficiently well yet to know which child belonged to which couple.

Her mother and her young sisters sat on the other side of the church, her mother unable to hide the delight she felt that Charlotte was going to be settled and happy. Eliza and Lucy sat with Jane in the row behind Lord and Lady Mountjoy and there were a few people she knew from the village taking up some of the rows further back. Two of Robert's close friends were also in attendance, having travelled down from London and stayed in the local inn the night before. The only notable absence was Robert's mother, who had sent her apologies, but was remaining in York for the summer and hadn't been able to make it back for the wedding.

Charlotte had asked him if he'd wanted to postpone and he'd shaken his head, telling her that nothing could make him want to delay their nuptials, least of all his mother who had been given two months' notice to make the journey south if she had wanted to. It made her feel sad that his mother could not put her son first on at least one occasion, but Robert had told her he had long ago stopped hoping his mother would change and instead had decided to build relationships with those who did care and did want to be involved.

As she stepped into the central aisle all eyes turned to her, but she was focused on one person only. Robert smiled at her, his eyes locking with hers as she paused at the back of the church. Slowly she began moving again, focusing on putting one foot in front of the other and trying to ignore all the eyes on her, just thinking of the man waiting for her at the end of the aisle.

'You look beautiful,' he murmured. 'Your dress is lovely.'

'Better than my breeches.'

'I do love it when you dress like that, but it may raise a few eyebrows in the church.' He was looking at her as though he wanted to kiss her and she could see the restraint it took to keep his distance.

Instead he took her hand as the vicar began the ceremony and Charlotte felt as though her feet were floating an inch from the floor. Everything felt like a dream, the most wonderful, exquisite dream, and she hoped she never woke up.

'Hello, Lady Overby,' Robert said as they walked down the aisle towards the door, all their friends and family beaming with happiness for them. 'Have I told you how happy I am you agreed to marry me?'

'Only once or twice.'

'Not nearly enough, then.' He kissed her as they stepped out into the early autumn sunlight and whispered in her ear. 'I have gone from being the unluckiest man in Somerset to the luckiest man in England and it is all because of you.'

* * * * *

COMING SOON!

We really hope you enjoyed reading this book.
If you're looking for more romance, be sure to
head to the shops when new books are
available on

Thursday 28th
April

To see which titles are coming soon, please visit
millsandboon.co.uk/nextmonth

MILLS & BOON®

Coming next month

A DANCE TO SAVE THE DEBUTANTE
Eva Shepherd

Sophia rubbed her handkerchief across her eyes to wipe away the last of her tears. This handsome stranger was going to save her. It wasn't quite what she had envisioned for her first ball, but it was certainly better than being abandoned, left to cry all on her own.

And hopefully he was right. Once they had danced together the Duke would become her Prince Charming and her Season would be just as she had dreamed it would be.

'This really is kind of you,' she said.

Oh, yes, he most certainly was a handsome stranger. Even, dared she admit it, more handsome than the man she hoped to marry. His brown eyes contained so much warmth that staring into them was raising her body temperature, and despite the growing heat of her skin she found it impossible to look away.

Instead, she continued to stare at his lovely, smiling eyes. The way they crinkled up at the corners was so endearing, showing he laughed often. He was so obviously a kind man, otherwise she would feel uncomfortable being alone with this stranger, but she felt safe with him.

She quickly lowered her eyes when he inclined his head and raised his eyebrows in question. She had been staring at him for far too long.

'So, shall we?' Those brown eyes were still smiling but he did not appear to be laughing at her.

She waited, unsure what he was asking.

'But before we return to the ballroom and drive your beau wild with jealousy, perhaps we should introduce ourselves,' he said, standing up. 'I'm Lord Ethan Rosemont.'

She rose to her feet and bobbed a quick curtsy. 'How do you do? I'm Miss Sophia Cooper.'

'I'm very pleased to make your acquaintance.' He made a formal bow. 'And I would be honoured, Miss Cooper, if you would grant me the next dance, but perhaps you'd like to freshen up first.'

'Oh, yes, I suppose I should,' she said, and then to her mortification hiccupped. Her hand shot to her mouth, but he merely smiled at her, as if she had done something sweet rather than extremely gauche. She lowered her hand and smiled back in gratitude.

'I'll wait for you by the French doors just inside the ballroom.'

'Oh, yes, of course,' she muttered, embarrassed that she had got distracted and actually forgotten what they were planning to do.

'When you enter, I'll be so dazzled by your beauty that I'll simply have to dance with you immediately. That should make him sit up and take notice.'

She gave a little laugh and departed for the ladies' room. It was all make-believe, but for the first time since the Duke had abandoned her, she really did feel like the belle of the ball about to embark on an exciting adventure.

Continue reading
A DANCE TO SAVE THE DEBUTANTE
Eva Shepherd

Available next month
www.millsandboon.co.uk